A NEST OF WASPS

MARK EZRA

NO EXIT PRESS

First published in the UK in 2026 by No Exit Press,
an imprint of Bedford Square Publishers Ltd,
London, UK

noexit.co.uk
@noexitpress

A CIP catalogue record for this book is available from the British Library.

ISBN
978-1-83501-246-8 (Paperback)
978-1-83501-247-5 (eBook)

2 4 6 8 10 9 7 5 3 1

Typeset in 11.2 on 14.25pt Minion Pro
by Avocet Typeset, Bideford, Devon, EX39 2BP
Printed and bound in Great Britain by
CPI Group (UK) Ltd, Croydon CR0 4YY

The manufacturer's authorised representative in the EU for product safety is Easy Access System Europe, Mustamäe tee 50, 10621 Tallinn, Estonia
gpsr.requests@easproject.com

Praise for *A Sting in Her Tale*

A *Love Reading* Book of the Month

'Mark Ezra's impressive debut creatively mixes biblical themes with echoes of Richard Osman's *Thursday Murder Club*… but is very much its own work' ***Financial Times***

'It's a well-written book. Punchy throughout' ***Spectator***

'Compelling and engaging' **Julian Fellowes**

'Anyone who enjoys Richard Osman and Mick Herron will love this taut, atmospheric spy thriller' **Charles Cumming**

'Quirky and inventive. Splendid stuff!' **Luke Jennings**

'A hugely entertaining spy thriller. Pacey and laced with dark humour' **Emma Curtis**

'Mark Ezra is an accomplished writer. There are distinct echoes of the classy Agatha Christie espionage novels' **Peter James**

'This entertaining layered story has a couple of clever twists, neat cultural references and a pleasing nod to the women of the Secret Service' ***Crime Time***

Also by Mark Ezra

A Sting in Her Tale

For Jenny

'The stinging wasp... ought not to be awakened from its sleep.'

Chanakya, 4th Century BC

1

2019

THE TROUBLE WITH MURDER, EVEN if you can get away with it, is that it often creates as many problems as it solves. There's a fair chance your crime will eventually be discovered and that you will, in due course, have to pay the price. Then there's the matter of your conscience. That can weigh heavily. In my case I considered the murder of the man I had known as Callan to be both just and necessary. As for my conscience, I'm glad to say it gave me no trouble at all.

There were things that needed tidying up. Not only in my West Sussex cottage whose basement, after its unexpected flood, had dried out in the last weeks of a surprisingly hot summer. I had not been responsible for the flood – not directly – but you will have to read my earlier account of events for the details. That account concerned a certain oligarch and former Soviet spy who came to a sudden demise in a reception room at the Russian embassy, cause unknown.

I waited a whole month before showing my face in the village. I had been warned that reappearing any earlier would be risky. Callan's associates would want revenge for the death of one of their own. Once that month was up, I was given the all-clear to return home.

I would soon be visited by my daughter, Eva, bringing her child, Alice, to stay with me for a long weekend. I don't think

I've ever looked forward to anything more. Not Eva's visit – she could be sharp-tongued on her best days – but Alice's. She was such a dear little girl. If I behaved myself I hoped to be accorded full grandmotherly privileges and babysitting duties whenever Eva, the television newsreader, and her wife Silvana needed child cover at short notice. I would be only too happy to pop up to town and sleep in the spare room, with the little girl tucked up beside me. I was counting off the days before I would see her again.

On my second day back Percy Bishop, that twinkle-eyed paradox of seducer of lonely divorcees and coldly efficient agent for those in power, invited me to the Chestnut Tree tea rooms for a catch-up. At least, that's what he said we'd be doing. In truth we hardly spoke of recent events. Instead, while our 'deluxe' cream teas were prepared, Percy amused me with tales of past adventures – both romantic and those in Her Majesty's Service – and, once tea had been served, and I had demolished a couple of sandwiches and a scone, rounded things off with this yarn.

'A man and his wife were out walking when they spotted a scruffy fellow waiting in a bus shelter on the far side of the road. "Good Lord," said the woman, "that looks like the Archbishop of Canterbury. Go and ask him if he is." So the husband crosses over to address the man, who responds animatedly, then crosses back to his wife. "What did he say?" she asks. "He told me to fuck off," says the husband. "Oh dear," says the woman. "Now we'll never know."'

I had heard the joke before. But I laughed appreciatively, allowing my gaze to sweep the tables occupied by envious old ladies, sipping their cups of tea with their little fingers stuck out at an angle. I did not do this myself, not only because I found the habit rather common, but because the last joint of my little finger had recently been severed. This had not been intentional on my part, but I had put the 'accident' to good use. Again, you will have to read my previous account to understand the full circumstances. Now I kept my little finger curled under my palm, concealing its scar tissue from prying eyes.

Percy wasn't laughing. Of course he wasn't; a good raconteur never laughs at his own jokes. He was staring at my chest in horror.

For an awful moment I thought a blouse button had popped open. Then I saw the red laser dot of a sniper's rifle settling over my heart. Before I could react, Percy had stood up, blocking the laser beam. He clutched his chest, uttered a cry of pain and lunged across the table. The impact knocked us both to the floor. I heard a sharp crack, the smash of crockery, cries of alarm and distress. Several customers had enjoyed Percy's favours in the past, and must have been distressed that the good times might be over.

'Stay there,' Percy hissed. He waited a few moments before he rose to his feet. I tried to follow, but he held me down.

'So very sorry, everyone. I thought I was having a heart attack. But I think…' He thumped his chest and let out a burp. 'It's merely a bad case of indigestion.'

The lady manager hurried over. 'I gobbled my food far too fast,' Percy continued, 'and now your delicious repast is having its revenge.'

I could see his eyes settling on the window and the street beyond, taking in everything. When he seemed satisfied the danger was over he helped me to my feet. He was careful to interpose his body between mine and the window. He turned to the manager.

'I do apologise, dear lady,' Percy said. 'I've made a total

hash of your delicious spread.' This was only partly true. He'd crushed a couple of cucumber sandwiches and knocked over a teapot. The rest was still perfectly edible. 'Perhaps I could place a new order for your deluxe cream tea for two? If you set it up in your back room, so your staff can clear up my mess, I'd be most grateful.' He ushered me through an archway into the back room and sat me behind its thick wall, well out of sight of the windows. The thought of eating again so soon after dodging a sniper's bullet made my stomach clench.

The manageress was delighted to provide another full 'deluxe tea' for two, and ordered her staff – two young people getting 'work experience' – to clear up. She was called over by an elderly couple who complained that their teapot had unaccountably smashed to pieces and spilled hot tea over their tablecloth.

Percy palmed a butter knife, walked back through the arch and approached the trio. 'I believe I'm responsible for that mess as well. Do let me offer you a fresh pot of tea.' He hovered close by, making encouraging noises as the tablecloth was mopped up and replaced. I heard scraping from where he stood on the other side of the thick wall. He was up to something.

Percy returned and sat facing me. He put down the knife. Its blade was bent out of shape. He reached into his trouser pocket, produced a folded handkerchief and pushed it over to me. I took it without question, unfolded it and found a spent bullet, its nose flattened.

'An unfortunate turn of events.' Percy was prone to understatement. 'Just when we thought things had settled down. But you should be safe for the time being. I'm certain they won't make another attempt on you here.' He exchanged his damaged knife for a fresh one and flashed me a smile. 'Let's enjoy our tea, while we consider the possibilities.' He saw I wasn't smiling. 'Not downhearted, are we?'

That was easy for him to say. Not so long ago I had been happy to die by my own hand. Now I was determined to live. I wanted to see baby Alice grow up and find happiness. I wanted the same for my children and, somewhat to my surprise, I wanted the same for myself.

'It's not safe for you to remain in the village,' he continued. 'It was my mistake to think that it was.'

'What do you suggest?'

'There are a couple of possibilities, but I believe I have just the place for you to go to ground.'

'Go to ground? For how long?'

'That will depend on the circumstances.'

Before I could reply, Percy produced his phone and sent a couple of WhatsApp messages. A moment later his phone pinged. He looked up and smiled encouragingly. 'All is in hand.'

Our second tea arrived: a pot of Darjeeling for Percy, Earl Grey for me. Arranged on a tiered cake stand were finger sandwiches, sultana scones and a generous helping of clotted cream and homemade strawberry jam. The waitress popped back with two glasses of Prosecco. I downed mine in one. It had an instant effect. Minutes earlier the thought of food had revolted me. Now the combination of adrenaline, alcohol and Percy's reassuring presence restored my robust appetite. I bolted down two cucumber sandwiches, buttered a scone, heaped it with cream and jam and took a big bite. Percy slid across his Prosecco.

'Perhaps you could manage this for me.'

'Going teetotal?'

'No, just need to keep my wits about me.' His words were chilling. He had done his best to relax me, but he was alert, aware of every movement. I pushed aside his Prosecco and we finished our tea in silence.

When the bill arrived Percy left a generous tip. As he walked around to pull out my chair he leant down and whispered, 'Take a look at the window.'

I glanced at the Georgian sash window facing the high street. Its central pane, about fifteen-inches high and nine inches wide, had a neat hole drilled through it. A small starburst framed the bullet's exit point. Nobody had noticed it yet, but they soon would. Questions might be asked.

'I want you to walk on my right. Don't speed up or slow down.'

Percy took my arm as we stepped into the street. 'Bend down,' he whispered. As I did so he snatched up a pebble. A huge lorry, far too large for the narrow high street, trundled down the road, rattling the old buildings. As it passed Percy flicked his pebble at the window. The pane, weakened by the bullet hole, shattered. Percy hurried us along behind the cover of the lorry. I glanced back. The manageress had come out to see what had caused the pane to shatter. She saw the lorry, shook her head and disappeared back inside.

'I'll send a glazier round tomorrow,' said Percy, 'but in the meantime…'

A car drew up. Percy opened the rear door, gently eased my head down to protect it from hitting the frame and bundled me inside. He stepped around the car and got in beside me. 'This is Pete,' he said. The driver, a broad-shouldered man with a shaven head, nodded without turning around. 'Pete's going to take us to your new home.'

Pete accelerated away. Between the shops on the high street

I caught a glimpse of my little cottage, with its overgrown front garden full of weeds. I knew I might never see it again. A new chapter of my life had begun.

As I said, the trouble with murder is that it often creates as many problems as it solves.

2

My safe house was off Ladbroke Grove, in that part of North Kensington that calls itself Notting Hill but isn't, unless you're a Conservative politician showing off. It was an off-white stucco terraced building with five steps up to the front door. Below that was a semi-basement, or garden flat. This lower flat may have been occupied. The two flats above me appeared to be empty.

As we pulled up Percy checked that I had switched off my phone. I should have done this long before we left West Sussex, and I had no excuse for not doing so. It was the shock and relief of avoiding assassination, I suppose, though I had experienced similar situations before and had managed to keep my wits about me every time.

I could merely have switched off the location services. You can still locate a live phone by triangulating its signals from nearby towers, but you need a court order to do so. Switching off your Wi-Fi is also recommended, as any public hotspot will give you away. Some agencies, the FSB in particular, use cell simulator sites which force phones to broadcast their locations, but you have to get close up to do that.

I surreptitiously switched off my phone. I suspected Percy was perfectly aware that I had only just done so, but he said nothing.

The interior construction of my safe house – a ground-floor apartment in this rather ordinary terraced building – was like nothing I had seen before. Apart from the front bay window, it enjoyed no natural light. It appeared to consist solely of one long, narrow enclosure, its walls and ceiling lined with wooden panels curving smoothly around the room.

'Designed by a boat builder,' said Percy. 'No sharp corners.'

'And scarcely any light,' I said. 'This is a holding cell, not a safe house.'

'Not at all,' he replied. 'Let me reveal its secrets.'

Percy strode to the centre of the room and tapped a panel in the wall. A smaller panel sprang open, revealing a brass ring set into the wood. Percy stepped away. 'All yours.'

'What do I do?'

'Try it,' he said, and stepped back further.

I pulled the ring and was surprised to see a wood partition unfold. I drew it along a rail set in the floor until it reached the far wall, where it locked into place. Lights came on in the ceiling, which was just as well, as I had divided the long room and cut myself off from the window.

'What do you think?' asked Percy.

'That I've just made a smaller cell for myself.'

'Think of it as a magic box. Nothing is quite as it seems.' He marched to the back of the room, counted three panels from the right and pressed inwards. In response, another small panel popped open. In the recess was a door handle. 'After you, my dear,' he said. I could see that he was enjoying himself.

I turned the handle and found myself pushing open a door to… a fully furnished bedroom with bookshelves and a bed. It overlooked an overgrown and untended garden, accessed by a locked French window, with sash windows either side. 'They are all bullet-proofed, as is the one at the front. Though if you have an emergency you can open them like this.' Percy depressed another panel and revealed a red button and a lever. 'Panic button, in case of intruders. There are three such buttons in the flat. And this lever, you simply pull down and the window pops out of its frame. You can slip out onto the balcony.'

'It's a bit of a drop into the garden.'

'See the bars on the right-hand side?'

The bars on the right-hand of the narrow balcony were horizontal, unlike the vertical ones on the other two sides.

'You lift them a couple of inches, push them forward and they drop to form a six-foot ladder. You climb down and let yourself fall the last three feet.'

'Hmm.' I wasn't convinced: at my age, even a three-foot drop could cause problems, but I let him continue.

'The garden has steps at each of the far corners. They're hidden, overgrown with ivy. But if you reach them you can disappear into a neighbour's garden and access the street beyond.' He strode around the bed and revealed yet another handle. This time he opened it himself. 'Bathroom, which doubles as a panic room. Though I cannot imagine you ever panicking.'

'You've never seen me baking a soufflé.' I was making light of things, but the place made me feel claustrophobic. It was a hangover from the time I was imprisoned in a cramped dungeon by a mad maharaja. My safe house was luxurious by comparison, but it wasn't that long since I'd been fighting for my life in my own cellar. I did not want the memory flooding back. Yes, the pun was intended.

'Steel door and frame to keep attackers at bay,' Percy

assured me. 'Running water and a cupboard stocked with food – all in cans, I'm afraid.'

'Better make sure there's a can opener.'

'You should be able to hold out for a week or so.'

The thought of being cooped up in this tiny panic room for a week filled me with dismay.

'But it'll never come to that,' he continued. 'Pressing any of those buttons will bring rescue within twenty minutes.' He shut the bathroom door and led me back into the main room. 'To escape any room you simply depress the correct panels to reveal their door handles. So familiarise yourself with their locations. They are not all easy to find. The intention, of course, is to confuse and delay an intruder with murder in mind.' He took a look around the room, as if to reassure himself he had forgotten nothing. 'Ah yes, there's also a kitchen with a well-stocked fridge and pantry, but I'll leave you to find that yourself. It shouldn't take you long.'

His tour and lecture over, Percy slid open the dividing partition, restoring the main room to its original size. 'I think that's all for now. I shall be in touch, dear lady.'

'How long am I going to be holed up here?'

'Only time will tell. But you won't be bored. You should expect a visit shortly. From someone you know.' He checked his watch. I only caught a glimpse, as he wore it high up on his wrist, hidden by his shirt cuffs, but I recognised it as an Omega HS8. The model had been mass produced for pilots of the Royal Navy Fleet Air Arm during World War Two. It was most probably an heirloom from his father, which gave me a clue to Percy. It was the same model that Dennis had worn, right up until the time… well, there was no point dwelling on the past. Percy gave me a swift hug and a peck on both cheeks, and then he was gone.

I was alone. More alone than I had been for a long while. It is one thing to cut yourself off from society and draw yourself into your shell. You do it to lick your wounds and to heal, with the intention of returning when you are ready for the fray. It is quite another matter to find yourself in hiding, like a hunted beast, in a strange and unfamiliar place. You wait for the danger to pass, with only a faint hope that you will ever see your loved ones again. At least in my case I was comforted to know that I had Percy Bishop on my side. And I was curious to know who my mystery visitor would be.

3

Matthew Fawcett waddled up the street, paused outside my safe house, looked both ways to check he had not been observed, then mounted the steep steps to the front door. I stood at the bay window, hidden from view behind a nicotine-stained net curtain, watching. Matthew proceeded belly first, propelling himself forwards and upwards by his own cantilevered mass. Grabbing the iron handrail, he hauled himself fist over pudgy fist until he stood, panting at this unaccustomed exertion, the conqueror of his own personal Everest.

He inhaled deeply. Under the strain a button pinged off his waistcoat and clattered down into the basement. He stared gloomily into the well, clearly wondering whether the hike back down to reclaim the button was worth the effort. The ring of his mobile phone made his mind up for him. He studied the incoming number and cut off the call. The phone rang again. This time he answered.

'I can't talk now. I'm in a meeting with the Prime Minister.' He flicked his phone to silent and pressed my doorbell. I waited a few seconds, then let Matthew into the small apartment that I now called home.

*

'The trouble with chicken,' said Matthew, balefully eyeing the cold drumsticks I had offered him, 'is that it tastes like frog.'

'What on earth do you mean?'

'Armadillo in Guatemala,' he continued, 'crocodile in Papua New Guinea, giant snail in Africa, diamond-back rattlesnake in New Mexico, termite fungus in China. Each and every time I was assured it would taste just like chicken. But the only one that had me half-convinced was the West African goliath frog. And now, every time I am offered chicken, all I can think of is that revolting great frog, a yard long with its legs outstretched.'

'And all in Her Majesty's Service.'

'The drawback to working undercover. You're obliged to hunker down and sup with the locals.' He sighed. 'I used to be quite slim you know.'

'I recall,' I fibbed. Matthew had never been slim. When I first met him in Athens he had been overweight. Now he was obese.

'I really should have asked you for a salad.'

'Any other complaints? Should I start a list?'

'You've given me beans. I can't eat beans.'

'What's wrong with them?'

'Greece 1973. My first posting. I took a young lady to a rather fine restaurant in Athens.'

'You, on a date with a *girl*? You surprise me.'

'We were all a lot more… flexible in those days. And I was prepared to make certain sacrifices in the service of queen and country.' He fumbled with his waistcoat buttons. 'I was hoping to elicit information about the girl's father, an opposition minister in exile.' Matthew undid the buttons one by one until his belly, enlarged by a thousand expense account lunches and now unleashed, flopped heavily over his belt.

'I had dined at the same establishment only two evenings earlier, with a couple of handsome young lads from the embassy, and the place had been a riot of fun: music, dancing, plate smashing, all the things that encapsulate the joyful prelude to satisfactory consummation.' He licked his lips at the memory. 'But that night there was just a single violinist scraping a slow dirge while diners digested their dinners in mournful silence.' He poked at the beans with a fork.

'I took it upon myself to liven up the room. I snatched up a plate, smashed it to the floor, did the same again and began dancing a lively sirtaki that I had picked up on my previous visit. The other customers ignored me. They carried on eating as if I were invisible.'

'Hard to imagine.' Matthew attempting to dance the sirtaki would have been impossible to ignore.

'I felt a heavy hand on my shoulder. I was arrested, handcuffed and taken to a police cell. Turned out that the Chief of Police, a dour, humourless fellow, had been dining at the very next table to us. What I hadn't known was that the junta had decreed that plate smashing debased the nation. They claimed it made the Greeks appear an unsophisticated and vulgar people.'

'What's all this got to do with beans?'

'I spent a week in that jail. All they gave me was beans. Boiled beans. For breakfast, lunch and supper. Seven days running. Now I can't bear the sight of them.'

'Those were Greek beans, these are French. But I'll take them away if they offend you.' I removed the plate. His pudgy hand locked onto it with the resolute grip of a lobster's claw.

'If you could provide a little warm butter to moisten them,

I might just manage to force a few down,' he suggested.

I let go and did as he asked, melting some salted butter with a little ground black pepper in a pan and pouring it, unfiltered, over the beans. Matthew devoured them in three large mouthfuls.

'Of course,' he continued, 'I could have used my "get out of jail" card. It would have taken just one call to the embassy. But I was operating undercover, and so I had to endure the indignity. Do you know, they stripped me.'

'Surely not, even under the junta.' The Greek government of the early 1970s, composed of military colonels who ruled with an iron fist, was notorious for ignoring basic civil liberties.

'Oh no, not the junta. My fellow prisoners. One of them took a fancy to my pink shirt. Insisted I hand it over.'

'Without a fight?'

'My dear, he was enormous. *Everywhere*. The outcome was inevitable.' Matthew stripped the chicken bones of their remaining flesh, much the way his fellow prisoner must have removed his pink shirt. 'A tissue, if I may, my dear old thing.'

I provided a tissue, but my instincts were alerted. Any endearment emanating from Matthew meant he was about to spring bad news. I watched with a sense of foreboding as he made a vain effort to wipe his fat fingers clean. The tissue dropped to the floor. I let it lie.

'I take it this isn't an entirely social visit?'

Matthew started to ease his bulk off the chair. Then he thought better of it and settled back down. 'The thing is,' he began, 'I have been approached to investigate a… a highly important matter.' He paused, so that I could appreciate just how important that matter might be.

'For the service?'

He stiffened, as if I had extracted the information against his will.

'I thought you left the service years ago,' I continued. 'As did I.'

'I am ever prepared to make myself available. For extraordinary circumstances.'

'And what would these circumstances be?'

Matthew shifted his vast weight from one cheek to the other, as if he was reluctant to say more. Which was nonsense, of course. Why else was he here?

'We have a traitor in our midst.'

'You mean a traitor in the service?'

'Got it in one.'

'And you've been recalled to discover... this traitor?'

'Traitor and murderer.'

'Murder?'

'This goes back to the 1980s. Our era.'

'I recall one murder very well. But that was an outside job. No traitor involved.'

'That is what we believed. But new information has come to light.'

'What new information?'

'Ah, on that matter, I'm afraid, dear heart, my lips are sealed.'

'A traitor in the service?' I mused. 'Do we know where we're to look?'

'We believe it's somebody quite high up. Someone with a seemingly impeccable record.'

'Someone... untouchable.'

'Exactly. That's why I've been brought in.' Matthew smiled. 'As somebody from outside, I can operate independently. I'm putting together a team. I already have my first recruit.'

'Who's that?'

'Why you, of course, my dear.'

I felt that Matthew, the swollen spider, had woven his web and I had stepped right into its sticky centre.

'What use do you think I could possibly be?'

'There is material to be studied that our past experiences, yours and mine, may illuminate. Things that are obscure to those closer to them than we are.' Matthew could always be relied upon to make an issue murkier than it already was.

'Then you'll need to get me out of here.'

'Alas, dear heart…' His voice trailed off.

'What?'

'The thing is, you've set the metaphorical tiger among the vultures.'

'Not a metaphor with which I am familiar.'

'Cat among the pigeons doesn't quite encompass the enormity of the situation. You can't go around town assassinating every billionaire oligarch to whom you take a dislike.'

'One particular billionaire. And he thoroughly deserved it.'

I could see Matthew considering further arguments. He dismissed each from his mind with a flick of his hand and a sad smile.

'What's done is done. *Sursum corda*. Let us lift up our hearts and move on.'

'You can move on. I'm stuck inside here, anticipating an assassin's bullet or a plutonium pill in my pottage.'

'At first,' he continued, as if I had not spoken, 'it'll simply be a matter of studying the files. But you may not be "stuck" in here as long as you fear.' He sucked traces of chicken fat from his stubby fingers and stood up. He had to use the armrests for leverage. The feat took him several seconds to achieve. I averted my eyes as he struggled to button up his waistcoat.

'I must be off, dear heart. You know, I believe your incarceration may yet prove a boon. I shall be in touch.'

4

MATTHEW EMPTIED MY FRIDGE OF its leftovers and departed. I watched him descend the steps and trundle off towards Ladbroke Grove. He didn't get far. He stopped at the bakery which sold Portuguese pastries: *pastéis de nata*. He selected two from a display shelf and dived inside. I waited for him to come out. He didn't. A man dressed in black, his features concealed by a hoodie, approached and looked inside. If Matthew was being followed, then his mission must have been every bit as important as he had implied.

The hooded man stepped back and glanced up and down the road. I could sense his frustration as he realised that he had lost Matthew. How the fat little man had given him the slip was a mystery to him, but I could see what Matthew had done. The pastries had been a delicious deception. When he darted forward it was not into the shop to pay, but into the side alley beside the shop door. I later checked an old A-Z map. The alley took a dog leg to the right and after a few yards another to the left which led to the street beyond. Matthew would have had a car waiting for him that would have whisked him away as soon as he appeared. The hooded man peered into the alley. He was too late and he knew it. Matthew, the canny old owl clutching his stolen pastries, had eluded him.

*

I sorted my few clothes in their two drawers. Percy had been good enough to arrange for a suitcase of underwear, blouses, skirts and slacks to be delivered shortly after he had left me. I had made a point of requesting whoever had packed for me – probably Dottie or Lottie, the two ladies Percy kept on hand for such eventualities – to include what I called 'Dennis's belt', though Dennis had gifted it to me years ago.

I went into the bedroom and tried to sleep. It was a pointless exercise. I could almost hear the cogs of my brain whirring. Why had they attacked me in the tea room when I was with Percy? It would have been far easier for them to kill me when I was alone. What exactly was this 'assistance' Matthew expected me to give him? Who was the man shadowing him and did he pose a danger to me? To all these questions I had no answers.

The afternoon sun came around – the bedroom faced south-west – and I gave up trying to nap. I got up, made myself a cup of tea – only Assam was available, but I was lucky, it was my favourite. The milk, what little Matthew had left me, was fresh. I took my mug and slipped out onto the balcony that overlooked the garden below. It was a mass of elder and stinging nettles. Though I knew it had been left that way on purpose, it was all I could do to resist clambering down and hacking at the weeds.

In the garden backing onto mine five brawny men, stripped to the waist, were erecting scaffolding around a house. There was a great deal of unnecessary shouting, it seemed to me, as if it was their first day on the job. 'Tighten yer nuts, Charlie, don't leave them dangling.' Charlie shouted back something inaudible, which raised a guffaw from his fellow scaffolders, then made a big show of tightening the nuts on the couplers.

I supposed they felt they were giving value for money. Scaffolding is expensive. If they put it together quickly and quietly it would seem even more so. The noise – the clanking and shouting in a mixture of cockney and Eastern European languages – was all part of the show, and half of what the clients were paying for.

A man stepped out onto the balcony next door to see what was causing the racket. I should have ducked inside immediately, but I was too late. He had already seen me. I recognised him as the presenter of a series of middle-brow arts programmes; the phoney type who got up my nose instantly. His were the type of 'documentaries' that suggest that the guest artists were lucky to meet such an important presenter. He was famous for embarrassing his subjects into gifting him samples of their work. He owned a small Hockney, a maquette of sculptor Anthony Gormley's 'Angel of the North' and a couple of pieces by Damien Hirst. The last I could do without. He and I nodded to each other and I was on the point of stepping inside when he addressed me.

'Just moved in?' He seemed delighted that I was old and white. If I proved a troublesome neighbour, I would not last forever.

'We're turning this house into a centre for Afghan refugee women and children,' I snapped back. 'Hope you don't mind a lot of screaming and shouting.'

Looking like he had swallowed a wasp, he backed swiftly into his house, slammed the door and locked it. I went inside and mentally kicked myself. I was supposed to be keeping out of sight; not attracting attention to myself. And here I was, stinging a stranger with a childish jibe.

There were three books on the shelves. One was the Koran in Arabic. The other two were a crime thriller and a

French-English dictionary. Had the previous occupant been a French-speaking North African with a strong interest in solving crimes? I somehow doubted it. I left the books on the shelf and searched for a television. Percy had pointed out the remote control but so far I hadn't found the screen.

I pressed a few buttons on the remote without result. Why can't these things be of a standard design? Who hasn't struggled in a hotel room to find the right channel? I tried another button, and suddenly a panel in the wall sprung open and a television monitor appeared. It came alive, blaring at top volume. That must have been my fault. My nerves jangling, I reduced the volume to a low murmur.

I never watch daytime television. I have more than enough to occupy my mind on a normal day. But this was not a normal day. I surfed the channels. I was disappointed by the rubbish classified as entertainment. I found nothing of interest until I caught the *BBC News*. I was hoping for a glimpse of my daughter Eva. Not because I missed her, but because she was my connection to little Alice. Eva presents the evening news, and the twenty-four-hour scrolling bulletins were read by people unfamiliar to me.

There was no mention of an attempted assassination of an elderly woman in a West Sussex tea room. Percy had done a good job. And if he'd missed something, I supposed someone high up had kept the matter quiet. Probably my son Bernard, the political high-flyer.

I watched until the end of the news bulletin – there was not much else to do – then curled up on one of two opposing sofas with the crime thriller. I got to around page thirty when I was interrupted by a telephone ringing. There was a landline in the flat. Unlisted, I presumed. I picked up the receiver. A female voice spoke. 'A parcel will arrive by courier shortly.'

'Shortly is a vague term.' The words were scarcely out of my mouth when the doorbell rang.

'He's at the door now,' the voice continued.

I went to the bay window. A young man stood outside, holding what appeared to be a large Amazon box. I opened the door, but stayed well back in the shadows.

'You'll have to sign for it.' He stepped in, handed me a pen and held out papers for me to sign. I had seen this form before.

'What is this?'

'Official Secrets.'

'I signed it years ago.'

'Never hurts to have a fresh copy.'

I signed the papers, together with a duplicate.

He dutifully folded them and put them in his breast pocket. 'All yours.' He handed over the box. The weight of it almost caused me to drop it. I needed both hands to haul it inside, kicking the door behind me as I stepped into the flat.

I extracted an enormous package from the 'Amazon' box. It was wrapped so tightly in brown tape that I had to get a knife and saw it open. As I peeled off the wrapping I found myself holding a heavy-duty cardboard box. It was stuffed with documents, many of them going back to the 1970s. Most, but not all, were in chronological order. I laid them out by date, starting with 1977 and progressing to the current year. When I'd finished I had made forty-two piles. Some contained only a few pages. Others from the 1980s and 1990s had close to two hundred pages per year. It was important to establish a progressive narrative. I was annoyed to find that the pages from one section, dated 1989, were interleaved with pages from the 1970s right through to the year 2015. I separated these out, but not before making a note of the order I had found them in. Whoever had interspersed them this way must have had a reason.

I am a fast reader. I tried speed-reading the documents as I sorted them. I cannot claim to absorb everything in a five-second scan, but I can pick up the gist of any matter and I was beginning to form an idea of what Matthew Fawcett might want. I was two thirds of the way through sorting these papers in order when I discovered a note written in Matthew's broad scrawl. It read: *Don't bother reading this stuff. Just keep it on file. Important stuff on its way.* Infuriating man!

The largest bundles of papers mostly concerned events in Greece in the mid-1980s, when I had been stationed in Athens. Many of the documents seemed unimportant: receipts, bar bills and the like. There was one list of larger sums, some of them considerable. This was typed and had no signature, but had been approved and stamped at our Athens embassy. Against each was a question mark. Whatever the question, it did not appear to have been answered. As I could provide no answers myself, I decided to set these papers aside and wait for Matthew's 'important stuff'.

I dipped back into the crime thriller and quickly identified the murderer. I skipped to the last chapter and confirmed that I was right. I wondered how I would have approached the story, and where I would have inserted a shoal of red herrings. I can't say I would have made a better hash of it than the writer. He had, it said on the back cover, sold more than twenty-five million copies of his books and was now living in Guernsey. That's the trouble with announcing your success to the public: the taxman reads that stuff too. Guernsey is a lovely place to visit and the fish restaurants are excellent, but I wouldn't want to live there. I didn't want to be stuck in this hole much longer either. But it would be unwise to phone out, and nobody was likely to call me. Not even my own children. Since early childhood they had become used to my disappearing for weeks on end.

An hour or so later I was going out of my mind with boredom. I paced up and down the room like a caged tiger. In frustration, I kicked the wooden panelling. A hatch flew open. Intrigued, I peered inside and found a mop and bucket. I had no intention of either mopping the floor or of staying cooped up alone here for one more day.

Then I remembered something I had come up with when establishing a safe house for others. If urgent communications were required, a book placed causally in the window would elicit a response. I positioned the French-English dictionary accordingly and settled down with the thriller, reading each chapter from the end of the book back towards the point where I had left off. It didn't matter that I knew whodunnit. I wanted to follow the writer's process in plotting his story.

It took less than forty minutes for the phone to ring. This time the voice was familiar: Matthew's.

'My dearest, I've hardly got back to my club and already you've found a connection, a link.'

'Not a bit of it. If you want me to do a proper job, I need those "important papers".'

'Ah, bit of a hold-up there, I'm afraid. Department is delaying their release.'

'Then I need to get out of here. I can't stay indoors another twenty-four hours.'

'It's not safe for you to go out as you are. You'll be recognised.'

'If anyone's actually looking for me.'

'Believe me, they are. We constantly monitor the airwaves.'

'I cannot stay here, and that's final.'

'Well, they always said you were a difficult woman. Let me think about it. There may be a solution.'

'Good.' I considered his words. 'Who said I was difficult?'

'Oh... people. Nobody in particular.' He rang off.

5

When I awoke the next morning I continued reading the crime thriller, which I found better backwards than I expected. The phone rang. I answered and was delighted to hear Percy's cheerful voice.

'How are you bearing up?' he asked.

'I'm going mad locked up in here, much sooner than I expected.'

'Well you'll be glad to know that relief is at hand.'

'So you've heard from Matthew?'

'I've heard nothing. You're due a makeover. A young lady will be with you in thirty minutes. She will ring the doorbell twice, and present her credentials.' Percy hung up.

I showered, dried myself and dressed. Well before the thirty minutes was up I was ready and waiting. The grimy net curtain created a barrier between me and the outside world. It was enough to keep me safe from prying eyes, but not from a sniper's infrared scope. It is all very well to think that your window is bulletproof. I've seen what a high-powered, rapid-fire rifle can do. I sat well back and read another few chapters of the thriller. I was beginning to enjoy it.

A small blue Citroen C3 pulled up outside. A young woman got out and hauled a make-up box from the boot of her car. She rang the doorbell twice. I went to the window and rapped once. She produced a warrant card and held it up for me to check. It said her name was Sarah Azizi-Ryan.

I unlocked the door – two deadbolts. She bustled in and set up her kit. Sarah had a finely chiselled nose – probably the work of a skilled plastic surgeon – hazel eyes with a dark rim around the iris, and full lips outlined with a brown lip liner. She wore a scarf over her hair. This might have been for religious reasons, but may just as likely have been to make herself less easily recognisable.

Sarah was familiar with the layout of the flat and in minutes had the bathroom looking like a hairdresser's salon. She got to work quickly, pushing my head back into a basin of warm water. 'You can have a head massage, if you like.' I accepted. The sensation of her lathering up and running her fingertips through my witch's mop of wiry grey hair, caressing my cranial bumps with all the concentration of an octopus flexing its suckers, left me feeling more relaxed than I had been in weeks. For a moment I even stopped pondering over the events that had brought me here. But only for a moment.

I lay back, enjoying this special sense of closeness to another human being.

'Just sit there and relax,' she said. 'I'm going to prepare the colour.'

'Do I get to choose?'

'No. Clients choose tints they are used to. I'm here to create a totally new look.'

'I see,' I replied doubtfully.

'Keep your eyes shut and let me get on with it.'

She ran a comb through my hair, rubbing in a thick substance and letting it set. Then she attacked my roots, dabbing on a dark formulation that soaked through to my scalp.

'We don't want to let your roots grow out white.'

'So that I look like a badger, or a skunk? Never bothers some people.'

'You'll have ten days, two weeks max, before your roots need topping up.'

I hoped I could get everything Matthew needed done before two weeks were up, so I kept my mouth shut.

This became harder to do when she ran a thick comb through my hair, so viciously that it brought tears to my eyes. The relaxing effects of her scalp massage evaporated quickly.

After what seemed an age she washed the dye and fixer out of my hair, gave it a partial blow-dry and started to cut it.

'What are you doing?' I asked.

'You don't want the same haircut, do you?'

I had been getting the same haircut since I retired – chopping it myself, ignoring the split ends – but I saw her point.

'What do you have in mind?'

'Let me surprise you.' She worked for another few minutes and I felt the occasional tug as she hacked away. I sensed a lightness about my shoulders as my straggling, knotted mane dropped away.

'Keep your eyes shut. I'm going to try something.' I felt a pair of glasses being slipped over my nose and ears. I reached up to help her. 'Keep still, I haven't finished.' She dried the last strands of hair, teasing them out around my face.

'You can open your eyes now.'

I stared into the mirror she held before me.

'Good grief! What the…?'

The woman whose face I saw reflected was a perfect stranger. Rich red hair – I believe they call it 'deep 35' – cut short and styled in a sort of bob more suited to a younger woman, over bright yellow and black striped glasses in enormous square frames. Suitably waspish, I thought.

'Looks nothing like me!' I exclaimed.

'That was the brief, wasn't it? I need to do your eyebrows, and then I have some clothes for you to try on.' She removed the glasses – tinted lenses – and began to pluck away. Her actions were bearably painful in a way that made me appreciate her diligence and attention to detail. After a few minutes of tugging she applied a pencil to both eyebrows. She replaced the glasses. Over the frames I saw she had reduced my scraggly grey brows to pencil-thin orange strips. She went to work on my lips.

'Pucker up. When was the last time you kissed somebody?'

'A long time ago, in the way you mean.' I didn't count the baby kisses I showered on little Alice. I puckered my lips.

'Perfect, hold it right there.' She applied a smear of lipstick and rubbed it in. 'A little liner to enhance their shape.'

She stepped back and studied me. 'You know, you must have been quite beautiful when you were young.'

I resisted a barbed comeback and kept my scarlet lips buttoned.

'Okay, we're done here. Now stand up and follow me.' I was beginning to enjoy myself. I hadn't employed a disguise since I'd left the service. They had all worked well enough for their purpose. But what this young lady had done for me was quite extraordinary. She reached into a bulging shopping bag and pulled out a bright red quilted jacket. 'This should be your size.'

I tried it on. 'I can't go out like this,' I said, staring at myself in the mirror. 'I'll stand out a mile.'

'But not as yourself. I've got a couple more outfits for you. Try these first.' She produced a pair of green trousers and dark slip-on shoes with gold reflective squares. 'I got these in two sizes. This is the larger pair.'

I tried them on. They were a little loose but I preferred them that way. Tight shoes are better for running in, but who wants to stand in them for hours on end?

'I'm giving you a couple of changes of clothes, all bright stuff like this. Also a sober outfit you can slip into, and a couple of wigs. Don't try them on now, or I'll have to redo your hair. The wigs are loose fitting and should work fine in an emergency.' I had put on the trousers and looked like some refugee from a New York fashion show. 'Just one thing, a photograph.'

'Is that wise?'

'It's for you to hold onto, so you can recreate your look. I'll leave the eyebrow pen and lipstick. You'll need them. Now give me a pose.'

I struck the sort of thing I thought she was after: a fashion model's pose – left foot forward, hand on arched hip.

'You'll find yourself on the cover of *Silver Surfer* with that pose, but you wouldn't want that for a record. I meant straight on. A mug shot, for easy reference.'

I straightened up and faced her. She produced a polaroid camera. I hadn't seen one of those for years, but we had often used them in the field in the last century. 'Last century' – that made it seem so long ago. The camera flashed. She watched the photograph develop.

'Shit, it's solarised,' she exclaimed. 'That's the problem with these things. Old photographic stock.' Faintly embarrassed, she slipped the polaroid into her bag. 'Don't want that hanging about.' She fired off another. It rolled out of the camera and she gave it a few seconds to develop. 'Perfect.' She handed it over.

'You've done a marvellous job. My own children wouldn't recognise me.'

'Well don't put it to the test. Should you need a top-up or more clothes, get in touch through the usual channel.' She gathered up her things and left.

I entered the bedroom and studied myself in the full-length mirror set in the wardrobe door. She had cleverly given my red hair some highlights, which made it look a really professional job, not something an old lady hiding out in a safe house might have done for herself. I slipped the polaroid photograph under a sheet of paper lining a shelf and, checking first that nobody was watching out on the street, headed for the front door, stepped outside and locked it behind me.

6

'WITH ONE BOUND SHE WAS free.' A sentence familiar to those of us who enjoyed romantic novels when we were schoolgirls. As I skipped down the steps to the street I found those words liberating. This wasn't the first time I had been locked up with no idea if I would ever again be free, but the last time it had been done by enemies of the state. To be locked up by your own colleagues and countrymen, in your own capital, albeit for your own safety, can leave you with a profound sense of despondency.

I strode towards Ladbroke Grove to catch a bus. I realised I had no money and no means of communication. I could not use my own bank and credit cards, nor my own phone. They could all be traced. Nor could I use any travel card in my own name, or at least in the name I had been living under for so many years. But I had a plan. One I had prepared years ago.

I joined the queue for the 52 bus southbound to Victoria. I only had to wait a minute before one appeared in the distance. All I needed was a way to pay my fare.

An elderly but active couple marched from a newsagent's and pushed to the front of the queue. People who had been waiting patiently bristled, but nobody uttered a word of complaint. Seeing the bus approaching, the elderly couple produced their Freedom Passes.

If there's one thing that annoys me, it's bad manners. Especially in people who think they are entitled to better treatment than anyone else.

As the bus pulled up and the doors opened I jostled forward, propelling the elderly man into the back of his wife. As he turned to glare at me I eased his Freedom Pass out of his hand without him noticing.

'No need to shove,' he grumbled, adjusting his blazer. But I had already boarded. I swiped his pass across the reader, which pinged green, and strode towards the rear, deftly flicking the pass out through the central door. His wife stopped at a bench marked 'Priority seats for people who are disabled, pregnant or less able to stand'. A young Italian couple was already ensconced. 'That's a priority seat,' the elderly woman snapped, 'get up.' She looked every bit as able to stand as I was.

The Italians, barely understanding her words, but in no doubt of their meaning, abandoned their seats. The girl was on crutches and had to be helped by her male companion. She hobbled over to the space where people prop their buggies. 'That's more like it,' crowed the woman. She placed her bag on the seat beside her to prevent anyone else from using it. 'Brian!' she called to her husband, dithering at the front of the bus, 'what's keeping you?'

'Can't find my Freedom Pass,' he bleated. 'This blighter won't let me on the bus without it.'

'Ignore him and take a seat.'

The bus driver produced his phone.

'If I don't get off he's going to call the police!' Brian got off the bus.

'But I've already swiped my pass!' his wife exclaimed. She stepped out through the central door and spotted the pass in the road. 'Look,' she exclaimed, 'there it is, you stupid old man!' As she bent to reclaim it the driver shut the bus doors and drove off down Ladbroke Grove. There was a general grunt of satisfaction from the other passengers as the young Italians reclaimed their priority seats.

Thirty minutes later I dismounted at Victoria and headed for a shabby Edwardian office block off Wilton Street. I rang the doorbell and was buzzed inside. The lift was listed as 'out of order' – its usual status – so I climbed the three flights of stairs and marched down the ill-lit corridor towards a thick oak door. I stopped beside a row of battered and dusty filing cabinets. I reached behind the cabinet labelled *E–J*. My hand touched something cold and metallic. I withdrew the key I had concealed there more than five years ago, anticipating that one day I would need it. That day had come. I knocked on the door.

A grill slid open. A wizened old woman peered out.

'Can I help you?'

'Box 374'.

'You have your key?'

I held up the key for her to see. I possessed an identical one, still in its hiding place in my cottage.

The woman handed me a slip of paper. I signed a name on it – not my own, of course, but the one registered in this establishment. I pushed the slip through to her. She took it and shut the grill. After a few seconds I heard a series of locks turning, followed by a heavy bolt being drawn across. The door swung open and I stepped inside.

Victoria Safe Deposit has been in existence almost since the day Victoria station began operating in 1868. Originally its premises had been within the station itself but, as the station expanded, the business moved to various addresses nearby, finally settling in its present location in 1908. It had hardly changed since then. Nor, it seemed, had the staff. Modern safe depositories had sprung up in Knightsbridge and Mayfair. This one had stayed much the same as always. It had lost out on the big new clients, but retained its old ones who preferred to store their wills, deeds and documents under the guardianship of familiar faces.

I was in a small anteroom. The only concession to the march of time was the CCTV camera set high above a second door – this one of solid steel and better reinforced.

The old woman turned the locks in the oak door through which I had entered, concealing her actions with her bowed body. There were five locks in all, but she only turned four. I understood her method. Anyone attempting to overcome her, steal something and escape in a hurry would, in all probability, turn all five locks, thereby inadvertently securing one lock and ensuring they were trapped. Sorting through the twenty or so keys on the woman's key ring would, in any case, delay any miscreant.

'You may go in.' She pressed a buzzer as I stepped up to the steel door. With a soft click the door sprang open. I entered a room about seven metres by five. Waiting was a withered little man – he might have been the old woman's brother. 'Good morning,' he said – it was still a few minutes before noon – 'if you have your key ready, we may proceed.'

He was already standing by box 374. We inserted our keys in the twin locks and turned them simultaneously. A metal panel sprang open to reveal my box inside.

'I shall leave you now,' the old man said. 'Press the buzzer when you are ready to leave.' He disappeared through the steel door and I heard it lock.

I set my box on a table and checked the contents: an envelope containing £5,000 in used banknotes, mostly twenties; a similar number of euro banknotes, an EU British passport in the name of Eleanor Farquhar, a French one in the name of Delphine Fabricant and a German one in the name of Helga Schmidt. The French and German passport photographs, one with dyed black hair and the other with silver locks, did not resemble my current appearance, of course. But Eleanor's hair was dark and closer in cut to my current bobbed style – I had worn a wig for the photograph – so I selected the British and French passports – I could always dye Delphine's hair if need be – and left the German one in the box. I took Eleanor Farquhar's driving licence, her London Freedom Pass and a credit card in her name, and identical items in the name of Delphine Fabricant. There were several other documents and proofs of identity, but I left them in the safe box. I took two Oyster cards for bus and tube travel, both in completely different names, a small notebook with two telephone numbers on the first leaf, and an old burner iPhone together with its charger. I plugged it into a wall socket and allowed it to charge.

I counted out £3,000 in cash, two thousand euros, and left the rest. For a rainy day? This *was* a rainy day, wasn't it? Well, no matter how bad things are, they can always get worse.

I shut the box, slid it back into the vault and locked it. I checked the charge on the phone. It was barely adequate, but it would have to do. I pressed the buzzer. The little old man reappeared through a hidden door set in the panelling. Did he have a separate entrance for the room from which he had emerged or had he passed through several doors in turn? Either way, this was a firetrap of the worst order and one day the health and safety people would force them to install a separate escape route.

With both passports, credit cards and my bank notes safely hidden about my person I walked from Victoria towards Sloane Square. I was pleasantly surprised by the sense of freedom my new identity gave me. Eleanor Farquhar was, I decided, a bright and optimistic person, full of goodwill to all mankind.

'Eleanor' smiled beneficently at young couples in the street. She said 'hello' and 'good day' to families with children and babies. She encouraged handsome young men to stop the traffic and help her cross the street.

This bonhomie came to an abrupt stop when 'Eleanor' crossed Sloane Square. I had only gone a few yards along the King's Road when I noticed a familiar figure striding into Blacklands Terrace. I hurried after Bernard, my son, recently appointed Secretary of State for Defence, who disappeared into the John Sandoe bookshop. I could not resist following him inside.

John Sandoe (Books) Ltd is one of the last independent bookstores in London. Started with, reportedly, 'three planks laid on bricks', it has spread up, down and sideways, to become a rabbit warren of stairs, corridors and book-laden shelves. It consists of three small shops – perhaps once cottages on the Blacklands Farm estate – all linked together. I entered the door at number eleven and passed the main counter in time to see Bernard heading up rickety steps to the floor above. I followed as silently as I could. The stairs creaked, but there were enough customers to cover my approach.

When I reached the top of the stairs it took me a moment to see where Bernard had gone. I headed towards the floor's southern end and found Bernard deep in conversation with another man. I was able to make out a few words.

'I need you to find out the source. Put a stop to it now,' Bernard was saying. He stopped talking the moment he saw they were no longer alone.

They were, I was amused to notice, standing directly in front of a display of James Bond thrillers: *Goldfinger*, *Dr No*, *Thunderball*, *Octopussy* and *The Living Daylights*. I had no idea there was still a healthy market for the works of Ian Fleming.

'Excuse me, could you pass me that Antonia Fraser please?' I spoke very clearly, with the cut-glass diction I had abandoned in my twenties.

Bernard's companion, tall, thin, with a receding hairline, selected the book and handed it over. I kept my face turned away from Bernard as I studied the book's cover. '*A Splash of Red*… not what I'm looking for, thank you.' I handed the book back as if Bernard's companion were a member of staff. He glanced at the cover and slipped it back on the shelf. I moved off towards the southern staircase. When I was out of sight I waited and listened. A woman who had been browsing nearby approached them.

'Wasn't that…?' she asked.

'Who?' asked Bernard's tall companion.

'That actress, the famous one.'

Bernard and the tall man said nothing.

'She played Catherine the Great. I know her name it's… Helen… Helen Merton.'

'Mirren,' corrected Bernard.

'That's the one.'

'I didn't see,' he replied, cutting off further exchange.

It's not unpleasant to be compared to a famous and, I might say, glamorous film star. It's true that we have similar eyes, but there the similarity ends. I could not imagine Ms Mirren dyeing her hair a deep vermillion except in the interests of a film.

I made my way down the stairs and hung around the counter as if I needed help. There were two elderly women taking an inordinate time to pay for their books, and I was happy to wait. One woman was writing out a cheque. The assistant behind the counter rolled her eyes in despair. She would have to make a special trip to pay the cheque into a bank – if she could find one that was still in business – but this was Chelsea, and full of rich old ladies with chequebooks, so it probably wasn't as out of the ordinary as all that.

Floorboards creaked overhead. Bernard and the tall man came down together. Bernard left through the front door. The tall man continued on down to the basement. I doubled back and descended the south staircase, curious. I was not concerned at being seen. If the tall man fancied another glimpse of 'Helen Mirren', he was welcome. I was basking in the triumphant glow of going unrecognised in public by my own son. Some Secretary for Defence he was.

There was no sign of the tall man, just a wood-panelled door marked *Staff Only*. I was certain he was not a member of staff. I picked up a picture book and flicked through the pages with one hand. With the other I set the camera on my burner phone to record video. A young man, hurrying down the stairs, stumbled slightly and regained his footing. He entered the staff room.

The door was on a slow spring, set to self-close. As I moved past I held up the phone to capture the inside of the room before the door slammed shut.

Once outside in the street I replayed the footage. The staff door had only been open for three seconds or less, but in that time the camera had caught the tall man stepping out from behind some shelves and furtively passing something to the young man. The door shut before I could see what it was. I wondered what Bernard was playing at when he should be in his office. It was none of my business, of course, but I'm a curious old bird and my training and instincts are to enquire and to investigate. I went to a phone box and called the number I had for Matthew.

'Where are you calling from?' he demanded. When I explained that I was no longer in hiding, he expressed exasperation. 'You're not safe. It's essential that you remain out of danger.'

When I told him I had no intention of being cooped up any longer, he realised there was no point arguing.

'You'd better come over and meet the others.' He gave me an address and swiftly cut me off before I could ask who these 'others' were.

7

THIRTY MINUTES LATER I WAS striding through Marylebone, searching for an address in Devonshire Mews South. I had swept out of Great Portland Street tube station and made my way at a brisk pace heading along Devonshire Street. Almost immediately on my right was the turning into Devonshire Mews North, so I crossed to the mews directly opposite. I expected this to be Devonshire Mews South. I was wrong. This was a maze named Devonshire Close. I resumed walking west along Devonshire Street, crossed Harley Street and found Devonshire Mews West, which ran… north. Opposite it I at last discovered what I was looking for: Devonshire Mews South. Somebody at the Howard de Walden Estate, owner of this large chunk of Marylebone, needed to get their compass out and rename their mews streets, fast.

I do not like to be the last to arrive. It puts one at a psychological disadvantage. I almost broke into a trot as I hurried down the mews. I forced myself to slow down and steady my breathing. I approached one of the last doors on the right, rang the video doorbell and waited. Almost immediately a woman's recorded voice answered, 'Can I help you?' I spoke the six-digit number which Matthew had given me. The door swung open and I stepped inside.

I found myself in an empty room lined with bookshelves. Stairs rose to the floor above. I called out, 'Hello?' There was no reply. I heard a soft click and a section of bookshelf swung open. Through the opening I saw a similar room and, at its centre, a table. Around it sat four people, three of whom I knew. One was Matthew himself.

'My dear,' he said, 'I would never have recognised you. Red hair. So very fetching. Do come in.'

I stepped through into the adjoining house – the wall between the two had been knocked through and dressed with bookshelves – and took my seat at the table.

'You know Ambrose of course.' I acknowledged my old colleague Ambrose Flynn, who stood to greet me with a peck on the cheek. We had first worked together in Athens in the mid 1980s, and several times since. Later he had served as quartermaster to many of us in the field – those currently operating and, in my case, those long retired. None of the others present knew that Ambrose and I had joined forces only a few weeks earlier, and that Ambrose had seen fit to execute an old comrade of mine. This righteous act had created a powerful and secret bond between us.

'And Jonathan Raikes,' Matthew continued. He indicated the man opposite me. Raikes had been my colleague in Cairo in the early 1980s and we had enjoyed a good relationship. But we never worked together again after the untimely assassination of the Egyptian president, Anwar Sadat, soon after he had signed a ground-breaking peace accord with Israel's prime minister, Menachem Begin. This treaty had earned Sadat the undying hatred of those who believed he had betrayed his country.

In October 1981 Khalid Al-Islambuli, an Egyptian military officer, approached Sadat during a victory parade, produced three grenades from under his helmet and hurled them at his intended victim.

The grenades must have been manufactured locally, for only one exploded, and it had fallen short. Gunmen sprayed the stands with machine-gun fire. Several diplomats were killed. Sadat himself died in hospital later that day.

Our ambassador Michael Weir, seated directly behind Sadat, escaped injury. This led to suspicions that the British were behind the plot. Total nonsense. If we had been responsible, I would have ensured that the grenades – Russian-made, of course, to put people off our track – were in full working order, and that our ambassador was seated nowhere near the intended target.

It had been our duty to monitor and analyse all communications relating to potential terrorist attacks and insurrection. In this Raikes and I had failed badly. Only after the event did we discover that Khalid Al-Islambuli had circulated details of his plot on rice paper, easily swallowed and digested. The whole mess had been an embarrassment, to say the least.

No blame was attached to us, not officially at any rate. But we both received a thorough bollocking, not to put too fine a point on it. In those deeply sexist days the man was assumed to hold command and any female was regarded as his subordinate. It hadn't been like that, of course. We were both equally responsible. But Raikes' subsequent posting to Ulan Bator in Mongolia, one of the coldest cities in the world, was hardly a promotion. I got off more lightly. I was assigned a tedious desk job back in London and then, when they felt I had been punished enough, sent on a variety of short and relatively uneventful missions, leading up to my posting to sunny Athens.

That had been the last I had seen of Raikes until today. I greeted him as an old friend. He greeted me coldly. Ulan Bator's chill still held him in its grip.

Sitting beside Raikes was a large woman.

'This', Matthew continued, 'is Bella Walsingham. I don't believe you've met.'

We hadn't, but Bella's reputation preceded her. She had a reputation of being a one-woman think-tank: someone who advised the government and the security services when they had a particularly sticky problem. A modern day Mycroft Holmes, they called her. She claimed descent from Sir Francis Walsingham, Queen Elizabeth I's spymaster. I once looked him up and discovered that Sir Francis had left no male heirs, so perhaps Bella's connection was pure fabrication. But Francis Walsingham had had a daughter, and perhaps his brother's heir had married a distant cousin. I was willing to accept Bella at face value, which was high.

She gave me a sharp nod and a smile.

'I hope you will forgive me,' Matthew continued, 'but I felt it was for the best that I inform the others of the unfortunate circumstances of your recent incarceration.'

Well, I thought, he could have put it more delicately. Or better still, not mentioned it at all. Narrowly avoiding death by a sniper's bullet – not that it was the first time in my life – was annoying enough without having it broadcast to all and sundry. I felt like a woman being informed that she had the back of her skirt tucked in her knickers. That was bad enough, but having it pointed out in public was so much worse.

I glared at Matthew but he was oblivious to my feelings. Typical.

Matthew took his seat beside Bella. He opened a folder and passed four sets of documents around the table. Each was stamped with the letters FYEO: For Your Eyes Only. 'First item.'

We dutifully turned to the first item. At the top of the page was stamped: OPERATION H.

The front page consisted of a summary of what Matthew had already told me. A British embassy staff member had been betrayed and killed in Athens back in the 1980s. His betrayer had never been identified nor his assassin apprehended. Attached to this was a list of staff working at the British embassy at the time.

I studied the list and committed it to memory. It was headed by the Ambassador, followed by the Deputy Head of Mission, then the Economic Counsellor, the First and Second Secretaries, starting with the Head of Chancery, down through Commercial and Information, then the naval, military and air attachés, followed by an administration officer and an archivist. These were all British. Ambrose, Matthew and I were all on the list – even though my presence had been kept off official records – and so was the name of the person who had been murdered.

Added to this list were locally engaged Greek nationals, who made up the rest of the embassy staff. Including secretaries, drivers, admin and maintenance, the total numbered some forty individuals.

There was a second list of agents who had been operating in Greece at that time. Most of them had been working undercover and had been recruited from the local population. Three of the names were redacted.

'What's the point of giving us a list with the names redacted?' barked Bella.

'*Some* names, only. These people, old as they may be, are still active in the field. You will be given their names when and if all the others are eliminated from suspicion.'

'And in the meantime, they have time to cover their tracks.' This was Ambrose.

Matthew sighed. 'You don't know they are on the list. And they don't know that they are on it either.'

'What's the second item?' I asked.

'There is no second item. Not until we have eliminated all these names. Those still living, at any rate. Ladies and gentleman, this is an unofficial mission. But it has been sanctioned from on high.' Matthew paused. He had always liked to sound important, and I could sense he was enjoying being back in the fray. Indeed, we all were.

'A word of warning,' he continued, 'if you believe you are close to identifying the mole, let me know immediately. It is essential that he or she does not know that they have been exposed. Leave that to the higher authorities.' He paused again, looking each of us in the eyes in turn. 'I need hardly remind you that all this is entirely *entre nous* and is not to be discussed with anyone outside this room, under any circumstances. You will report directly to me and to no one else. Understood?'

We all understood and agreed.

The meeting was short and to the point. The others were each given one name from the list to investigate.

'Felicity,' Matthew continued, 'will be working from home.'

I was stunned. 'What on earth do you think I can achieve cooped up in there?'

'When it comes down to it, you may very well be the key to solving this puzzle. And I mean to keep you safe until we do.'

That was true enough. I had been close to the murdered

victim. Indeed I had probably known him better than anyone else.

'There's just one problem,' I said to Matthew as we parted.

'What would that be?'

'I need a computer, broadband connection and access to all relevant documents.'

'Of course you do. I'm surprised you haven't found your computer already.'

'My computer? Where?'

'Telling you would make it too easy. But it shouldn't take long to work it out.'

8

I LEFT DEVONSHIRE MEWS SOUTH with a deep sense of frustration and foreboding. Matthew had been quite obtuse – or should I say opaque? He had provided each of us with a name from his list, each of us, that is, except me. I was to return to the safe house and wait. Wait for what? And how could I be of any use? My skills were honed for use in the field. Matthew said I would find a computer, but my ability to wield one, other than as a weapon to brain someone – was at best adequate, no more.

As I headed west along Weymouth Street I had a distinct feeling that I was being followed. I crossed Marylebone High Street and caught a glimpse of someone behind me reflected in the window of the Oxfam shop opposite. Experience and instinct alerted me: the pace of a passer-by and that of a pursuer are quite different. I dashed into Moxon Street, scurried past The Marylebone pub, the expensive Fromagerie and the Ginger Pig butcher, then ducked right into Garbutt Place. I broke into a trot – a run would have been undignified and well-near impossible, my legs are not what they were – passing the blue plaque honouring the educator Octavia Hill. Anyone unfamiliar with Garbutt Place would see the high iron gate at the far end and mistake it for a dead end. But there was a hidden alley, Grotto Passage, which angled off it. I hurried through a paved courtyard, and took a sharp right, passing the Grotto Ragged and Industrial Schools (established 1846). The alley narrowed to no more than the width of a human body. I emerged into the sunlight of Paddington Street. I crossed over and entered Opso, the Greek restaurant on the corner, and under the pretence of booking a table for lunch, took my time observing the narrow exit of Grotto Passage for signs of my pursuer. The restaurant beside the exit was a branch of The Real Greek. It seemed appropriate that the day's Greek theme was continuing.

I first asked the manager to reserve a table for two, then changed it to four, then asked for a restaurant business card and promised that I would, in due course, ring and confirm. In the three or four minutes I delayed there, the only creature to emerge from Grotto Passage was a disreputable-looking tomcat with a torn ear, which sat in the sun and licked its bottom. Satisfied that I was not being followed I continued on into Luxborough Street and reached the Marylebone Road. I strode west, opposite the cream facade of Madame Tussauds and the green dome of what used to be the London Planetarium, until I reached the Baker Street tube station entrance at the top of Chiltern Street. I passed through the gate and managed to catch the Hammersmith-bound train on the point of departure.

The carriage was almost empty. An announcement came over the tannoy that the train was being held at the station. After about a minute the sonalert warned that the doors were about to close. Just as they did so a figure squeezed through the doors and plonked itself right beside me. It was an old trick, and one I had used myself in the past, but I was annoyed to be caught out that way by Jonathan Raikes.

'I lost you at Moxon Street, but I guessed that if I headed for the tube station I might catch you.'

'I thought we were not on "speakers",' I replied, somewhat frostily.

'That's what the others believed, so I felt it best we keep up the show. I bear you absolutely no grudge for what happened in Egypt. The failure was entirely mine and I've done all I can over the years to make up for it.'

The train moved off noisily. As we were out of earshot of the other passengers, most of whom were listening to music or watching videos on their phones, we spoke openly.

'What do you think of the situation?' Raikes continued.

'You three have each got a person to investigate. I get to sit hunched over a computer for hours on end.'

'It's a lot safer.'

'And bloody boring.'

'What the three of us are doing is dangerous. People don't like being investigated. Even the innocent ones.'

'Why did you follow me?' I asked. 'Something is bothering you.' Something was definitely bothering me, but I couldn't quite put my finger on it.

'Matthew is playing a long game, only giving each of us one name at a time. Why can't we all put our heads together and figure this out as a group?'

'I would have thought that was obvious.'

A smile twisted his lips. 'You mean he's gathered four of the smartest agents together to investigate a possible mole… who could very well be one of them?'

'It could quite easily be one of us.'

Raikes turned towards me with a wicked smile and whispered, 'Is it you?'

'Well, I know it wasn't you, stuck in Central Mongolia.'

'Don't remind me. Worst years of my life.'

We reached Edgware Road. Some passengers got off, others got on. None of them sat near us. We waited until the train moved off. Raikes spoke first.

'Aren't we all a bit old for this sort of thing?'

'Speak for yourself.'

'Ambrose seems past it.'

'Don't let him fool you. He's sharp as a Tojiro knife. He was Matthew's superior in Athens.'

'And now Matthew's calling the shots. Doesn't that seem odd?'

'Matthew took some big gambles in his career, but he came up smelling of roses. He's exactly the sort of person they would put in charge.'

'Yes. He's had instructions from the very top.' He sat and thought for a moment. 'Well if it is one of us, Matthew's taking a very big risk. It could all backfire horribly. It's not you and me I'm worried about. It's the other two. I don't know anything about them.'

'I can vouch for Ambrose.'

'And Bella Walsingham?'

'Her credentials are impeccable.' Even as I said so an element of doubt crept into my mind.

'Four people dragged out of retirement to help solve a thirty-five-year-old mystery.' He shook his head.

'Do any of us really retire?' Ambrose certainly hadn't, though he had been drawing his official pension for years. And the same must have been true for Matthew. 'We are all ready to return to the fray if we're needed. And the truth is, being needed is the one thing we miss in our lives.'

Raikes nodded. 'You're right. The fact is, I am rather

enjoying it all. I know we were told not to, but I think you and I should stay in touch.'

I saw no good reason to disagree, so I gave him my landline number. I had discovered it by the simple expedient of dialling 17070 from the line itself. A woman's recorded voice had recited my number to me.

'Thank you. This is my stop.'

We had reached Paddington. The moment the doors opened Raikes disappeared into the waiting crowd. A few people got off, many more boarded, wheeling on suitcases with their Heathrow labels still attached.

A male passenger took the seat beside me and spent his journey talking loudly to himself. That's the impression he gave. In fact, he was engaged in a telephone conversation with his Apple AirPods wedged firmly in his ears. Most of his call consisted of informing the person on the other end of the line that he was on the tube, and yelling that they should speak up, as the carriage was noisy. Of course it was; he was the one making the noise.

Eventually, on the pretext of searching my handbag, I nudged him hard in the ribs. He extracted a pod from one ear and demanded, 'What's your problem?'

I turned to him. 'Alexander Graham Bell created the telephone so that people could speak to each other over long distances without having to shout at the top of their voices. You appear to have missed the purpose of his invention entirely.'

He was about to respond when I continued, 'If you held your phone up to your ear and spoke in a normal tone of voice, nobody would object.'

'Nobody else is complaining.'

A large man opposite leant forward. 'Why don't you effing shut up and give the rest of us some peace and quiet?'

Our tormentor sulkily reinserted his AirPod and selected some music on his phone. The way he suddenly jerked back his head indicated that it was playing at full volume. He clawed at his ears, extracted the pods, turned his music down and stared at the floor. When I alighted at Ladbroke Grove he gave me an injured, accusative look as if his discomfort had been all my fault.

I walked down to street level and strode briskly south towards my flat. As I turned the corner I stopped sharp. The street was blocked with fire engines and police cars.

A duty policeman was doing his best to direct the gathering crowd.

'Nothing to see here. There's nothing to see here.'

There clearly was something to see. An ambulance, blue lights flashing, blocked the middle of the street. From the basement next to mine came two paramedics, carrying a gurney between them. On it was a body, its face covered. A straggle of wiry grey hair poked out from under the blanket. I experienced a horrible feeling of déjà vu: another poor old lady mistakenly murdered in place of me.

As they loaded the body into the back of the ambulance the blanket fell away to reveal the victim's face. It was an old man with a mass of thick hair and a beard stained yellow with nicotine. Inwardly, I sighed with relief.

Police were knocking on doors, asking if the residents had seen anything suspicious. So perhaps this was a case of suspected arson. Or maybe something designed to flush me out. A man pushed past the duty policeman. 'I live in this street,' he said. 'I need to get home.' I followed close on his heels, as if I were with him. The policeman, young and inexperienced, let us pass. The pushy man went up the steps of a house on the north side, diagonally opposite my safe house. I carried on walking. The fire was no business of mine. I did not hurry – that would have attracted attention. I disappeared into a group of rubber-necking neighbours. A dead body is guaranteed to bring out the gawpers.

As I continued on to the far end of the crescent I glanced back. That was when I spotted him. A man sitting in the driver's seat of a parked car. A man with two prominent moles on his cheek. I had seen him just a few weeks earlier, planting a bloodied car jack in my chest of drawers, captured on the CCTV in my cottage. He was looking in his rear-view mirror, observing the police, and had failed to see me. He was bound to fail. He was watching for an old lady with unkempt white hair.

How had he traced me here? Only Percy and Matthew knew my whereabouts. A cold sensation hit me. Could either of them have betrayed me? The two people in whom I had placed my entire trust… Then I realised that others also knew my location: the 'Amazon' delivery man who had got me to sign the official secrets document, Sarah Azizi-Ryan, who had given me my makeover. Perhaps there was a whole back room of assistants who knew exactly where I was. A safe house is not always as safe as it seems.

Then I realised that it was probably I who had led him here. He could have traced my phone right up to the moment I had switched it off. He would not know my exact address. Nor that I had spotted him and knew exactly who he was. I held the advantage, for the time being.

A loud siren startled me. The ambulance had pulled out past the double-parked line of police cars but 'two moles', as I named him, was blocking it. The duty policeman stepped up to wave him forward. My would-be assassin started his car and moved off, turning left at the crossroads. The ambulance overtook him and sped away, its siren blaring.

I considered my options. If I returned to the safe house I would be noticed and questioned by the police. What had I seen? Who was I? How long had I been living there? Could I prove it? Another option would be to enter the house by climbing the wall round the back. Out of the question – my safe house was impregnable. The third, and best, option was to wait it out.

I headed round to the next street, then crossed Ladbroke Grove and strode off to Portobello Road to potter about the market. As I passed Electric House – a private club whose members work in the media – I contemplated entering and claiming that I was Helen Mirren with an appointment to meet some upcoming director. A bit of creative thinking always helps when dealing with tricky situations. But what if Dame Helen was already in the club? It was a possibility. Instead, I crossed to the east side and bought mushrooms – porcini and chanterelles – from the man on the corner stall. He also sold large flat-cap mushrooms beside which he had scrawled the word 'Portabello' in white chalk on a blackboard.

'That's a spelling mistake, young man,' I informed him.

He looked at me blankly. Some stallholders put apostrophes on their labels: 'grape's, pineapple's, etc.,' to attract pedants like me who, having pointed out their grammatical mistakes, felt obliged to buy more of the stallholders' produce than they required. But this man needed correcting.

'It says Portabello mushrooms,' he answered in a surly manner, 'because that's what they are.'

'Well,' I replied, 'if you care to turn your head just a little you will see a street sign on the wall behind you, which gives you the Kensington and Chelsea Council's version of the spelling.' There was a very prominent street sign reading 'Portobello Road'. 'The council and I are in complete agreement on the matter.'

He made no answer, but when I passed by again some fifteen minutes later, the mis-spelt word had been scrubbed out and 'Portobella' scrawled over it.

At other stalls I bought onions and sourdough bread. After popping into Tesco for double cream I headed back to the house.

I was lucky. The police convoy had gone and the crowd had dispersed. There really was nothing to see here. The duty policeman was ringing doorbells and questioning neighbours. The street formed a convex crescent so as soon as he reached the next building he was out of sight. I entered my safe house and locked and bolted the door behind me.

I searched the flat carefully, Matthew's words ringing in my ears. What was it he had said when I asked about a computer? 'I'm surprised you haven't found it already.'

There was nothing in the main room to give me a clue. I went into the bedroom and studied the almost empty bookshelf. I was reminded of Matthew's long bookcase. There were only the three books here. None of them concealed a hidden lever. I started at the left corner and worked my way to the right, tapping all along the woodwork. It wasn't until I'd got a third of the way along that the shelving shifted. It was almost imperceptible, but it definitely moved inwards a couple of millimetres. I gave it a sharp push, there was a click, and it swung open towards me, revealing a desk with a computer and a router, together with a small office chair and several foolscap notebooks with pens. I switched on the router, gave it a moment to connect and then started up the Apple MacBook Pro. It demanded a password to unlock it.

That was all I needed: wrestling with possible passwords until the computer shut me out. Then I saw it. A small note slipped under the laptop. On it were the initials IBDJDOB. Eliminating the DOB, or date of birth, I guessed that IBDJ referred to Ioseb Besarionis dze Jughashvili, the birth name of the Soviet leader Joseph Stalin.

The date of birth of that murderous bastard was 18 December 1878. I typed 181278. The laptop failed to open. I tried again, this time including the year in full: 18121878. The laptop remained locked. What was I doing wrong?

I sat and pondered. Matthew loved to play cryptic games. I had got the date right, I was certain of that. Perhaps there was something wrong in the way I had entered the figures. In a flash I remembered. When Stalin had been born, many Eastern European countries – including Georgia, his birthplace – still followed the old Julian calendar, not the Gregorian one we use today. That meant that Stalin was born on the 6th, rather than the 18th of December. I typed 061278 and the laptop opened its secrets up to me.

There was a single email waiting. It contained a number of links. I hesitated before opening them. Any link could harbour a virus. Well, so what? The laptop wasn't mine, so it wasn't my problem, was it?

The links led to several useful sites. Some connected directly to the Foreign Office and the SIS, or MI6 as it is commonly known. How Matthew had managed to secure access to these was beyond my comprehension. He clearly had some very powerful connections. The first thing I did was to open the Athens files for 1984.

9

Greece, 1984

I HAD FLOWN INTO ATHENS on 29 February 1984. It was a Wednesday, which gave me a couple of days to get the hang of embassy protocols and the weekend to familiarise myself with the city's geography. I had been to Athens before, of course, but then I had been on missions to other countries, such as Cyprus during their war with the Turks in 1974, and I had never enjoyed more than a brief stopover in the ancient capital itself.

Nobody met me at the airport, which proved to be par for the course. I had been given the position of secretary to a relatively junior official in the embassy. In reality, this was no more than a pretext. Just as well, as my shorthand was terrible.

I found a taxi and gave the driver instructions to take me to the Athens Hilton, situated a few hundred metres from the British Embassy. I always travel light and only carried a small suitcase with me. The driver set off in a westerly direction. I sensed he was doing his best to increase the journey time and his fee.

'This isn't the way to the Hilton,' I said.

'There is big traffic jam at Kolonaki,' he insisted. 'I save you time. You are tourist, no? I show you nice sights.'

'I work for Interpol. I am investigating taxi drivers who rip off foreign tourists.'

Without another word the driver executed a hard U-turn into oncoming traffic and joined the tree-lined avenue heading into the city. As we approached the centre I saw no sign of his 'traffic jam' – just the usual snarl-ups and congestion you expect in a city that size. We made it to the Hilton in fifteen minutes flat. I handed over the drachmas for the journey and added a substantial tip. Suspecting a trap, the driver refused the tip, which was a first for me anywhere in the world.

I set off for the embassy. It was a warm, breezy day and the bright sky held no hint of the smog that would cloud the city from late spring through to mid-autumn.

There is something about Athens that always raises the spirits. Perhaps it is the pride the Greeks have in their history, perhaps it is their joyful enthusiasm for life and all it brings them, be it happiness or tragedy. As I approached the embassy I could make out the magnificent Parthenon atop the Athens Acropolis. When a nation's architects design and construct such beautiful buildings, when its sculptors create such wonderful works from simple blocks of marble, and when you count among your ancestors the likes of Archimedes, Pythagoras, Plato, Socrates and Aristotle you have reason to be proud.

Mind you, it's a lot to live up to. It was hard, as I approached the embassy, to recognise those great philosophers and scientists represented in the faces of sweaty drivers angrily hooting in their overheated cars. Besides, few of those great thinkers ever fathered children, so perhaps the modern Greek is descended from quite different ancestry altogether.

The original embassy building, which remains the British ambassador's residence, is probably the finest neoclassical house in Athens. Its garden is an oasis of calm in a hectic city of smog and hooting horns. I was headed for neither the residence nor the garden. Instead I presented myself at the more modern block next door, completed in 1968. I entered through the consular entrance as if I were an ordinary tourist enquiring about a visa. In those days there was nothing like the security we endure today. Which was a shame, considering the events that were to come.

A doorman held open the door, checked my passport and indicated that I should join a queue.

It was all very different from the first time I had visited. Back in 1969 it had been crowded with young people in colourful, flower-patterned clothes. The Brits were complaining that their belongings – sleeping bags, guitars and political books – had all been confiscated, while the Americans were applying for visas to Britain, so they could pursue free love and get themselves laid. The women were long-haired and wore tasselled waistcoats of faux leather, beads and sunglasses. The young men had been shorn of their locks, as evidenced by their pale white or fierce red, sunburned necks. After travelling through liberal France, Italy and Yugoslavia, they had encountered the repressive regime of the Greek military junta. They would have been given two options: bugger off back to whence they had come or submit themselves to the mercies of a military barber and his electric clippers. The colonels who made up the junta needed tourists to boost the state coffers, but under their own terms. Free love and hippie hair had to be abandoned at the border.

This day in 1984 the hall was full of sedate, elderly couples who had, somehow or other, encountered problems with their visas.

Instead of joining the queue I leant forward and whispered the words, 'I'm here to see Mr Flynn—'

The doorman reacted as if a firework had gone off inside his head. 'Of course, ma'am,' he gasped, before I had even finished speaking. 'I shall fetch someone right away.'

Flynn was what was known in British embassies as 'the friend'. This was a euphemism for the Secret Intelligent Service's man in the embassy. Only three people were supposed to know his identity: the ambassador, the 'friend' himself, and his number two. In this case the knowledge, in clear breach of protocol, had trickled down to the doorman.

He hurried off to a desk where a dozy young woman sat manning the phones. He instructed her to make a call. Moments later he returned. 'Someone will be right down to see you. Will you take a seat?' All the seats were already occupied by old ladies and their even older husbands.

'I'm happy to stand,' I said.

A few minutes later the lift doors opened and an awkward man in his late thirties or early forties – it was difficult to tell – stepped out and beckoned me forward. The doorman gave a small bow as I passed him, which was hardly an aid to my working undercover and unnoticed.

We travelled up two floors in the lift. My companion made no comment, just let a gentle smile play around his lips and bright, intelligent eyes.

The lift doors opened onto a marble-floored hall. My host led me along a corridor, past a series of offices whose open doors revealed members of staff working quietly at their desks. He took me into a larger office at the far end. As he opened the door for me he addressed a young man in the next door office. 'Lemon tea for two, Tristan. And a few biccies.'

Young Tristan looked up in annoyance. There were two women seated at desks nearby and he clearly thought that making tea was below his status and a more suitable use of their time.

'And don't take too long about it.' He ushered me into his office. The door shut and we were alone together.

'We can talk freely. My name is Ambrose Flynn. I shall be your contact at the embassy from now on. Ambassador Bingham has been informed that we are meeting today, and has asked that only he be kept appraised of your reports, which you will deliver directly to me.'

'You're concerned about leaks.'

'Unintentional ones. There are several young Greeks on our staff. The Greeks are a charming and sociable people. But an innocent remark, a slip of the tongue over a coffee or a drink at dinner, may reach the wrong ears. So let's keep things simple and stick to the rules. That way we won't find we've let something slip and have a dozen possible suspects on our hands.'

'And my immediate superior?'

'He's away on compassionate leave. Mother died unexpectedly. So you don't need to worry about him just yet. In fact, I already have a mission for you.' He stood up suddenly and threw open his office door. Satisfied that nobody was eavesdropping our conversation, he shut the door. 'I have to sweep this office for bugs twice a day. Even more if I leave the office.'

'So leaks *are* a problem.'

He turned back to me. 'I've had information that a terrorist group – could be 17 November, could be another – is planning an attack on somebody in the embassy. The ambassador himself is the most likely target, but it could be anybody. Perhaps even me.'

I had heard of the 17 November group. They had named

themselves after that day in 1973 when the Greek military junta crushed the student occupation of the Athens Polytechnic, the top engineering university. With their rallying cry of '*Psomi-Paideia-Eleftheria*' (bread-education-liberty), the students, together with construction workers and disillusioned farmers, had taunted the junta with threats to bring down their corrupt government. In the early hours of 17 November the Junta responded by sending a military tank to smash through the university gates.

According to the junta's spokesperson, no student was killed in the ensuing chaos, but he acknowledged that at least twenty-four protesting civilians had lost their lives that day. The truth was that many more had been murdered in the crackdown, and several hundred seriously injured. That day a terrorist resistance movement was born.

'The junta was deposed ten years ago. What do 17 November hope to achieve now?'

'They purport to seek the collapse of the Greek government and the destruction of Western influence, particularly that of the USA. But I'm not sure even they know what they want, except to destabilise the country and grab money for themselves. They've followed the Baader-Meinhof and Red Brigade playbooks with kidnappings, bombings and bank robberies. Any sense of moral superiority evaporated when they murdered the American CIA station chief, Richard Welch.'

I studied Ambrose. 'So you want me to keep an eye on you?'

'I am the least of your concerns. It is the ambassador you must protect. He is well aware that he may be next on the terrorists' list, but he doesn't like being molly-coddled. He's not to be made aware of your presence.'

'How on earth am I supposed to manage that?'

'It's not going to be easy, but I've heard you are a resourceful woman. The ambassador has accepted a week's holiday on the yacht of Vasilis Mavros.'

'The shipping magnate?'

'The same. You're familiar with the names of shipping tycoons?'

'Everyone's heard of Mavros. He's in the gossip pages every other week.'

'I didn't think you were the type to read the gossip pages.'

'I'm not. But while stationed in London I shared a flat during weekdays in Earl's Court with two young women who read them all. I defy anyone to live like that and not pick up on how millionaire socialites squander their money.'

'Squander? That's not how Ambassador Bingham sees it. He's greatly looking forward to his cruise. He and Lady Mary don't want to be bothered by secret service hulks hovering around them. Besides, there isn't a spare cabin for bodyguards to bunk down in.'

'So how do you imagine I'm going to get aboard and stay undercover?'

10

Exactly one week later I reported for duty on board the MY *Fantasy* berthed at Marina Zea in Piraeus. The MY stood for Motor Yacht – or gin palace as my mother would have called it. And as for fantasy, well, to my eyes it certainly was fantastic. Built by the Sanlorenzo shipyard in Viareggio, where I had once holidayed as a child, it was some 38 metres long – a little over 120 feet – with a simple but elegant interior.

I had been taken on as second steward. Ambrose had arranged for the young woman who usually held the job to be offered a better-paid position elsewhere. I had no qualifications or experience in that kind of work, but the fact that I spoke English counted in my favour.

The Chief Stewardess (Chief Stew), Kate, was also English. A jolly, confident woman of around thirty, she greeted me as I walked up the gangplank.

'Thank God you could come at such short notice. For a while I thought I'd be managing this cruise on my own. Come on, I'll show you our quarters and, when they're back on board, introduce you to the crew.'

She led me to the front of the yacht and down steep metal steps into the crew quarters housed under the foredeck. She threw open a door on the port side. It led onto a tiny bedroom, about two metres wide and about five-foot deep.

'This is where we sleep. I'm on the top bunk, you below me. There are two footlockers below the bed – my stuff's on the left.'

She took one pace back so that I could step inside. Her bed was unmade, littered with hair and make-up accessories. To the right was a small wardrobe with an inbuilt chest of drawers. I opened it. Inside I found a vibrator and a pack of condoms. I turned to Kate and raised an eyebrow.

'Those are Fanny's – the last girl,' she said, by way of explanation. 'Though she didn't need the vibrator, she did need the condoms.' She did not go into details. 'We've got some tidying up to do, and then you can meet Captain Grigori. He's catching up on his sleep.'

I could hear loud snoring emanating from a cabin at the end of the small corridor.

'I hope he sleeps alone,' I said.

'The second deckhand, a Sri Lankan, has to suffer that racket. Fortunately Captain Grigori is up early and Sunil can sleep in for an hour or so to catch up.'

'Doesn't sound like this Sunil gets much sleep.'

'None of us do when there are guests aboard.' She led me into the crew galley, where a young Frenchman was preparing lunch. 'This is Jean-Louis,' she said. Jean-Louis hastily wiped his hands on his apron and shook mine warmly.

'Call me Jean. Or Louis.' He laughed. 'Just Jean is fine.'

'What are you making, Just Jean?' I asked.

'What I am always asked to make. Something Greek. I, a Michelin-starred chef, who have worked in some of the greatest restaurants in the world, am stuck here making *stifado* and kebabs.'

'That's not true,' said Kate. 'Jean-Louis's done some pretty fancy Greek dishes. What's on the menu today?'

'Souvla – lamb on ze spit – with a Greek salad and chips. I'm also making roast potatoes, English style, crispy on the outside and fluffy in ze middle. For our English guests.'

'English guests?' I wasn't supposed to know our ambassador would be joining the cruise. And he wasn't supposed to know I would be watching out for him.

'It's a secret,' Kate said. 'Keep it under your hat.'

Ambrose had provided me with excellent references, supplied by the British Council in Athens. According to them I'd been working for the Council, teaching English as a foreign language, and now wanted a taste of adventure. I was no spring chicken and Kate had probably balked at having an older woman as her assistant. But now that she had met me she could see I was keen to please and unlikely to cause her any problems.

At noon we were told to get into our 'whites' – our smartest uniforms – and assemble on the rear deck. We stood barefoot as a Bentley R-Type Continental from the 1950s rolled into the marina and Vasilis Mavros stepped out. He wore battered, faded jeans, an old white T-shirt with a tear at the right shoulder and dirty flip-flops. He looked less like a shipping multi-millionaire and more like a reject from the 1960s hippy trail. His eyes were masked by aviator sunglasses. His thick black hair, tumbling down to his shoulders, was so glossy it looked as if it had been soaked in extra virgin olive oil. Or chip fat. From this distance, it was hard to tell. He gave a wave to the crew, dismissed his driver, and headed up the gangplank.

Captain Grigori, a bulky man with a massive bull-like neck and head, greeted Mavros effusively. Unlike the rest of us, Grigori was not wearing whites but some sort of cod-military khaki which bore little resemblance to any uniform I had ever seen. Kate had filled me in on Grigori's background. He had been a captain on one of Mavros' bulk carriers and, having frittered his wages away on women and gambling, could not afford to retire. So Mavros had given him the job of captain on his private yacht. A gamble, in my view, given Grigori's penchant for whisky.

Mavros assessed the line-up. Alongside Grigori stood Jean-Louis, then the bosun, Lefteris, a grim-faced man who never smiled once. Next to him were the two deckhands, Stavros and Sunil. Kate and I were last in line. Mavros peered at me and gave Kate a questioning glance, as if to ask if I was any good. Kate smiled back. Mavros nodded to me in acknowledgement and stepped into the saloon.

Captain Grigori barked an order and we dispersed to carry out our duties. Twenty minutes later we were again made to line up on deck. This time Mavros himself joined us. He had showered and wore loose tan slacks, a well-cut yellow polo shirt and deck shoes. His aviator sunglasses sat perched on his head.

A small unmarked car drove onto the dock. The driver hopped out to open a passenger door. Lady Mary Bingham stepped out. She was dressed as if she were about to open a country fete: billowing floral-print skirt, white blouse, a double string of pearls and a broad-brimmed straw hat with a blue bow. Her husband, Sir Roland, got out on the other side. He wore navy blue trousers with a blue and white striped matelot sweater that his wife must have told him made him look nautical. He caught sight of Mavros on deck, waved and bounded up the gangplank, carrying a heavy briefcase. Lady Mary tottered up after him in unsuitable heels.

'Roly!' cried Mavros, delighted his guests had arrived. 'We're leaving in ten minutes and we'll have lunch in a couple of hours. So why not get comfortable and let Kate show you around the boat? And Mary…'

'Yes?' queried Lady Mary.

'Perhaps some flats, if you have them?'

Kate held out her hand to take Lady Mary's high heels, which she placed in a wicker basket by the gangplank.

'But they are Christian Dior!' she exclaimed.

'They'll be quite safe,' said Kate, as she led the guests up to the top deck. She indicated I should follow.

The deck featured a fold-out dining table surrounded on three sides by built-in sofas covered in some sort of towelling material. This was just one of three dining stations. At the forward end of the deck was a large area designated for sunbathing and a modified bridge with a full set of controls for the captain to stand at and steer if he needed a clear view of port.

When we had heard enough of Lady Mary cooing over the beauty of the yacht and muttering her regrets that none of her friends were around to envy her, we went down to the main deck. The long saloon was lined with built-in sofas facing each other. At the far end was a bar and a large indoor dining table, with seating for ten, for when the weather was bad. Beyond it was the captain's control room or bridge. At the open rear of the main deck was a third dining table where most of the guests' meals would be taken. Among all this expanse of perfectly turned woodwork there was not one sharp edge that might injure a passenger in bad weather.

Kate led the way down to the cabins. Mavros had the master suite to himself. Along either side of the corridor were two more suites with king-sized beds. The Binghams were given the one on the starboard side, as this was generally less noisy when in port. The deckhands had already brought the Binghams' luggage down. Kate offered to unpack for them.

'Oh, would you? That's so darling of you,' said Lady Mary. 'But let me change first.'

Kate and I headed back up to the main deck. The deckhands cast off from the dock. The captain eased the yacht forward to raise the twin anchors. Once they had slipped into their housing and been locked into place, Grigori edged the yacht out of the marina and into the main channel. He fired up the twin engines and we cruised past oil tankers, reefers and bulk carriers all waiting to be let into the port of Piraeus to discharge their cargoes. Once out to sea we sped up and were soon charging down the coast at 27 knots. The deck crew and we 'stews' went down to change out of our whites and into our working clothes: navy blue polo tops and white shorts for the stews, while the deck crew, who were more likely to soil their clothes as they laboured, wore navy blue shorts and white T-shirts with the yacht's name emblazoned across their backs.

A few minutes later Sir Roland Bingham reappeared. He had ditched his 'nautical' outfit and was wearing the standard uniform of the English gentleman abroad: a pink shirt from Turnbull and Asser, and pale yellow slacks over tan deck shoes with cream tongues. He carried a Panama hat and held an unlit cigar. In all the time he was aboard I never saw him light it.

'Would you care for a cocktail, or champagne?' asked Kate.

'A martini would be nice,' he replied. He took a seat by the dining table at the rear of the deck. Although it was early March a mild wind carried heat from the south. It felt like an English summer's day: warm enough to sit out in the light breeze.

Kate whispered to me that once Lady Mary returned I should go down and unpack their bags. She had no sooner spoken than Lady Mary reappeared. She had unwisely chosen a navy blue polo shirt and white shorts. These made her look as if she were a member of the crew. She stared at our attire in dismay. 'I've left my handbag downstairs,' she bleated and disappeared down to her cabin.

By the time Kate had prepared Sir Roland's martini to his liking, Lady Mary was back. This time she had got her outfit right. She was in a fuchsia pink linen blouse, cream slacks and soft beige pumps: almost a mirror image of her husband. The breeze had cooled.

'What on earth are you doing out on deck?' she demanded. 'It's freezing.' While Kate led them into the saloon and returned to fetch Sir Roland's martini, I took the opportunity to go below deck and unpack for them.

Lady Mary's clothes were strewn across the bed. Unlike me, she did not travel light. She had come with two enormous suitcases and had ferreted through both of them to get her final ensemble together. I straightened her blouses and skirts, placed them on hangers and put them away in the wardrobe. I took her long dresses and smart trousers and put them away too. She certainly had brought a lot of clothes for what was supposed to be a cruise of just a few days. Her camisoles, slips and knickers went into the drawers and her shoes – five pairs in a variety of styles – I stored in the pull-out drawer under the bed.

I turned my attention to Sir Roland's small suitcase. It contained a pressed cream-coloured suit, which I hung on a hanger and left in the shower to lose its creases. As the wardrobe was full of Lady Mary's clothes, I stored his folded shirts and trousers in the drawers beside the bed. I then turned my attention to his wide and heavy briefcase.

My instructions were to keep Sir Roland safe, not to snoop. But something didn't feel right. If he was taking a break, why had he brought along such a large briefcase? Of course unexpected events could erupt at any time. A decade earlier the Greek junta had attempted to assassinate the President of Cyprus, Archbishop Makarios. Shortly after that the Turkish army had invaded Cyprus, and the junta had fallen. And just a few months later a civil war had erupted in Lebanon. The whole Eastern Mediterranean could erupt into conflict at any time. Even so, the way Sir Roland had guarded his briefcase and kept it close to him suggested that it held something important inside.

The briefcase had twin three-number combination locks, each of which would open a catch. There were one thousand possible combinations for each lock. At present they were both set to 737. I guessed I had about five minutes to work out the correct three numbers, get the case open and study the contents. I tried to remember Sir Roland's birthday, and then Lady Mary's, as a clue to the right combination. Then I had a sudden idea. A simpler one.

I pushed aside the two catches. With a click the briefcase opened. Sir Roland had omitted to lock it.

I checked inside carefully. I wasn't expecting poison gas to spurt out like in a spy movie, but opening it might trigger an alarm. In which case I would have claimed that I had simply been stowing it away and that it had sprung open. In the event, there was no alarm.

Slipping on the thin white gloves I kept for serving lunch, I opened the case's compartments and extracted two bound documents. One was labelled Option A. The other: Option B.

That was when I heard Lady Mary's voice.

'If we have to eat outside I'm fetching myself a shawl.'

I slipped the documents back in the briefcase, shut it and replaced it where I had found it. I gave the locks a quick wipe with my gloves, which I slipped off and pocketed. As Lady Mary entered I was rising from the drawers by her bedside carrying a large green pashmina. She looked startled to see me.

'I thought you might need this,' I said.

'Exactly what I came for,' she said, recovering. 'How clever of you. My, you've unpacked everything.' She looked in the wardrobe. 'I couldn't have done better myself.' She accepted the pashmina and I followed her back upstairs. At least now I knew the combination to Sir Roland's briefcase.

11

THE MY *FANTASY* MADE ITS first stop at Cape Sounion, the final promontory of Athenian coastline before we headed for the islands. While Jean-Louis prepared a late lunch, Mavros took his guests ashore to admire the Temple of Poseidon, perched on the cliff above. Captain Grigori wanted someone to go along with them. The crew were relieved when I volunteered. I had never visited the ancient temple. More importantly, I needed to watch Sir Roland Bingham's back.

We left the yacht by tender – a rigid inflatable Zodiac – which Mavros piloted himself. We reached a shingle beach and Sunil, the second deckhand, leapt into waist-deep water to tie the tender to a large rock and draw it into the shallows. Mavros helped Lady Mary out and I offered Sir Roland a hand. He would have been happy to jump onto the shingle on his own, but I didn't want to risk accidents. It was a strenuous climb up the hill, but Mavros kept up a running commentary along the way. He informed us that Poseidon's temple, built sometime around 440 BC, had been destroyed by an invading Persian army. It had been partially restored in the nineteenth century once the Greeks had driven out the Turks with the help and encouragement of Lord Byron.

By the time we reached the top, Sir Roland and Lady Mary knew more about the temple than they cared to. Mavros was scarcely out of breath, although his guests most certainly were.

It was too early in the season to attract more than a scattering of academic tourists but, in any case, Sounion never drew the sort of crowds that the Acropolis did. I felt I could relax. Sir Roland would be safe here.

Mavros skirted around the side of the temple to show his guests Byron's signature, scratched into the marble. Some wags claimed that the signature had only appeared in the 1950s, but that didn't bother Mavros. He beckoned his guests to marvel at it.

It was then that I saw the man.

If you've ever witnessed an assassin preparing to commit an outrage – and I've seen a few in my time – you'll know that the attacker holds himself in a particular way: body bent forward and head held high. This is to ensure that, in his first mad rush, he will reach his victim before he can be stopped. He is completely focused, as is his hard and determined expression.

This was exactly the look I saw the man adopt as he dashed across the open space towards Mavros and his two guests. With no thought to my own safety I sprinted across the temple floor. But the man had a twenty-five yard lead on me. He reached Sir Roland first.

I saw no gun, no knife. But I saw Sir Roland's look of alarm as the man spun him around and screamed in his face… just as I slammed into his back and we fell to the dusty ground.

I put the man in an armlock with one hand while I frisked him for weapons with the other.

'Let the man up,' Sir Roland ordered. Our ambassador was furious.

'He threatened you, sir,' I protested.

'He did nothing of the sort. He simply wanted us to pay the entry fee. They need it to maintain the temple in good order.'

I studied the man writhing beneath me. He wore a navy blazer and trousers and displayed a badge that declared him to be a museum guard. I helped the fellow up.

'I'll deal with this,' said Mavros. He spoke a few words to the museum guard and thrust a thick roll of banknotes into his hand. The man counted the banknotes, glared balefully at me and stalked away, dusting down his suit and pocketing the money as he went.

Mavros smiled. 'Don't worry. Easy mistake.' He turned to his guests. 'Lunch is ready.'

We made our way back down the hill. I was worried that I had given myself away, but Mavros and Sir Roland both seemed to accept that it was a crew member's duty to put themselves between their guests and danger. Lady Mary gave me a warm smile of gratitude, but Sir Roland kept his distance and refused my help getting back on board the Zodiac. Mavros guided the tender back to the MY *Fantasy* and Sunil tossed the bosun a line. While Sir Roland and Lady Mary went downstairs to freshen up, I hurried to our shared cabin to dig out a plaster. When tackling the museum guard I had scraped my knee on the ground. I had to wash dirt and grit out of the wound. I cleaned it with disinfectant and searched the shower cabinet for plasters or a small bandage. I found nothing.

Then I remembered that Kate, the chief stew, had a plaster on her right index finger. Perhaps she had a pack of them somewhere. I opened the top drawer of her bedside cupboard. I found several letters and her service contract. As I pushed them aside I felt something hard and metallic under a silk scarf. I lifted it aside. At the bottom of the drawer Kate had hidden a new model Beretta 81 handgun. I replaced the scarf carefully, along with the contract and letters, and left the cabin.

12

I HAD BETTER LUCK FINDING a sticking plaster in the kitchen. Jean-Louis had already prepared the first course: small souvlaki, hummus, melitzanosalata and flakes of feta with some mini pittas, which he had baked himself (or so he claimed, though I saw him frequenting island bakeries on our trip). He had ditched his first idea: souvla with Greek salad and roast potatoes. He now had a large gilthead bream, purchased from a local fisherman, roasting in the oven, along with a pile of small-cut potatoes in the top tray, so he was able to deal with my injury.

Jean-Louis kept a store of plasters in case he cut his fingers, which he never did despite demonstrating his ability to chop a thick bunch of coriander into tiny pieces in under fifteen seconds. He carefully snipped away at a loose flap of my skin with tiny kitchen scissors, cleaned the graze again with a dash of stinging vodka and applied a padded plaster over the wound. He neatened it with a couple of snips and looked up at me with a gallic smile.

'You could go far on zeeze legs.'

The last thing I needed was a good-looking and highly-sexed young Frenchman distracting me, but I smiled back at him and hopped down from the counter.

'If these are ready,' I said, indicating the starters, 'I'll take them out.'

'The guests are seated,' he said, checking the video monitor. There were three cameras aboard, one in the engine room, in case of fire, and the other two covered the dining areas on the main and top decks.

As I picked up the three plates, balancing one on my forearm, Kate came down to ask me to serve lunch. She was impressed to see me ready prepped. She followed me with a bowl of fresh salad, over which Jean-Louis had sprinkled dried oregano, or 'pencil sharpenings' as Dennis, my old SIS instructor and part-time lover, insisted on calling them, being less enamoured of Greek cuisine than I was. Kate also held a bottle of Assyrtiko wine, which she uncorked and poured for Mavros to check if it was sufficiently chilled.

'Excellent,' he pronounced. Kate poured the guests wine and we stepped back to see if there was anything else they needed. I glanced at Kate. Why did she keep a gun in our cabin? Why had she concealed it in her bedside cupboard?

She turned to speak to me and I looked away quickly. 'Please tell chef to prepare the main course.'

I nodded and disappeared back to the galley. Had she seen me studying her? If she had, she couldn't possibly think it was for any reason other than my desire to learn the ropes.

In the galley, Jean-Louis had removed the gilthead from the oven.

'Now I let it cool and rest a little. Hot fish has no flavour.' He poured extra virgin olive oil into a bowl. He squeezed the juice of two halved lemons, straining the pips with his fingers. He whisked the oil and lemon juice into an emulsion, added salt and pepper to taste, then whisked it all up again.

Jean-Louis took the crisp potatoes out of the oven and sprinkled them with oregano. He sliced the bream – it must have weighed three or four kilos – into steaks. He extracted pin bones with tweezers, then plated the fish up with the potatoes. I carried up two plates while Kate took up a third, together with a salad of tomato and Greek basil.

The guests had finished their first courses and Mavros was in the middle of telling a story.

'You have to remember that I was only nineteen years old at the time. I had borrowed millions against the… how do you say, the bottom—'

'The rump?' suggested Sir Roland.

'The rump of my father's business. We were almost bankrupt, no money coming in and his two old banana boats rusting, but the banks didn't know it.' He took a sip of wine, and paused, checking his guests were paying their full attention. He waved his left hand at us. He was not to be interrupted.

'So I arrived in Japan to take delivery of my first oil tanker. I already had contracts, which I had to put in place immediately or I would not be able to make the interest payments and the banks would call in their loans. And I flew in a Greek crew, because I thought I could trust them.'

He paused again, took another sip of wine.

'So I proudly showed the crew my new ship. She was beautiful. But when they looked around their quarters they were unhappy. They talked together and then the captain told me, "The crew won't sail this ship. Their quarters are sub…" how do you say?'

'Substandard?' ventured Lady Mary.

'Exactly. I said, how can that be? Everything is the best, the most up-to-date. You must to accept the ship.'

'Then the bosun came forward. He was a bastard. A dirty communist. And so was the cook. He said, "The beds are no good." The beds were built for Japanese men, just over five-feet long. The crew could not sleep well, so they refused to take the ship. I telephone the Greek consul. He confirmed what they said. Under Greek maritime law if the beds are not suitable the crew are not obliged to sail.'

He let this sink in. Sir Roland and Lady Mary were leaning forward. Even I was interested in hearing how the story ended.

'So now I had no crew. And I was obliged to pay each man one month's salary and provide return tickets to Athens. I was at… how do you say it? My wit's end.'

I glanced across at Kate. She stood there patiently. I guessed, rightly as it turned out, that she had heard this story before. If Mavros' story went on much longer the fish was going to be cold.

'I went back to my hotel. I was in despair. Then I had an idea. I called the consul and asked if I was permitted to send the crew their month's payment straight to their accounts in Greece. He said yes. I asked about their return tickets to Athens. Must they be direct flights? They could be in any form, he told me. Just as long as they got back to Athens. So I sent payments to their bank accounts, bought them tickets, and called the crew to meet me.

'The Captain, he was a decent type, he apologised. He said he would be happy to sail for me any time but the bosun and the cook were union men, and he couldn't go against the union. So I showed the crew that I'd paid their salaries into their accounts, and presented their return tickets. They went away happy.

'Minutes later, loud knocking on my door. How can I

help you? I asked. "What the fuck's this?" – sorry for my language, Lady Mary. The bosun, he waved his tickets in my face. I explained: it is your return ticket from Yokohama, via the slow boat, stopping at every port, to Vladivostok. From there you take the trans-Siberian slow train all the way to Moscow. It will be very cold. And you will have to buy your own food. If you have any roubles on you. Then you make many transfers of trains and buses that will bring you to Athens before the end of the month.

'Their faces were white. They went into the corridor to discuss the matter. There was again knocking. I opened the door. The captain spoke. The crew was now willing to sail. Okay, I said. But not you, I said to the bosun, or you, the cook. You two go home the long way. So piss off.'

Mavros sat back, spread his hands wide.

'And that, Sir Roland, was the foundation of my shipping empire.'

Lady Mary dutifully clapped her hands in applause. 'Bravo.' Mavros waved his hand, beckoning us to serve lunch.

Kate laid a plate before Lady Mary, who beamed. 'Fish, my favourite!'

'Not any fish,' replied her host. 'Tsipoura. The best the Aegean has to offer.' He poured the wine and dismissed us.

Kate and I took the dirty dishes down to the galley. The rest of the crew had eaten, but Jean-Louis had put aside some fish for us, along with roast potatoes and a fresh salad he had knocked up.

'I wait to eat with you,' he said, setting out our plates. Jean-Louis had given himself the front belly of the fish – a sacrifice, as it could hold traces of bitter liver – while he had saved the broad tail sections for us. It was delicious. So were his roast potatoes.

About a minute later the internal phone rang. Jean-Louis answered, listened, and replaced the receiver. 'Boss wants more fish for his guests.'

I looked in horror. I was just finishing the last portion.

Jean-Louis winked at me and pulled a baking tray from the oven. He'd kept back three large portions. He arranged them on a dish and, indicating I should keep eating, took them up on deck.

'This is his big moment,' said Kate. 'Just see.'

On the monitor we watched Jean-Louis hold the dish as the guests helped themselves to that delicious gilthead bream. Lady Mary spoke and Jean-Louis gave her a courtly bow.

'He loves the compliments.'

Jean Louis offered the last piece to Mavros, who declined it. In all the time I saw him, he never had a second portion of anything. He was too occupied with his health and how he looked, with his slim muscular body and mane of glossy, windswept hair.

That evening we stopped at the little island of Tinos. Mavros led his guests ashore to make their 'pilgrimage'. Kate accompanied them. She wore the crew regulation T-shirt and shorts, so I could see she was not carrying her gun. But I was frustrated. How could I keep my eyes on Sir Roland from the boat? Jean-Louis came to my aid – not that he had anything other than seducing me on his mind. He offered to show me Tinos, as long as Captain Grigori gave us permission. We found the captain flat out on the top deck, snoring. As Mavros and his guests would be eating in town that night, Grigori had the chance to get at least three hours sleep. He would have to be up with the deckhands before dawn, ready to cast off and head for the next island before the guests were awake.

Jean-Louis stood over the snoring captain, blocking out the sun, and asked if we could go ashore. I did not expect an answer, but Grigori waved an arm in approval and grunted his assent. He was the only man I knew who regularly snored while awake.

Jean-Louis guided me through the streets and up the hill to the Holy Church of the Virgin Mary. As we approached the wide square I saw an extraordinary sight. Lady Mary was on her knees at the base of the broad sweep of steps up to the church. She raised her right knee and ascended one step. Then she raised her left knee and climbed the next. She continued up another four, one step at a time.

'That's quite enough, Mary,' said Sir Roland. 'At this rate we won't be eating until midnight.' He helped her to her feet. She had forgotten she was wearing her Pretty Polly 'stand easies'. Now they were shredded at the knees. Only too aware of their distressed appearance, she dangled her handbag in front of her, as Mavros led them into the church.

'About half the tourists try climbing the steps on their knees,' Jean-Louis told me, 'but most give up after a couple of steps. You should be here at Greek Easter, then you'll see serious pilgrims climb the steps all the way up. Do you want to see inside?'

Of course I did. I needed to watch Sir Roland's back. 'But I'm supposed to be on duty on the boat.'

'The boss won't mind if he sees you're with me. The perks, you may say, of my job.'

We entered the church and Jean-Louis narrowly missed knocking his head against a silver boat-shaped ornament hanging low from the ceiling. A monk hurried forward to apologise. He had been raising the boat, but had stopped to pay his respects to Mavros, a notable church donor. The monk hauled on a silver chain and the little boat rose to a safe height above the heads of the visitors. Watching him was a family – a gnarled fisherman, his wife and two very plain daughters.

'Votive offerings to St Mary,' explained Jean-Louis. 'She is the patron of seafarers. If you survive a storm or a shipwreck, you thank the blessed virgin with a silver boat or a cash donation. But if you survive an illness you'll donate something more appropriate. Take a look.'

I needed to keep an eye on Sir Roland, down at the altar end of the church, but I made a show of admiring the silver offerings – legs, arms, hands and fingers – that hung from silver chains slung above the church aisles. I saw Lady Mary make a cash donation while Sir Roland glanced at his watch.

I noticed someone else in the shadows. A tall, bulky man with dark bags under his eyes. He wore a charcoal grey suit that was too tight for him and light brown shoes that did not go with his suit. He might have been a churchgoer, but the way his eyes followed Sir Roland around the church told me his presence was not entirely spiritual.

After my mistake at Cape Sounion I had no wish to embarrass Sir Roland again. I slipped deeper into the shadows and kept my eyes firmly focused on the man in the suit.

Mavros sensed that Sir Roland had had enough. He pointedly checked his watch and led his guests out of the church. Jean-Louis reappeared at my side.

'They will be going to a little restaurant the boss likes down near the harbour. We could go for a drink, the two of us. I know a little ouzeri just around the corner.'

'That's kind,' I said, 'but perhaps we could have a drink down by the harbour? Then I can be sure I'm back on board before the boss.' And I should be able to keep an eye on Sir Roland. It was a lot more appealing than sitting in a dark alley accompanied by a Frenchman with only one thing in mind.

We strolled down towards the harbour and Jean-Louis pointed out the old taverna where Mavros and his two guests were dining. The owner, a woman, made a big fuss of the three of them.

'See those two eating at the next table?'

Two uniformed men sat at the table.

'That's the local chief of police and his second in command. Both armed. In case you're worried.'

'Who says I'm worried?'

'You are taking a lot of interest in Mavros. It's as if you are his guardian angel.'

'I don't know what you mean.'

'There have been a lot of kidnappings and threats to Greek shipowners. I thought perhaps you were watching him for one of those insurance syndicates in London.'

I laughed and relaxed. 'I didn't know kidnapping was a big issue here.'

'You bet. Communists and extreme left groups.'

'Who gets the payout if he's kidnapped?'

'It's used to send in a crack team of ex-army mercenaries, or Foreign Legionnaires. The kind of people who kill for a living.'

'Well I'm not one of those.' No, but perhaps Kate might be. That could explain her gun. 'So we're not in danger on the boat?' I was playing the naive stewardess.

'Don't worry, I'll keep you safe from any kidnappers.'

Jean-Louis moved in to put his arm around my shoulder.

And who would keep me safe from Jean-Louis? I spun away. 'That looks a nice place.'

I headed to a bar by the harbour's edge. I found a seat at a table. Jean-Louis sat facing me. Now at least we had the table between us.

A waiter approached us.

'*Mia Mpyra, parakalo*,' I said, ordering myself a lager. The waiter turned to Jean-Louis.

'*Enas Mythos, parakalo*.' Jean-Louis had gone for his preferred brand of beer. The waiter nodded and went off to fetch them. 'Your Greek is good.'

'Hardly,' I laughed. 'I've just used it all up.' That wasn't quite true. I had a smattering of Greek, enough to get the gist of what people might be saying but not enough to get me out of trouble. 'What about you?'

'Enough to do the shopping. Fish, meat, vegetables, all that. And enough swear words to keep the crew out of my galley. My first week in Greece I thought "*Malaka*" meant "milky coffee". It was only when I took a crew member shopping for vegetables that he told me the stallholders were calling me a "wanker". After that, I stopped trying so hard to beat them down on their prices.'

As we chatted, I noticed the bulky man in the ill-fitting suit striding down to the waterside. He carried a small suitcase in one hand and a briefcase in the other. A ferry was waiting to pick up passengers. He marched up the gangplank and spoke a few words to a crew member. He glanced at the taverna where Mavros was entertaining his guests with more stories. The man turned back and disappeared into the bowels of the ferry. Finally I felt able to relax.

13

Notting Hill, 2019

OVER THE NEXT THREE DAYS I received several more bundles of files. I had hoped to receive them by email attachment. Since the turn of the millennium all records were supposed to have been converted to digital. But the filing staff had started digitising the most recent documents first before slowly working their way backwards through the 1990s. If they were any good at their job they would be promoted out of the filing department, leaving the slackers to get on with the chore. The result was that full digitisation had not yet reached the first half of the 1980s.

The most recent delivery had arrived in three large boxes, each some two-feet deep. When I had worked in the secretarial pool in Bonn in 1976 the filing, with some exceptions, had been near perfect. The exceptions had mostly been caused by me, when I had contrived to hide information from those spying for communist East Germany. By contrast, the material presented in Matthew's boxes was in an appalling mess. Files, photographs, pages that had come loose, receipts and chits were all bundled into arbitrary piles, some held in place with rusting bulldog clips. It was almost as if someone was trying to prevent me from discovering anything relevant or helpful.

I emptied all three boxes and spread the contents over the floor. It took several hours to sort them out into their correct date and order. I did my best to absorb their contents as I went. By the time I had arranged everything into a system I could understand, I had learnt that the service was unwilling to meet any receipt of more than fifty pounds without first querying it and demanding a full explanation in triplicate. This much I already knew from personal experience.

The receipts were relatively easy to sort out as almost all were dated and, in most cases, had signed request chits attached. I was able to put these together with the individual files on our various agents operating out of the Athens embassy in the late 1970s and early 1980s. Some of the cardboard wallets that should have contained details of our agents were empty. Others were full of heavily redacted pages. Photographs had been damaged with coffee stains or worse. If Matthew expected any progress on my part, he was going to have to provide me with better material.

Through one stapled receipt I made out a faint scrawl. I flipped it over and recognised a name. Ray Turnberry had held a lowly position in our Athens Embassy in the 1980s. In my recollection, he was never going to be a high riser and promotion would always be elusive, but the man himself might have some useful information. He had not been on Matthew's initial list.

I went to my laptop and typed the name: Raymond Turnberry. I found several entries, mostly for young sportsmen and university graduates in America. I also found a Scottish golf course.

I backtracked and added the words 'Companies House'. It's an old spy's trick. Even the most secretive of former agents may have forgotten their directorship of a long-dissolved company linked to their address. I pressed the enter button and came up with two answers. The first, a Raymond Emeric

Turnberry, was twenty-eight years old and some kind of YouTube star. The cash in his company account was over two million pounds. I resisted the temptation to watch any of his YouTube videos, and clicked on the other Raymond Turnberry. This one's middle name was Charles, and his date of birth was 1950. This looked hopeful. He was a director of Turnberry Tortoises, and the company secretary was Esmé May Turnberry, presumably his wife. The company director and secretary shared an address in Cobham, Surrey. Matthew had not forbidden me from investigating on my own. I decided to pay the Turnberrys a visit.

I had no problem in hiring a car in the name of Eleanor Farquhar. I might have expected some snag since the photograph on the driver's licence looked nothing like me in my current disguise, but the young woman at the reception desk showed no interest in it at all. Demonstrating all the lethargy of a special awareness driving course, she accepted my credit card and presented me with a long document.

'Sign there and there, where I've put a cross.'

'Shouldn't I read it first?'

'Please yourself. Nobody else bothers.'

I ran my eyes down the list of clauses. 'Mind if I photograph the car before I drive off the forecourt? To check any bumps and scratches.'

She gave an impatient sigh and rolled her eyes.

'I take it you won't mind, then,' I said. 'Which car is it?'

'I can't give you the keys till you've signed the contract. Do you want it or don't you?'

I signed the document where she had marked, and stepped out onto the forecourt where a middle-aged man was hosing down a blue Mercedes B-Class hatchback. I was on the point of filming the exterior when I remembered that my burner phone's battery was flat. I switched on my regular phone, found Settings, tapped Privacy and Security, tapped Location Services and turned them off. My phone could only have been trackable for a few seconds at most. I hoped nobody would be tracking me at that precise moment.

I walked around the Mercedes, filming all sides of the vehicles and getting close-ups of the wheel arches and the state of the tyres. I had been caught out before, and handed a massive bill for a supposedly damaged wheel arch and tyre. I had no intention of getting ripped off again when I returned the car.

The man with the hose watched me. 'Don't blame you, love. They'll rook you if they can. Key's in the ignition.'

I thanked him, got in the car, turned on the ignition, put the car into drive and left the forecourt.

Cobham is about an hour's drive out of London – if there are no hold-ups – down the A3. I charged up my burner phone and, following the instructions on my Waze App – by far the best, in my opinion – took the turn-off to Cobham. The route took me under the A3 and along a country lane until I came to a set of metal gates. A modest wooden board proclaimed this to be the entrance to Hazelnut House, my destination.

I wound down the car window, leaned out and pressed an intercom button. After a few moments a thin voice – it was hard to tell if it was a man's or a woman's – answered.

'Hello, can I help you?'

'I've come about the tortoise.' It was a response guaranteed to gain me entry. There was a buzz. The metal gates opened and I accelerated up the gravel drive. The gates clanged shut behind me.

The drive led me through a curving alley of tall, dark laurels that opened out to reveal a large stucco villa. Opposite the villa's front entrance was a small lake. Around it stood a flock of pink flamingos. Beyond the house a well-manicured lawn stretched off towards a wooded area. Nibbling the grass were several strange mammals, resembling crosses between large hares and small deer. They were accompanied by large humps, resembling enormous brown molehills.

Raymond Turnberry stepped out the front door and down the stone steps. Following him were two large boxer dogs. They matched their owner well. Raymond looked much as I remembered him, but age had taken its toll. His exophthalmic eyes still bulged above his snub, upturned nose with its wide nostrils. His lower jaw jutted forward, giving him a permanently pugnacious expression, though Ray was one of the gentlest men I ever knew. He wore a padded green gilet over a checked shirt, and the country squire's obligatory red cord trousers over semi-brogue, well-polished brown shoes.

'I was expecting you yesterday.' The high-pitched voice had been his. 'I wish you had phoned to let me know.'

'I do apologise,' I lied. 'My car broke down, and it took me forever to get someone to come out and fix it.' As I had hoped, Raymond had mistaken me for a tortoise fancier and had failed to recognise me. Both boxer dogs sniffed at my pockets, checking that I was not carrying any treats, and swiftly lost interest.

'Will you come in and have some tea?'

'I'd be delighted.' I followed him up the steps into the house. The boxers trotted in after me.

As we entered Raymond indicated a large drawing room on the left. 'Would you like to wait there? Or you can come into the kitchen while I brew up. I think you'll find it interesting.'

'I'll come and watch, if I may.' I was intrigued.

Raymond led me along a corridor and down three steps to the kitchen at the back of the house. Lining the corridor were a series of terrariums, each containing a variety of snakes and lizards. I stopped to watch a large green chameleon stalking a locust. It swayed back and forward as it closed the distance between itself and its prey. Its hypnotic movements mesmerised the insect, which froze. Suddenly the chameleon's long tongue darted out, wrapping itself around the locust and whipping it back into its gaping mouth. The chameleon's bulging eyes – not unlike Raymond's – blinked as it swallowed its prey.

'Hermann's or Sulcata,' Raymond called from the kitchen. I followed the sound of his voice.

'Oh, Sulcata tea will do for me.'

'What?' asked Raymond.

'Sulcata.'

Raymond stared at me as if I were mad. 'Sulcata, the African spurred tortoise,' he explained. 'Hermann's, the European variety.' He did not give me time to answer. 'You're not here for a tortoise, are you?'

He reached into a drawer as if he was looking for a spoon. When he withdrew his hand it held a gun.

'What do you want?'

'Well, the fact is I'm here to see you.' I took a step forward.

'Don't move.'

'Raymond, it's me, Felicity. We were both stationed in Athens.'

'Felicity?' He peered at me with narrowed eyes. I could see he recognised me, but his expression did not change.

'You can put that gun down,' I said.

'I'd rather not, if it's all the same with you. I've heard what you can do to an unarmed man.'

'Well, let me sit down, and you can make me that tea, if you don't mind. What variety is it?'

'Assam.'

'Good. Then we shall sip our tea and you can hear me out.'

Raymond let the tea brew and poured two cups. 'If you like it stronger, I can let it stew. Esmé takes it weak.'

'Your wife?'

'She's out feeding the birds.'

'Wild birds?'

'Oh no. She's the president of the Avicultural Society. Like her father. We have a wonderful collection of rare tropical birds.'

'Do you breed them?'

'Not only breed them. We return them to the wild. We've had great success with sunbirds, turaco and hummingbirds.'

'Impressive.'

Raymond flashed me a wary smile. He kept his pistol close at hand.

'And expensive,' I added.

'Well, Esmé is fortunate.'

Of course she was. Her father had been the banker Sir Esmond Ellice. He had increased his fortune with investments in Japan after World War Two and had invested heavily in art and commercial property in London. He had also enjoyed his own private zoo.

'How long have you been married?'

'Esmé and I have been together ever since I left the service. But we only got married last year.'

That was the year that Esmé's elder sister Ethel had died, unmarried. Esmé would have inherited a sizeable fortune to add to her own.

'So if you haven't come here to buy a tortoise, what have you come for?'

I let him stew a minute, like his tea.

'You remember that spot of bother we had in Greece in 1984?'

Raymond went pale. 'It's never been out of my mind.'

'I need to go over everything. In detail.'

14

'I was thoroughly debriefed. There is nothing I can tell you that you won't find in the files.' Raymond sat back and pursed his lips, as if that would prevent revelations from slipping out.

I narrowed my eyes. 'As we were colleagues, I thought perhaps you might be prepared to give me more detail. Anything that comes to mind. Anything that you might have missed or thought unimportant at the time of the original inquiry.'

'Such as?'

'Was anyone else there who you remember? Anyone on a street corner who might have been acting on point duty?'

'I didn't see anyone.' He looked up. 'Oh, hello.'

I turned and saw Esmé struggle into the kitchen. She was using a Zimmer frame, pushing it ahead of her then stepping painfully forward before pushing it on again. She was a short, rotund woman. Her lips were painted a bright red and she had doused herself in too much Chanel Number 5, which preceded her like a stale fog. Her right hip jutted awkwardly as she moved.

'I heard you had a guest,' she said in an accent that rang more of the sharp crystal of Knightsbridge than the home counties. 'How do you do?' This was addressed to me.

'This is the lady about the tortoise,' Raymond lied. 'But there's been a bit of a mix-up.'

'You should show her around.' Esmé produced a pair of raw lamb chops from her dress pockets. They were covered in fluff. She offered them to the boxers, who snaffled them up. 'I shall be out on the lawn.'

'We'll join you shortly,' Raymond replied. He had kept his gun out of sight. Once Esmé had gone, he laid it on the table. 'Can't be too careful.'

'I'll need a lot more than "I didn't see anyone" if you want me to leave you alone.'

'This isn't official, is it?'

'It's as official as it gets. Do you want me to provide confirmation? It'll mean more detailed inquiries, more poking about in your affairs. Even the most diligent of us has things they'd rather not have surface. I know I have. I'm trying to keep things simple. Just between the two of us.'

'I have a completely new life here,' Raymond whined. 'I've put my time in the service far away in the back of my mind. You can't expect me to remember all the details after so long.'

'We're not talking about routine here: the tedium of daily chores, assessing intelligence reports which are always less than they seem. I'm talking about the murder of a colleague in broad daylight.'

'I've never understood why the phrase "in broad daylight" is supposed to make something sound worse. Surely "at dead of night" is no better?'

Sometimes silence can do your work for you. I sipped my tea, watching Raymond over the rim of my cup. After a minute he started to shift. His right leg suddenly shot forward. 'Bloody cramp!' He writhed in pain as he put his weight into stretching his leg.

'Do you have tonic water?' I asked.

'In the fridge.'

I found a can. I popped it open and handed it to him. He glugged it straight down and let out a burp. He glanced over at me. 'Does it work?'

'I've heard it does. Feel any better?'

'I believe I do.' He flexed his leg and stood up. 'Now, before I ask you to leave, I shall do what my dear wife suggested, and show you around.'

He led the way from the kitchen, through a large music room and out through French doors into the garden. He had left his gun in the drawer in the kitchen, but his guard was still up.

'We have about five and a half acres here. Over on this north side are cages housing breeding birds, and some of the tortoises.' He continued along a path to the side of the lawn and stopped by the first cage. 'Turaco. A mated pair. The male – with a crest – comes from the Amsterdam zoo. The female is from Brussels. They send them to us and we get them breeding.'

I couldn't see the birds. With good reason. The wood-framed cage was about twenty-feet wide by fifteen deep, and about fifteen-feet high. Unlike most bird cages – barren deserts with compacted mud floors and a couple of dead branches for perches – this cage was packed with living, flowering plants and shrubs that climbed up to the roof. The perches were branches of thriving shrubs. I recognised tropical hibiscus, guava, strelitzia and passion flowers.

'I don't see any birds.'

Raymond uttered a call, similar to the honk of a goose but shorter and with a higher pitch. Two bright green birds suddenly appeared on the nearest branch.

'They'll think it's feeding time. Sorry to disappoint you birdies.'

I saw movement on the floor of the cage. A large tortoise – about a foot long – had appeared from the dense undergrowth and was munching on a cabbage head.

'That's a young Sulcata. They get a lot bigger than that.'

'What happens in winter?'

'We have the staff erect glass panels all around the cages; keeps them frost free.'

We passed several more cages, all richly planted. Each had small streams and pools of clear water running through them. I pondered how I could get Raymond to open up. If I couldn't, then my visit would be wasted.

As we rounded a thicket we heard faint cries coming from across the lawn. I peered into the hazy distance and saw that one of the giant 'molehills' was moving.

'My God, it's Esmé!' Raymond gasped. He set off at a fast trot across the lawn. I followed.

It took me a few seconds to understand exactly what had happened. Esmé's Zimmer frame had overturned on the grass. Through its metal struts I could make out an enormous tortoise – almost five-feet long and three-feet across, thrusting at something large that lay beneath it. That something was Esmé, face down on the lawn, whimpering.

'I've been calling out for fifteen minutes! Get him off me!'

Raymond grabbed the beast's massive carapace above its neck and heaved, to no effect. The giant tortoise was in a state of high arousal. Between the creature's rear legs something long and pink protruded. I stepped gingerly around it. The creature kept on thrusting. I took hold of one massive foreleg, which had been clawing at the old lady's corpulent body, to get a better purchase. I tugged backwards with all my might.

This only produced a combination of angry hissing and snapping jaws.

'Tank won't bite,' said Raymond, before adding, somewhat uncertainly, 'I don't think so, anyway. His eyesight's not that good.'

The hissing was certainly off-putting. I took hold of the front of the carapace with one hand and got a better grip of the foreleg with the other.

'One, two, three… heave!'

We both heaved together and managed to topple the great beast onto its rounded back, where it lay hissing and thrashing its trunk-like legs. Raymond struggled to raise his wife off the ground, but she was too weak and shocked by her ordeal to stand. Together we managed to lift Esmé into a wicker chair. She sat there, palpitating.

'Oh dear,' she exclaimed. 'I think I've broken my pearl necklace. What a bother!'

15

Our journey to the Royal Surrey County Hospital in Guildford was completed in under twenty minutes. That was because I was driving. Raymond was in no fit state to do anything but hold Esmé, whom we had wrapped in a blanket. Both her legs had received long gashes from the giant tortoise's long claws. Despite this, she seemed remarkably unaffected by her ordeal.

'I haven't been into Guildford for weeks,' she said. 'Perhaps we can go shopping afterwards.'

'Let's see what the doctors say,' Raymond cautioned. His face was white and he was trembling. After we'd rescued Esmé it had been up to me to roll the helpless tortoise over onto its front, so it could stalk off with what little dignity it still possessed. I had taken Raymond's key to his estate car – a Volvo – driven it up onto the pristine lawn and helped bundle Esmé into the back.

At the hospital I found a parking space, displayed the car's blue badge on the dashboard with my time of arrival, helped Esmé into a wheelchair and hurried her through the emergency doors. She was on blood thinners, so her bleeding legs looked much worse than they were. A paramedic asked what had caused her injuries.

'A tortoise attacked me!' Esmé declared, with some indignation.

The paramedic took control of the chair and wheeled her out of sight.

'Of course, he thinks she means a domestic tortoise, something about eight inches long.' Raymond sighed. 'They'll think she's mad. I suppose we both are, a bit.'

I took his hand. It was still trembling.

'I don't know what I'd do if I lost her.'

'She's had a bit of a shock and a few scratches,' I said. 'But as far as I can see she's more resilient than you are.'

I kept hold of his hand. He seemed ready to speak. I was prepared to be patient, but his words tumbled out.

'There was something,' he confessed. 'I dismissed – no, ignored it – at the time.' Raymond struggled to control himself. 'It seemed nothing. Just a silly remark.'

I waited a while. 'A remark? From whom?'

'Jim, his name was. Or Jamie. I can't really remember.'

'Surname?'

'That's just it. I don't recall. He wasn't with us for long. I think he fell ill. Infected mosquito bite or something.'

'What was it he said?'

'Something about the ambassador's car having sand in its fuel tank.'

It did not take long for Esmé's wounds to be dressed. She was given an antibiotic injection and, because of her 'advanced age', a bed for the night. I snorted in disdain: she was younger than I was. Raymond said he would stay and see her settled in. That meant I had to get a taxi to Guildford station, wait for the train to Cobham & Stoke d'Abernon (a thirty-minute trip, if the train is running) which, it so happens, is nowhere near Cobham, then wait for another taxi to get me back to Hazelnut House. As I was dropped off I realised that I had no way of getting in past the gates. I called Raymond, but there was no reply. I was on the point of checking the high fence around the estate for breaks when Raymond called me back.

'So sorry, I'm not supposed to make phone calls in the hospital. I've had to come out in the street to call you.'

'How's Esmé?'

'Asleep. She can drop off whenever she feels like it. Lucky her. I think I've remembered that chap's surname. Sanders. Or Saunders. Something like that. Or maybe Sanderson? No, I'm pretty sure it was Saunders. He went back to London.'

'I need to get in to fetch my car.'

'Of course, how stupid of me.'

He told me the passcode, I keyed it in and the gates swung open. I hurried over to my car and managed to get inside just as the two boxers bounded up, snarling. They were a lot less friendly without their owners present. I turned the car around, only to find the gates had shut again. I had to edge the car up to a release button set in a wooden post. I wound down my window, reached out and almost got my fingers bitten off.

I like dogs. Most dogs, that is. I've looked after several in my time. Some were difficult animals with bad reputations. I managed to win them all over with a bit of care and understanding. I understood these boxers. They thought they were protecting their master and mistress, and that I was an intruder. I lowered the passenger window and called out to them. The dogs dashed around to the passenger side of the car, ready to give battle. At the same time I reached out and pressed the button. The gates opened and I edged forward, careful not to injure the dogs.

Once the gates had closed behind me and I was off their territory, the dogs lost interest. I headed back to London to drop off the car.

I drove carefully, so as not to attract attention. The A3 narrowed to a single lane as they were working on 'improvements'. A large SUV tailgated me and hooted persistently, trying to get me to speed up. As there was a fifty-mile-an-hour limit and I was already going at fifty, I ignored him. He kept hooting until the road returned to three lanes. He revved his engine and roared past me, yelling profanities. A hundred yards on he had to stop at traffic lights. As I pulled up beside him he wound down his window and shouted, 'You stupid old bat! What the fuck do you think you're doing, holding up the traffic?'

I rolled down my window and beamed my most winsome smile. 'I am a high court judge,' I replied. 'Now that I've had a good look at you, and have recorded your number plate, I shall remember you. If ever you ever appear before me in court I hope I shall not allow this incident to influence my judgment in deciding your length of sentence. But I cannot promise you anything. We are all human, after all.'

His mouth dropped open. The lights changed to green and I drove on. He remained where he was, his engine idling. Horns hooted behind him. In my rear-view mirror I saw him execute a sharp turn across the oncoming traffic, doing his best to put a wide distance between himself and me.

I was still congratulating myself on dealing with this hooligan when I entered the rental company's offices. The unhelpful young woman was not at her desk. Instead a man sat there, his head bowed over a pile of documents.

I dropped the car keys in front of him. 'I'm returning my hire car.'

The man stood suddenly. In that instant I noticed two things: the gun in his hand and the two large moles on his cheek.

'You will turn around and put your hands behind your head,' he said in a thick Eastern European accent.

'Say please, and I might comply.' I was furious with myself for not remaining alert. And for turning on my iPhone to film the car for scratches.

'Turn and put your hands behind your head,' he repeated. 'Please.'

I did as he said, wondering whether I could spin around and knock the gun from his hand. I decided against it. I heard a dull thump coming from a locked cupboard. So that's what had become of the receptionist. Perhaps she could brush up on her customer relations skills while she was waiting to be released.

The man stepped up behind me.

'Now put your hands down. Please.'

I lowered my hands and turned just as something hard and metallic hit the back of my head. I stumbled forward, my head spinning. Before I could recover I was struck a second time and lost consciousness.

16

Greece, 1984

At around six in the morning I was woken by the yacht's twin engines roaring into life. That was my cue to rise and shower. I did this quickly while the boat drew up the anchor chains with a loud and heavy rattle. I was dressed and ready before we reached the open sea and left Kate asleep in her bunk.

I found Jean-Louis in the crew's mess, nursing a hangover and preparing Greek coffee 'metrio' for himself and the deckhands. They had been up for an hour, casting off, lifting the fenders and coiling up the mooring lines.

'What happened last night?' Jean-Louis groaned.

'Between us? Absolutely nothing, I'm glad to say. I enjoyed a small lager and left you after forty minutes, when the boss and his guests were heading back to the boat. The last I saw of you, you were ordering a bottle of retsina and inviting two Italian ladies to join you.'

'I remember that. Not much more. Not even how I got back on board.'

We sat drinking our coffees in silence. The deckhands were busy above us, removing the covers on the sun deck.

Captain Grigori came in and slumped at the table. He carried the big bottle of whisky that Sir Roland had brought him as a gift. It was already half empty. Jean-Louis fetched him a glass. While Grigori poured himself a large slug of whisky, Jean-Louis cooked him scrambled eggs with feta crumbled over the top. Grigori wolfed the lot down in a few seconds, burped loudly, then lay down on the crew's bench and fell asleep almost immediately.

'Scrambled eggs, porridge, yoghurt, fresh fruit, or all of them? What do you want? You have a busy day ahead.'

'I'll take them all,' I said. 'But why does the boss keep Grigori around? He doesn't strike me as much of a captain.'

'Ah, that's a story. When Mavros' father Dimitris was starting out in the business, Grigori was his first captain. Despite terrible weather and near mutinies from the crew, Grigori always delivered his cargo and got Dimitris out of trouble many times. So his son is paying Grigori back with this job. To Mr Mavros, loyalty means everything.'

I studied the snoring figure.

'This is Grigori's final year at the helm. Then he'll be pensioned off.' Jean-Louis plated up the scrambled egg with pitta bread, crumbled feta over it and passed the plate over. 'But you should see the office back in Athens.'

'Go on.' I shovelled in a forkful of egg. Delicious.

'Two or three people do all the work. But there are a dozen guys hanging around – how do you say, *se tournant les pouces*?'

'Twiddling their thumbs.'

'*Exactement*. Their fathers were all captains in the Mavros fleet. Good ones. They begged Dimitris to give jobs to their useless sons. Now the boss has inherited them. He won't trust them with a ship, so they hang out in the office, get paid for doing nothing and enjoy long lunches.'

'Sounds expensive.' I opened a carton of Greek yoghurt and spooned in a glob of Attiki honey.

The deck crew arrived for breakfast. Sunil woke Grigori, who staggered up to the bridge to take over from the bosun. A few moments later Lefteris, scowling as usual, joined us. He shook his head and gestured with his thumb to his mouth that the captain was drunk.

I finished my breakfast and gave my seat to Kate.

'The guests will be up early. These diplomatic types always are,' she said. 'So go up and lay the table.'

We were travelling at around twenty-five knots, so as I laid the table at the rear of the deck I ensured that none of the lighter objects, such as paper napkins – we used linen ones for lunch and dinner – would blow away. When I'd finished I went and stood at the bow.

Mykonos island, shrouded in a watery haze, rose like a brown shadow out of the sea.

Nothing can match a yacht travelling swiftly between the Greek islands at dawn. The air rushes through your hair, the sea changes from steel grey to blue, the sun rises in a cloudless sky, shearwaters glide behind you and dolphins race each other at the prow as the boat powers through the waves, sending sprays of salt water to sting your face. The intensity of it all gives you such a sense of joy and freedom that you feel you will live forever.

17

London, September 2019

WHEN I CAME TO IT was night. I found myself strapped to a heavy oak chair in a small basement room lit by a single bare lightbulb. My hands were bound behind my back with zip-tie cuffs. My head hurt, but not as much as I expected. As I raised it a shadow fell over me. A rough hand slapped me so hard it almost knocked me back into unconsciousness.

'Good, you are awake,' the mole-man said in a voice so similarly accented to that of the late Josef (whose head I had recently blown apart) that, even in my befuddled state, I suspected he must be his brother or at least a close relative.

'Who are you and what do you want?'

'As you will not live to pass this information on to anybody else,' he replied, 'I shall tell you. My name it is Aleksi, and I want to know what happened to my cousin, Josef.'

His cousin. Close enough. 'I have no idea.'

'He lost his ear because of you. So I will take your ear. For my collection.'

'Your collection?'

'We have a game. When we kill someone, we keep something, a memento. A cigarette lighter, a shoe. Something to remind us. So I keep your ear.'

He studied me a while. 'And after that, I take your life.'

'Why should you want to kill me? I've done nothing to you.'

'This is true, but Josef has disappeared. You killed him.'

'What's this Josef look like? I don't believe I know him.' I was stalling for time and he knew it.

'Yes, you do.' He smiled. 'To tell you the truth, I never liked Josef.'

'Then why do it?'

'Family honour,' he said and headed out of the room. He stopped in the doorway and grinned. 'Don't go away.'

There wasn't much chance of my going anywhere. My ankles were strapped to the chair legs and my arms were held in place by the high back of the chair. It was far too heavy for me to move or tip over.

I could hear Aleksi ferreting about in the room overhead. I had only a short time to figure out a means of escape before he returned.

My hands, though restricted by the zip-tie cuffs, could still grasp the back of my belt. Made for Dennis's grandfather, a colonel in the Indian army, the belt consisted of strips of embossed leather linked by silver hinges. One night, when I was recovering from a gunshot wound at Dennis's house in Fulham, we had stayed up late and watched an old black-and-white thriller from the 1940s. In a pivotal scene, our hero was strapped down with his hands tied behind his back, while his female assistant (and love interest) was assaulted by the villain. Our hero struggled in vain to free his bonds.

'What he needs,' said Dennis, 'is an Ever-Ready.'

'A battery?'

'One of those old-fashioned, single-edged razor blades, the type you use to scrape paint off windows. If he had one stuck in his belt he could use it to cut his ropes and rescue his girl.'

'Who on earth has a belt full of razor blades?'

'Just one would do,' replied Dennis.

Two days later he produced the belt. 'It may come in useful one day.'

I checked it. The belt's square clasp opened and closed to lock a silver pin into the belt holes. Behind the clasp was a secret compartment, released with the flick of a catch.

'You can hide anything small in there. Codes, messages, microfiches.'

'A cyanide pill?'

'If that's what you want.'

Well, I did want. I was once provided with two such pills on an unofficial mission. One of them came in very useful. But it wasn't I who swallowed it.

'Check the back.'

I turned the belt around. The central strip of leather had been unpicked and re-sewn to leave a small slot from which protruded a short strip of steel.

'Take it out.'

I eased the strip free.

'Carefully.'

The steel strip proved to be the blunt end of a single-edged razor blade. I slipped it back in its sheath.

'Ingenious.' I kissed Dennis. He took it as permission to go further. I did not discourage him.

When I left the service I took off that belt – for good, I thought. Now, as Aleksi re-entered the room, I was glad to be wearing it.

He carried a Sabatier chef's knife. It was long, pointed and, if I knew Sabatiers, extremely sharp. Aleksi made a point of testing the blade with a show of deep concentration. He was beginning to irritate me. The back of my head was throbbing. My legs, tightly bound, were cramping up and my wrists chafed.

'If anything happens to me, people will come looking for you.'

'They can come looking, but they will not find me. I shall not be here.'

'It isn't so easy for a man with two large moles on his face to escape detection.'

Aleksi laughed: a short, sharp bark like that of a fox. He laid the knife on a table. 'They will be looking for a man with two moles, like these.' He reached up to his right cheek and tore the two moles off his face in one swift movement. 'Now that man is gone.'

It is not often that someone surprises me.

'You are not the only one who is able to change their appearance. People see the moles, not the face. It even fools facial recognition cameras.' He tossed his 'moles' to the floor and snatched up the knife. 'Now, the fun begins.' He leant forward to raise my hair off my right ear. He seized it in his left forefinger and thumb and bent it away from my head, so as to make it easy for him to remove it.

While Aleksi had been upstairs I had managed to extract the Ever-Ready razor blade from its sheath. It had not been easy. For a start, my back was pressed firmly up against the chair. My fingers, once so nimble, were now clumsy, mildly arthritic things. For one heart-stopping moment the blade had slipped from my grasp. In silent panic I rescued it from a fold of my coat. It sliced into my thumb but the pain was an insignificant sting. At least I had the blade.

As Aleksi taunted me I sawed away at my plastic ties. I

kept my movements to a minimum. As he leant forward to slice off my ear I felt the last sliver of plastic break apart. My tormentor held his blade pointing upwards, cutting edge poised above my ear. I grabbed his knife hand with my right and grasped his thinning hair with my left, forcing his knife hand up and his head down. The point of the blade pierced his throat between the angle of his jaw and his chin. I forced it upwards, into the roof of his mouth, and held it firm.

I'm no doctor, but I believe a knife thrust between the gums does little lasting harm. There may be some nerve damage, the ability to taste may be affected, but there will be little permanent damage. I had avoided his tongue. I needed him able to talk.

Aleksi had gone rigid. He knew that any movement might make things worse. I was only too happy to confirm his fears.

'Now,' I informed him, 'it only needs a small upwards thrust for the blade to enter your brain.' I was on shaky ground, but I presumed Alexis's knowledge of human anatomy was shakier than mine. 'Once it ruptures your brain, there's no hope. You understand?'

'Yeth,' Aleksi lisped. He could barely move his tongue.

'Good. Now you're going to undo the straps around my legs.'

Aleksi shifted his head. 'Careful,' I warned. 'I don't want to give you a lobotomy.' His eyes bulged at the thought. I lowered my hands and he bent to free my legs.

'Now I shall stand up and we shall walk to the door together.' As I stood, I almost stumbled. He tried to pull away, but I jabbed the knife point upwards. He yelped. 'Careful, now, we don't want any accidents, do we? I might easily slip and do you some permanent damage.'

We made it to the door. 'Where's your gun?' I demanded. He raised his left arm to reveal his holster. That meant he was right-handed. 'With your left thumb and forefinger, carefully lift your gun out of your holster and put it on that shelf by the door.' I could see he was thinking there might still be a way to overcome me, but I had an idea.

'Stand on your toes,' I said. He was now backed against the wall by the door. Even if he tried to use his gun, I was in a better position to ram the knife home. He took hold of the gun as instructed, between thumb and forefinger, and placed it on the shelf. It was a Smith and Wesson TRR8, an eight-shot pistol easily operated with one hand. I pressed the knife deeper into the roof of his mouth.

'Now listen. I didn't start this fight. But I am ready to finish it. I could kill you, but I won't – unless you do something stupid. You caught me out once. You won't do it again. Nod if you understand.'

He nodded very slowly.

'Very well, step over there.'

As he moved towards the corner of the room I withdrew the knife from his jaw. Blood flowed freely. He clasped his hands to his throat, his face white.

'Don't worry, you won't die. Just remember what I said. If I see you again, you're dead. Now step into that corner.' As he did so I snatched up the gun, stepped out of the room, shut the door behind me and turned the key. He would find a way out soon enough. But by then I would be far away.

18

Greece, March 1984

Mykonos town has the most intriguing layout of all the Cycladic islands. The *chora* was originally built as a maze of narrow alleys and passages to confuse and defeat Ottoman pirates. By the time we arrived, what had once been fishermen's cottages and net lofts had long been converted into smart boutiques and cafés.

Kate and I accompanied Lady Mary on her shopping trip. Kate knew her way around and I tagged along to familiarise myself with the town. It would have been easy to get lost in the back lanes if the streets had been crowded, but at this time of year, so early in the season, many of the shops only opened after midday, as they would remain busy well into late evening. Lady Mary bought several outfits from 'exclusive' shops at exclusive prices. I suspected that, even with the discounts Kate managed to get her, the prices were probably higher than they would have been in London, Paris or Milan. But Lady Mary was enjoying herself.

At around two in the afternoon we lunched in a taverna booked by Captain Grigori. Mavros and Sir Roland were already waiting for us and had cracked open a bottle of very good wine. A middle-aged couple had joined them. At our approach the couple stood and the woman hurried over to embrace Lady Mary and kiss her on both cheeks. They proved to be the Belgian ambassador and his wife. Their encounter had been pure chance, but it gave Mavros another opportunity to play the generous host. He knew both the restaurant owner and the chef, and when they brought fish on a tray for him to select, Mavros allowed the Belgian ambassador's wife to choose.

Kate and I were assigned a small table on the street outside the taverna, where tourists passed. As we sat chatting an oaf snatched a hunk of bread from our basket and made off with it, munching as he went. I stood to go after him, but Kate grabbed my hand and pulled me back.

'Tourists off the cruise boats,' Kate said with a shrug. 'They bring their own sandwiches, don't eat in the restaurants, don't spend any money. One day they'll be banned and that day won't come too soon for me.' She held onto my hand a little longer than seemed necessary.

Mavros had ordered for us: octopus with a split pea mash and a salad, followed by classic baklava in honey. Although Kate was something of a closed book I managed to get her to open up about herself. She had no intention of remaining chief stew all her life. She wanted to settle down, preferably with a successful superyacht captain who understood the nature of her work. She gave me no clue about why she kept a gun in our cabin, and I did not bring it up.

After lunch we returned to the yacht, which was anchored just outside the port. Captain Grigori sent Stavros over with the Zodiac to pick us up. He had to make a second trip for Lady Mary's shopping.

The moment we were all aboard Captain Grigori upped anchor and headed for Delos, the historic sacred island three kilometres to the south-west. For some reason I was delegated to accompany the group – it was probably Lady

Mary's idea of rehabilitating me in Sir Roland's eyes – along with Jean-Louis who, like me, had never visited the island before.

The Zodiac dropped us at the Delos landing point, built to accommodate day visitors alighting from a ferry. It was too high for us to reach comfortably, especially with choppy waves rocking the tender. We had to remove our shoes and jump across barefoot. As Lady Mary landed she scraped one foot on the concrete. I could see it bleeding, but she was made of sturdy stuff and slipped her deck shoes back on. Mavros told Lefteris to return for us in ninety minutes, then led us at a fast pace round the sacred site.

Delos is, according to Mavros and various Greek guidebooks, the birthplace of Apollo. This appealed to Mavros who, when asked about his family's origins by Sir Roland, proudly declared that all Greeks are descended from the gods.

The brisk breeze kept us moving. We had just reached the House of Dionysus, a villa whose spectacular *tesserae* depicted the god of wine and ecstasy riding a fearsome tiger (which to my mind more closely resembled a leopard), when Lady Mary stumbled and let out a cry. She removed her deck shoe. Two of her toes were bloodied and raw, with a thin flap of skin hanging loose.

'So silly of me,' she said. 'I thought I could manage, but walking around in these shoes has only made things worse.'

'Why don't you go back to the dock,' said Sir Roland. 'Vasilis and I can finish our fascinating tour, and these two can take you back.' He meant Jean-Louis and me.

'I'm perfectly capable of making my own way back.' She looked Jean-Louis up and down. 'Well, perhaps this young man can help.' She held out her hand for the chef to hold for balance, slipped her shoe back on, and hobbled away.

Mavros and Sir Roland continued the tour, leaving me to go wherever I wanted. I headed back towards the landing point, holding well back so that Jean-Louis could flirt with Lady Mary as she limped along.

I skirted around the site, passing the terrace of the Lions, with its row of sculpted beasts, their mouths open in silent roars. It was hard to believe that their creator had ever seen a real lion in the flesh. Like the mosaic of the tiger, these lions appeared to be a cross between a leopard and a cheetah, which may have been the sculptor's true model.

I noticed a person hiding behind the final lion. As I approached a man suddenly stepped out. It was the man in the suit I had spotted in Tinos, and he was sweating in the sun. As I carried on after Lady Mary and Jean-Louis he simply smiled and nodded to me. He remained where he was, partially masked by the lion statue, watching Sir Roland and Mavros. As he was a fair distance from them, and did not look as if he could move fast, I felt it safe to continue on my way. But I kept a wary eye on him.

I found Lady Mary and Jean-Louis sitting by a little bay close to the landing point. Lady Mary was dangling her injured foot in the clear seawater.

'Come and look at this, my dear,' she called to me. I went over. 'Isn't it remarkable?'

A prawn, some two-inches long, was snipping with its tiny claws at the torn skin of Lady Mary's second toe. She found it charming, even though the prawn was devouring the skin as it snipped.

'Neater than a surgeon,' she laughed.

A call of greeting from Sir Roland got her rising to her feet. The Zodiac was approaching to pick us up.

As the tender pulled up to the landing stage Lefteris threw out a line for Jean-Louis to catch. Lady Mary stepped onto the rib and was helped to her seat. The rest of us clambered on board. Jean-Louis threw back the line and leapt aboard, carrying Lady Mary's deck shoes. Lefteris put the Zodiac into reverse, turned the wheel and powered away. As we headed for the MY *Fantasy* I scanned the bay. There were no other boats in the vicinity. I could see no way the man in the suit had got onto the island nor how he would get off. But whatever he had been doing there, he was no tourist.

19

London, 2019

BEFORE I RETURNED TO THE safe house I stopped off at Westfield shopping mall in White City (extended late night shopping) and bought two changes of clothes. With my alias as Eleanor Farquhar now blown, I disposed of her bank card and driving licence and paid in the name of Delphine Fabricant.

I chose items that I would not normally consider part of my wardrobe: a plain white T-shirt, bright blue slacks and an orange cashmere sweater to drape over my shoulders. I carried other purchases, together with Eleanor's outfit, in a large carrier bag. I popped into Waitrose for some supplies and took a taxi back to Notting Hill. I had meant to cook myself a simple pasta dish – *spaghetti al burro e aglio* – but I was so exhausted by my exertions that I went straight to bed and fell asleep almost immediately. I woke up hungry at three in the morning. Foxes were rummaging in bins, motorcycles delivering cocaine to wealthy customers, and top-of-the-range car alarms beeping loudly as opportunist thieves tried to steal their catalytic convertors. The familiar sounds of Notting Hill at night.

I got up with the intention of snacking on cornflakes with a good dash of milk. But I struggled to get the screw lid off the plastic bottle. It was too tight to twist off, and I wasn't going to risk my teeth by clamping my jaws on the lid and rotating the bottle. Eventually I found an adjustable wrench in a kitchen drawer, which did the trick. I am all for food safety and hygiene, but manufacturers should jolly well consider the elderly... by which I mean anyone older than myself.

I then spent a horrible thirty minutes dyeing my hair brown. Horrible because I managed to drop great globs of brown dye all over the bath mat. And I flinched when I touched the bruises where Aleksi had struck me with his pistol. It made me wish I had disposed of him for good.

The phone rang. Who on earth was ringing me at this hour?

I wrapped my hair in a towel and rushed to answer the phone. But by the time I reached it the line had gone dead. I tried dialling 1471 to discover the number, but the caller had withheld it.

I spent a fruitless fifteen minutes attempting to wash the dye out of both the bath mat and the towel I had wrapped around my hair. I discovered a hairdryer in a drawer and spent another twenty minutes combing out my hair. The results would have been passable had I not managed to dye my hands and neck with large brown blotches. The process had seemed so straightforward in a professional's hands. How people ever have the patience to do this at home beats me.

My neck stains were not a problem. The dye would soon fade and in the meantime I could style my hair to conceal the blotches. My hands were another matter entirely. I googled a solution: vinegar and baking soda. I had neither in the kitchen. I would have to sort that out in the morning. Exhausted and damp-haired, I went back to sleep.

I woke at around eight o'clock when the school run began. Polish builders had started clearing out a basement flat in the house opposite. As eight was the exact time they were allowed to start making noise, they started up enthusiastically, hurling broken plaster and rotten floorboards into a large skip.

I hauled myself out of bed, took a quick shower in cold water and was at the computer by 8.13. I keyed in the name Raymond had provided: *Saunders*. It had not been on Matthew's list.

The name produced no results at Companies House nor on the online telephone directory. I also checked Facebook and LinkedIn. As I scrolled through I was distracted by loud thumps from across the road. The builders were tossing piles of books and telephone directories into the skip. Some of the books appeared to be leather-bound antique volumes of considerable value, now all consigned to the scrap-heap.

At 8.30 on the dot I rang Matthew from the landline. He did not answer the first time, nor the second, but the moment I put the phone down it rang. The display showed No Caller ID. I listened but said nothing.

'Come on, I know you're there,' snapped Matthew. 'What have you got for me?'

'Does the name Saunders mean anything to you?'

'Sanders?'

'No, Saunders.'

'Let me think.'

I waited.

'No, I don't believe it does.'

'He was in Athens, apparently. At the embassy.'

'Was he?' Matthew sounded genuinely surprised. 'Before my time.'

'During.'

'Well, he must have been pretty insignificant. Or didn't last long. Have you contacted him?'

'Not yet.'

'If you can find an address for him, let me know. So we can keep the files updated.'

'How are the others doing?'

'So-so,' he replied. 'Nothing of note.'

'You must have your own suspicions.'

'If I did, then I wouldn't need you, would I?' There was silence.

'I'll get on, then.'

'Toodle-oo.' The phone went dead.

Typical Matthew. No encouragement, no support. I thought of putting a call in to Ambrose, then thought better of it. He had enough on his plate. I would only speak to him if absolutely necessary. I got to work tracking down this Saunders, or Sanders, or Sanderson. If he was still alive.

I tried keying in variations of his name, but found a load of young people, male, female and indeterminate. Then I had an idea.

I went out into the street, again in my white T-shirt but with a light coat over it. This was of a distinctive bronze colour with a shawl collar and belt – quite fashionable really – which created an appearance so different from either my usual one, or the one that Sarah Azizi-Ryan had selected, that I felt safe to show my face in public. I had given Aleksi the fright of his life and I believed – hoped – that he had taken my advice and high-tailed it back to Bulgaria, or wherever he came from.

I was just in time. A lorry had arrived to remove the skip.

'Wait a minute,' I called, as the lorry backed up. 'I've forgotten something.'

The driver braked hard, setting the loose chains on his lorry rattling. He lowered the hydraulic arm over the skip, then dismounted to fix the chains to the skip's lugs. While he was occupied I clambered into the skip and began ferreting through the debris. I was searching for the old telephone directories.

'Hey,' shouted the driver. 'You're goin' to mess your nice cloves.' He was right. Smashed plasterboards gave off clouds of musty powder every time I shifted them. But I only had a few minutes to act before he'd lose patience. 'An' it's illegal to remove fings from a skip. It's stealin'.'

'Not if they're your own belongings,' I shot back. 'I made a terrible mistake getting rid of these old telephone directories. Some of them are real collectors' items.'

'Yeah?' He was curious now. I unearthed the directories and found several full sets: one from 1988, one from 1995 and the most recent from 2001. The others were from earlier decades and of no interest to me. I hauled up the volumes listed S–Z and climbed out of the skip.

''Ere, I'm tellin' you, you can't take those!'

'These are the ones missing from my husband's collection. He's got duplicates of all the others. You should look out for the 1960s E–K sets. They really are valuable. I think I saw some down the bottom there.' With that I hurried away. The driver lost interest in me. He clambered into the skip and dug into the waste and muck at the bottom. I returned to the house without him noticing where I was living.

As I plonked my three directories on the kitchen table I heard shouting. I peered out the window. The Polish builders had swarmed around the skip. One knocked the directory the driver was clutching out of his hands. The others were insisting he get out of the skip and replace it with a fresh one. They looked close to coming to blows.

20

I MADE MYSELF ANOTHER POT of coffee and sat at my desk to enjoy it before I set to work in earnest.

Raymond had told me that James Saunders had returned from Athens to London, and had remained there, which is why it made sense to check the London directories.

I started with the earliest directory (S–Z) for 1988. I made a note of everyone with the surname Saunders and the first initial J in the London area and jotted down the telephone number alongside it. Then I went through the next directory and straight away I realised I had a problem.

Ever since 1966 the old prefix for London phone numbers had been 01. In 1990 the prefixes changed to 071 for inner London while outer London became 081. Then in 1995 they changed again and became 0171 and 0181. And in 2000 they changed one more time to 0207 and 0208 respectively. Even if I was able to find the correct number I would have to judge whether it was in an inner or outer London area. This is not as easy as it seems. While most of Kensington and Chelsea was designated as Inner London, North Kensington, where I now lived and worked, had been designated Outer London. I had no idea how many other boroughs followed suit, but the truncated postcodes in the directories gave some clues.

Another problem was that many Londoners had opted to go ex-directory, and that meant there would be no record of them in the phone book. Besides, many users had abandoned their landlines entirely in recent years and gone digital. I just had to hope James Saunders wasn't one of them.

I made a note of any Saunders, Sawnders and Sanders (just in case Matthew had been right about the name) in the 1988 directory. James may have been his first name (though it could have been Jimmy, or Jamie), but some people call themselves by their second given name. So many possibilities.

I found twenty-one with the first initial J. I jotted down the addresses and telephone numbers.

Then I went through the 1995 directory and did the same. Some of the names and addresses from the first book were no longer to be found in this one, while some new ones had been added. I wrote these down and put question marks against the first list for those names which did not reoccur in the second.

Once I had gone through the 1995 and 2001 directories, using a process of elimination, I had eleven likely names which I put on one list. I kept a second list of names which I considered lesser possibilities. On the first list I went through the numbers and swapped the prefixes 01, 071 and 0171 to 0207. Any 081s or 0181s became 0208. I telephoned each number in turn.

Of course I needed a cover story. Or several, as it turned out, depending on the ages of the people answering or the responses I got.

The first three numbers no longer belonged to people called James or Saunders in any form. Those people had all long moved on. The fourth yielded a bit of information. The current holders were the children – and grandchildren

– of one James Saunders, now in a retirement home in Bournemouth. Pressed, they admitted he suffered from frontal lobe dementia, was unable to articulate and could not even remember his name, let alone any details from his life forty years ago. The fifth person I called admitted to being James Saunders but refused to speak to me. I ticked his name as a possible and moved on down my list. Two numbers gave off a single tone, which indicated their phones had been cut off. Another call led to the recipient admitting that his real name had been Jerzy Sandowski and that he had changed it by deed poll some thirty years earlier. As had his brother Janek. So I crossed both those J Saunders off my list.

By the time I had finished I had three names that might be possible leads. One, in Highgate, North London, sounded a little too young to belong to the James I wanted. When I told him that I was researching the name Saunders – its original meaning being 'son of Alexander' and having possible (highly tenuous, in my opinion) connections stretching all the way back to Alexander the Great – he enthusiastically offered to meet me at his house, where I was welcome to study his family tree. Voices can be deceptive – I know mine is – so I gave his name and address a single tick, to denote it might be worth following up.

The second number was in Wimbledon, south-west London. This elderly gentleman accused me of being a vile, cold-calling 'phisher' and slammed the phone down. I called him back and managed to get him to hold on long enough to listen to my explanation that I was searching for my long-lost cousin James who, the last I heard of him, had been stationed in Greece in the 1980s. He heard me out, informed me that he had never been to Greece in his life, that Brexit had been the best thing that had ever happened to this country and that Edward Heath should never have taken us into Europe in the first place. None of this ruled him out, of course. He could easily have been the James I wanted. After all, anyone entering the diplomatic service needs to be a bloody good liar. But I sensed that he was not the man I wanted.

The third Saunders turned out to be a spinster. I told her I had got the wrong number and checked my list again.

The James who had refused to speak to me – the fifth of my calls – resided conveniently near me in Bayswater. In the first directory he was listed as living in a flat in Leinster Square. In the second directory he had moved to Moscow Road, but had retained his telephone number. He might have moved on from there since but I hoped that, having made the journey from Leinster Square to Moscow Road, a mere hundred yards away, the excitement had proved too much for him and that he had settled there for good.

I took a number 7 bus, using one of my spare Freedom Passes, from Ladbroke Grove to Westbourne Grove, where I got off and strode down Hereford Road. Reaching Moscow Road, I turned left and headed towards the Greek cathedral of Santa Sophia. On the opposite side of the road were some flats. I crossed over and rang a doorbell. After a few seconds a young woman's voice answered. 'Yes?'

'I've got a package for James Saunders.'

'He don't live here no more. 'Asn't for years.'

I sighed inwardly. This was going to take me longer than I had hoped. There was a small commotion at the other end of the intercom, and an older woman's voice spoke. 'I got his new address, if you want.'

At last, a chink of light. 'Yes please.'

'Though maybe he moved.' There was a pause. 'S'not far.' She gave me the address – a house just around the corner.

I made my way to Bark Place. James Saunders clearly preferred to remain in familiar surroundings. I marched briskly down the narrow street and found myself outside a pretty pastel-coloured house. If James could afford a whole house in this part of Bayswater, he must have come up in the world. Then I noticed that the steps down to the basement led to a small self-contained flat.

Guessing this was more likely to be James's residence, I descended the few steps, passed a window blacked out with a thick curtain, and rang the bell.

Nothing happened for around twenty seconds, which can feel a long time when you're waiting for a door to open. Then I became aware of a corner of the curtain being lifted and a pale face peering out at me. As I turned, the face drew back and the curtain dropped.

I rang the doorbell again and rapped hard on the window. There was no answer. I bent down, poked open the letterbox in the door and shouted, 'I know you're in there. I'm not going away until you open this door.' A minute went by. I plucked a twig from a bush in the tiny front garden, depressed the doorbell and jammed the twig into it so that it would not stop ringing.

After another thirty seconds or so I heard a bolt on the inside of the door being drawn back and a key turn in a lock. Then another key turned and another bolt was drawn open. The door opened a crack. It was held on a thick chain to prevent entry. Peering out at me was that same pale face I had seen behind the curtain, and a pair of hollow, haunted eyes.

'What do you want?' His voice was thin and weak.

'James Saunders? I have something for you.'

'Is it a notice of eviction?'

'No.'

'What is it, then?'

'Can you open the door please?'

'Are you alone?'

I looked back up the steps and into the street. 'As far as I can ascertain, I have not been followed. Now are you going to let me in or do you want me to call Special Branch and get them to break down the door?'

James Saunders slammed the door in my face. I heard the chain slide off and the door reopened. 'Come in. Quick,' he said. He stepped back. I walked past him into a dark corridor. As I waited for my eyes to get accustomed to the gloom James placed one foot onto the step outside, looked up at the house, and then ducked back inside. 'I don't think she's seen you.'

'Who is this "she" you're so frightened of?'

'My wife.'

21

Greece, March 1984

THE FOLLOWING DAY SIR ROLAND encouraged Lady Mary to go shopping again. She was put ashore to join her friend, the Belgian ambassador's wife. Kate accompanied them. She did not seem happy about it, but Captain Grigori made the rules and she had to obey.

Mavros was keen to move on. The MY *Fantasy* edged out to sea, following the lie of the anchor chain. As soon as we were well away from the fishing caiques and sailing boats the captain opened the throttle until we reached our cruising speed.

There was a tense, heightened atmosphere, very different from that of the previous days. Mavros retreated to his state bedroom while Sir Roland busied himself at the back of the boat, using the dining table as a work desk. He checked through documents, made notes and corrections, then put them away in his briefcase and locked it securely. But he had a distracted look, as if something was weighing heavily on his mind. He requested a gin and tonic, which I prepared with a little ice and a slice of lime. He hardly touched it as he sat watching the sea go past.

The journey lasted little more than three hours. Jean-Louis prepared lunch, and I hovered around the kitchen, keeping him company. Every so often I returned to Sir Roland and asked if I could get him anything. He requested a second gin and tonic, then changed his mind and asked for a tonic without ice. He dismissed me. I sensed my attentions were getting on his nerves.

When we reached Chios we did not sail into the harbour, as I had expected, but dropped anchor just outside the port of Mesta. And there we waited. And waited.

I went back to the aft deck to collect Sir Roland's glass. Before I could ask him if he needed anything, he shook his head and turned away from me. I disappeared back into the galley and waited.

The boat rocked gently. The sky became overcast.

From the north came a yacht – smaller than ours, but faster. As it turned in towards us I saw there was no ensign on the stern, denoting its nationality. I guessed, rightly as it turned out, that it was Turkish.

Lefteris reacted to a call from Captain Grigori. He rushed to the side of the yacht, alerted the two deckhands and the three of them laid inflated fenders against the hull. Mavros appeared on deck. He looked serious.

The Turkish boat swung around wildly, its captain unskilled compared to ours. Lines were thrown across from one yacht to another and both deck crews hauled hard to bring the Turkish yacht alongside. Our crew tied up properly, the Turkish crew more slackly. Two men stepped across onto the MY *Fantasy*. The first, to my surprise, was the man in the dark suit whom I had seen shadowing us on Tinos and Delos. Following him was a shorter man wearing new jeans and a zipped black windcheater over a checked shirt. He wore sunglasses – although it was not sunny – and a white floppy hat that masked most of his face and his head with its greasy locks. He was unshaven. He had that look about him of a man who allows a straggly growth to linger around his face, never long enough to develop into a full beard, never short enough to suggest that he'd ever familiarised himself with a razor.

To my surprise, Mavros welcomed him cordially with the words, '*Salam Alaikum*,' and received the traditional response, '*Wa Alaikum Salam*.'

He led his guests into the salon, where Sir Roland, his papers laid out on the table, rose and nodded. He did not hold out his hand to either man.

I followed them into the salon to enquire if they would like any refreshments. Mavros whipped round and snapped, 'Leave us alone.' Then, more softly but sternly, 'I shall call if we require anything.' I turned on my heel and slid the door closed as I returned to the aft deck. As I made my way around the boat to the galley, Mavros shut the salon's venetian blinds, so that no crew member could see in. He even closed the door to the galley, which was almost always latched open.

Jean-Louis and I went to the foredeck and shared a cigarette. It was a Gitanes, his usual brand. He lit it, took a couple of long drags, passed it to me and I, without thinking, took a long drag… and choked and coughed. Jean-Louis snatched the cigarette back and watched, smirking, as I regained control of my body.

'I don't know why I did that,' I said. 'I never smoke.'

'It's the boredom,' he said. 'We shall be here all day, doing nothing. Unless you want to come to my cabin.'

'They may need me.'

'Then they will call us on the intercom.'

I declined his offer but kept it in mind. He was an attractive man and waiting to be summoned was mind-numbing. We bobbed about in the sea for more than an hour before we heard a word from the salon. Then the galley door slid open, Mavros popped his head in and demanded three coffees, black. Jean-Louis prepared them and I took them in on a tray, with a small jug of milk in case anyone changed their minds.

The stranger had removed his hat. His hair was thinning and his hairline receding. His eyes, no longer hidden by his sunglasses, were dark angry pits in a pale face that looked like it hadn't seen daylight in a long while.

'I said black coffee,' Mavros snapped as he pushed the milk jug away. 'And bring us a fresh pot.'

It was not just Mavros who was in a black mood. The stranger and Sir Roland were pointedly avoiding looking at each other, like a couple of tomcats spoiling for a fight.

I headed back to the galley. 'And leave it outside, I will fetch it myself,' Mavros called out, his voice muffled as I shut the door behind me.

Less muffled was the argument that broke out almost instantly in the salon. Jean-Louis had gone down to his bunk and I was left alone brewing the coffee. As it percolated, curiosity got the better of me. I took a glass from a cupboard and held it against the salon door. I put my ear to the glass and listened. At first all I heard was indistinct Arabic – that was the stranger and the man in the suit talking between themselves. Then the man in the suit spoke in accented English, difficult to make out. Easier to hear was Sir Roland's angry voice, a clear baritone, pointedly refusing the stranger's demands, whatever they were.

The percolator started to bubble up and I stepped away from my listening post to check it. I was just in time. The door flew open and Mavros marched in.

'Cancel the coffee. Our guests are leaving. Inform the captain.'

I did as I was asked, and a few minutes later the stranger and the man in the grey suit clambered back aboard the Turkish boat. Its engines revved and it attempted to speed away before our crew had finished untying the lines. There was a sharp crack as the Turkish lines snapped. One line whipped past Lefteris' face. Another inch and it might have taken out his eye. In that split second Stavros managed to untie our line. It ripped through his bare palms, eliciting a cry of pain as it flayed his skin.

The Turkish boat throttled forward and bounced across the waves, trailing our line in its wake. Sir Roland retreated to his cabin and Mavros to his own. Whatever the meeting had been about, it had gone badly.

22

London, 2019

I SAT IN THE CHAIR James Saunders offered me. It was covered with hairs and the stink of cat urine pervaded his gloomy basement.

'Do you keep cats?' I asked.

'No,' he shot back. 'I'm forbidden from keeping a cat. Why do you ask?'

'No particular reason.' I hunched up so the least part of me touched the chair – or anything else in the flat. I counted hard dry lumps under the chairs and tables. They looked like the sort of faecal matter a cat might deposit. 'May I ask why you are so concerned about your wife?' I wondered if she had been in the service, as we both had.

James leant forward, a haunted look in his face. 'She's trying to get me evicted.'

'Can she do that? If you're together?'

'Together!' He let out a bitter laugh. 'We haven't been together for years. We've *never* been together.'

'I'm sorry to hear that.' I was sorry I'd asked. I wasn't interested in his private life. I needed to keep him on track. But James needed someone to talk to. And I fitted the bill only too well.

'She only married me to fulfil her father's will and free up his money.' He clasped his hands together, agitated. 'We met in the coffee shop. The Greek one on Moscow Road. Over their *Portokalopita*. You know what that means?'

'Orange cake.'

'I mean my marriage,' he replied bitterly. 'It was a sham from the beginning. But you're right about the translation. Though their word for "orange" is actually two words. *Portokali* means "good from the port" because the ancient Greeks were not familiar with sweet oranges, and when they were first imported, that's what they named them.'

'You speak Greek?'

'A smattering. Picked it up during my time there.'

'That's what I want to talk to you about.'

James looked surprised. 'I thought you were my lawyer.'

'Whatever gave you that idea?'

'I called a firm to help me sort out my situation. Explained I couldn't leave the premises. They said they would be sending someone round. I thought you might be her.'

If he gave his lawyer the kind of suspicious rebuff he had given me, I could not see him advancing his case. I needed him back on track.

'I believe we were both working for the British government in Athens at the same time in 1984.'

'I don't recall ever seeing you.' He started to stand. I gently shoved him back into his chair.

'That's because I was working undercover. When I arrived a few minutes ago I threatened you with the Special Branch. Wasn't that a clue?'

'I thought you were joking.' He looked at his fingernails, bitten down to the quick. He studied a thumb carefully and began to chew it.

'I was only in the service a few months.'

That may have accounted for his name not being on

Matthew's list: someone in records had slipped up.

'Why did you leave?'

He hesitated. 'I'm bound by the Official Secrets Act.'

'We both are. But since I am working for your old boss, you are, of course, authorised to speak to me.'

'I shall need that in writing.'

'Then I'll have to come back tomorrow. And it'll involve a couple of other people sitting in. This might attract your wife's attention and maybe even give her just cause. Or we can get it done quickly now and she won't be any the wiser.' It was a long shot and I was clutching at straws, but he bought it.

'What do you want to know?'

23

Greece, March 1984

After the debacle at Chios, we had high-tailed it back to Mykonos where we picked up Lady Mary and Kate, weighed down with Lady Mary's purchases. At first I thought her ladyship had been extravagant, but as I stowed the purchases for her in her cabin, I saw that they were all items of exceptional quality and hard to acquire elsewhere. Checking the price tags I saw, to my surprise, that they were not as expensive as I had expected. As the season did not begin in earnest until Easter, Lady Mary had been able to snap up items in the early sale, where boutiques offloaded last year's remainders at favourable discounts.

I knew Kate wanted to hear what had gone on while we had been away, and I was happy to share what I knew of it – well, some of it – but first I had a job to do.

Sir Roland's briefcase was stowed in his bottom bedside drawer, as I had expected. The numbers on the locks were set at 123. I scrolled through each lock to 737, opened the briefcase and took a look at the papers.

The documents were not the ones I found on my last trawl. These related to some agreement between Her Majesty's Government and… well, it was hard to make out. Various names had been written in ink, in a rough, coarse hand – not Sir Roland's – and then crossed out, replaced and crossed out again. To make it worse, some of the words were in Arabic. I guessed the greasy-haired stranger had tried inserting a variety of names – his own, perhaps, or those of associates with business fronts – none of which had been acceptable to Sir Roland, as Her Majesty's representative. Further alterations had been inserted into the text, then firmly crossed out. Here I detected Sir Roland's forceful hand. It was hard to understand the context of the agreement, but its gist was that Her Majesty's Government had been asked to consider providing a laissez-faire, or laissez-passer, to members of Fatah, the militant Palestinian group, in return for them agreeing not to attack their enemies on British or Commonwealth soil. As a piece of diplomatic manoeuvring, it was about as dodgy a case of appeasing a group – designated as terrorist by Israel and the United States of America – as I had ever seen.

But that was just the point, I realised. Sir Roland had not signed it, had not even agreed to its more acceptable terms. Looking at his crossings out, I deduced that he had turned the greasy-haired stranger down flat. I hoped the UK would never consider appeasement of a terrorist group and it seemed, from the frosty conclusion to the meeting, that the British government, or at least its designated representative in Athens, agreed with me wholeheartedly.

I heard voices and footsteps on the stairs. I replaced the documents, spun both locks back to 123, had the briefcase back in its drawer and was turning down the corner of the twin beds just as Sir Roland and Lady Mary entered. They were surprised to see me.

'All put away, your ladyship,' I said. 'You've gained some wonderful bargains.'

It wasn't my place to comment on her purchases, but a compliment never hurt. Lady Mary smiled, gave her husband an 'I told you so' look, and left the door open for me to depart. Sir Roland sighed and lay back on the bed, staring up at the ceiling. It was as if the will to live had left him.

24

Back in Athens I found myself twiddling my thumbs. Sir Roland had his own security team who shadowed him wherever he went. One member accompanied him in his official car, while two others drove in a second car to either precede or follow his, depending on circumstances and intelligence reports. There had been several terrorist attacks, including one on the Iranian embassy in London four years earlier, and we took no chances. Even Lady Mary had her own female bodyguard and, looking back, I guessed that Kate, the chief stew on the MY *Fantasy*, had been armed for just that purpose. But then, it was only a guess.

Ambrose did not want to lose me to the UK, for reasons best known to himself, and kept me on in Athens. When his second in command returned from his mother's funeral, Ambrose introduced us.

My first impression of Matthew Fawcett was that he would rise far in the service as long as he kept his appetites in check. One look at him told me that this was unlikely. Even then Matthew was a podgy fellow. He was about my own height – tall enough for a woman but short for a man – aged around thirty-five or so, full-cheeked and with a stomach that was already beginning to bulge. He held a merry twinkle in his eye, suggesting that life was not to be taken too seriously, which he masked convincingly during briefing meetings. When Ambrose introduced us – in a small, anonymous apartment a short distance from the embassy – Matthew clasped my outstretched hand in his pudgy ones, leant forward and gave me a big fat kiss.

'We should go for dinner one evening. Enjoy the sights of Athens.'

'That would be nice,' was my answer. I wasn't convinced that it would be.

'Matthew will be your liaison at the embassy from now on,' said Ambrose. 'And you can meet in this flat if you need to talk. It's completely secure.'

Our dinner-a-deux took place a couple of evenings later. In the intervening two days I had learnt that my misgivings about Matthew's chances of rising up the ranks were misplaced. In fact, back in Whitehall, Matthew was considered something of a golden boy.

In 1983 a Russian KGB agent by the name of Mikael Polyakin had approached the US embassy in Athens and offered his services to the CIA. He had offered to provide the identities of KGB operatives working out of the Soviet Union's Athens embassy, together with the names of Greek citizens working for the Soviets. In return he expected payment and passage to Israel.

The Americans sent Polyakin packing. He wouldn't have been the first false defector, planted by Ambassador Igor Andropov, son of the late Soviet Leader, and Zharov, director of the GRU back in Moscow. James Angleton, former head of US counter-intelligence, had been paranoid about Soviet agents claiming to defect then feeding the CIA so much false information that much of American foreign policy became counterproductive. Angleton retired in the summer of 1975 but when his replacement, Richard Welch, was assassinated in Athens that same year, American paranoia proved to be entirely justified.

A week after his dismissal by the Americans, Polyakin turned up at the British embassy. He repeated his offer. The British were more receptive. That is not to say they opened their arms to him.

Polyakin was thoroughly debriefed and his claims and credentials checked. Distant cousins in Israel were questioned. He was asked to supply samples of information as a gesture of goodwill before the British would consider his request. He provided the names of several Soviet agents operating in Athens. This was a coup, by any standards. But as most of those agents were reaching the end of their careers and were soon recalled to Moscow, their exposure meant less to us than it might have done.

Andreas Papandreou, the socialist Greek prime minister, had been developing economic ties with the Soviets while at the same time attacking US foreign policy. When the names were leaked to him he made no attempt to expel any GRU agents in the Soviet embassy. As he was probably already familiar with most of the Greeks working for the Soviets, they were allowed to carry on as they had been.

Polyakin was treated well on his arrival in London. He was given a safe house to live in and a generous pension. His desire to emigrate to Israel suddenly evaporated. The fleshpots of London had proved too alluring. Then it all came to a sudden and brutal end.

One of Matthew's informers – he had several working in the field and was even reputed to have a contact in the Soviet embassy itself – revealed that Polyakin was exactly what the Americans had always said he was: a false defector sent to lie for his country. Suddenly all the information Polyakin had provided became suspect. The British agent who had vouched for him and checked his story suddenly found himself posted to Papua New Guinea, where he later died in suspicious circumstances that were never fully investigated. Polyakin was forcibly returned to Moscow, protesting wildly that he would be tortured and executed upon his arrival. Well of course he would say that, countered our masters in Whitehall – he had to keep up his act.

The whole affair – an unmitigated disaster – was hushed up. And Matthew, the rising star who had saved the British government from embarrassment and humiliation, was on the road to being fast-tracked towards a possible ambassadorship. That is, as I said, if his appetites did not get the better of him.

I waited for Matthew in the trendy Kolonaki district, a few streets from the embassy. I had chosen a dark corner in Taverna Filippou, which claimed to be the oldest in the area. I wasn't too concerned about being spotted – most embassy staff knocked off at five in the evening, and that went for spies, too – but it was best to be cautious.

Matthew was twenty minutes late. This was something I had to get used to in our regular meetings. Most of them were about trivial matters, and I came to believe that Matthew only used them as an excuse to get out of the office.

He was out of breath and sweating, although it was not a particularly warm evening. He had been exerting himself somehow, somewhere. Now he fully intended to replenish his resources.

'Have you taken a look at the menu?' he asked. I nodded. 'It's all good here,' he continued. 'Will you let me order for both of us?' This was long before anybody bothered to ask if you had a food intolerance or allergy. Allergies are a serious matter, and after a lifetime of trying to ensure I haven't been poisoned or drugged (I have: poisoned once, drugged twice) I have every sympathy for customers who are misled about the ingredients of the food they are served. As for the faddists… why don't they grow up and get a life?

At my school the nuns fed us the most ghastly stuff. One day we received a visit from a school inspector. He made the mistake of staying for lunch. A large bowl of 'stew' was dumped at the head of our table, to be distributed by the novice nun who was supervising us. As she dug into the mess with a ladle she extracted a web of stinking bones connected by ligaments and gristle. It was so revolting that even she noticed. Depositing it onto a plate, she instructed the nearest pupil to take it up to the Mother Superior and query what was on the plate. The school inspector quailed at the sight of it. He pushed aside his own dish and refused to eat any more. Thenceforth the food improved a little, but the novice nun was admonished severely and shortly afterwards she left the order. Some years later I saw her on television burning her bra alongside a group of feminists. A few years later she was on the TV news again, protesting about American nuclear arms housed on British soil at Greenham Common. She seemed to be much happier with her friends than she had ever been with us. Everyone needs to find their proper calling in life.

When our food arrived I realised that Matthew had not only selected a variety of meze, or starters, as I had expected, but also a number of main courses. He wanted me to try them all, though he was delighted when I only picked at some of them. 'All the more for me,' was his repeated refrain.

The dishes kept on coming. For meze he had chosen melitzanosalata, taramasalata, tzatziki and shrimp sautéed in ouzo, all served with two types of bread: a homemade sliced loaf and a pitta-style flatbread from a local bakery. This was all washed down with a bottle of Cypriot retsina, the island's pine-resinated wine.

Just as I was getting my second wind, our main dishes arrived: pork in lemon sauce, grilled octopus with fava beans, pork souvlaki, a whole roast grouper and a large chunk of lamb souvla roasted on a spit, which Matthew must have ordered in advance, as it wasn't on the menu. Accompanying these were roast potatoes, chips, a Greek salad and a dish of plain boiled greens, *horta vrasta*, which Matthew slid towards me and ignored.

I picked from each of the dishes. They were all delicious. Matthew managed to devour everything, as well as polishing off most of two bottles of wine, one white, the other red. 'What a pleashure!' He had a habit of inserting an 'h' into certain words which contributed to the impression of the voluptuary in everything he did.

'That's going to set you back a bit, isn't it?' I asked.

'You're on expenses, aren't you?' he shot back.

'Yes, but modest.'

'You won't get a meal as good as this anywhere else in Athens,' he said. 'You pay this time, my treat the next.'

I am no pushover, but I didn't feel it would be helpful to antagonise Matthew so early in our relationship. I proffered my Barclaycard and paid the bill. If I was lucky, I'd recover most of it from Ambrose.

As we left, Matthew took me by the arm. 'You know, it's a lonely old business, this thing we do. I'd rather not go home straight away. Would you oblige with me with a stroll in the park?' It was dark now, and I wanted to go back to my own place, a set of rooms Ambrose had arranged for me. Matthew persisted and I, feeling a little sorry for the fellow, indulged him. He was right. Our business was a lonely one. We had to be self-sufficient, on our toes at all times, and it could be exhausting. So I walked with him.

The nearest park, the Zappeion Gardens, were south of the impressive Zappeion Hall, just a short walk away. We linked arms and began our stroll down into the gardens.

I am not one for opening up to a colleague on short notice – or even extended notice, if it comes to that – so I was glad that Matthew was disinclined to talk. We had done enough of that over dinner, mostly on the subject of what we were eating and its historical context in Greek and Mediterranean cuisine, a subject on which Matthew was a self-proclaimed expert.

We passed the hall and entered the gardens. They were poorly lit for this time of night and, though I am skilled in various forms of self-defence, I remain reluctant to take unnecessary risks in a strange city. I had Matthew with me, of course, but I could not imagine him putting up much of a fight if we were mugged. Nor could I imagine him running fast enough to escape pursuit. Matthew's splayed, flat feet were not the kind that would bear his weight for any length of time.

I suggested we move towards a better lit area, but Matthew, eyes darting left and right, was adamant that we should stay on his chosen path, which would lead us past dark thickets of trees. Various men hung around, or strolled nonchalantly past, some young and virile-looking, others most certainly decrepit. One muscle-bound-type strode uncomfortably close to Matthew and jammed a cigarette above his own right ear.

'I've pulled,' said Matthew, pushing me away from him. 'You can find your own way back, can't you, dear?'

'What?'

'An old friend. Be a shame to keep him waiting.' With that he scampered after his muscle-bound 'friend' and disappeared into the trees.

25

England, 2019

The week after Dennis died was probably the worst I ever endured. Oh, I've been cruelly tortured, been locked away in solitary confinement for weeks on end, suffered deprivation, starvation and many other hardships, all in the line of duty. But in almost every case I was not alone. By that I mean that I knew there was someone out there, some colleague in the Service, looking out for me and doing their utmost to get me freed and safely back home. Most times that colleague had been Dennis. And now he was gone.

It had been such a stupid accident.

In retirement we met once or twice a week. Usually at a fair distance from my village – I didn't want to set tongues wagging. Besides, we were discouraged, as former colleagues, from fraternising. But I was never one to follow rules, especially those with which I did not agree.

Dennis and I had a special relationship. He had been my first instructor, had brought me home when I had almost died in West Germany, and had taken care of me while I recuperated. We had also been lovers, though that side of things had petered out quite early. My adult children, on the rare times they visited, treated him with respect and a degree of affection – a great deal more than they ever showed me. All these elements contributed to the strong bond that had developed and remained between us.

Dennis did on occasion visit my West Sussex cottage. He made a point of bringing a toolbox, as if he was coming to do repairs or maintenance work – which was often exactly what he was doing. He never stayed the night. Well, almost never. But that was by accident, not by design. The tongues wagged nonetheless but, as I never mixed with the locals, the village soon lost interest.

Dennis was exceptionally fit for a man his age, and I made every effort to keep up with him. Sometimes we did yoga together – though I was considerably more flexible than he was. Dennis had sustained many injuries in the field, and they included a broken back. A steel plate holding his vertebrae together prevented him from adopting the most difficult poses. But it didn't stop him doing a hundred push-ups, followed by fifty pull-ups on a bar.

I could never match him for push-ups. Although my body had a strong core, my arms lacked the muscle to get anywhere close. But I was able to hang onto the bar and raise my knees to my chest as many times as he could. Perhaps my slim body and lighter weight helped.

Early on he challenged me.

'However many push-ups you can do, I can do one more.' Anyone familiar with betting knows this trick. You, the 'mark', do as many push-ups from the floor as you can. But all you are doing at this stage is challenging yourself. Once you've completed fifty, for example, you may feel you've done enough to win the bet. You have made a psychological mistake. Unlike you, your opponent has a target to aim for. He just needs to hit that target and then complete one more push-up. I only fell for this trick once, and the bet cost me a jolly supper of fish and chips, which we shared on the seafront at Brighton, along with a couple of cans of cider to wash it down.

In our early days we would run perhaps ten or fifteen kilometres across country. My long strides matched his and when we reached our chosen destination – a country pub or a café – I was scarcely out of breath.

I kept up the workouts and runs right until the day Dennis died, though when I reached seventy we cut back on the distance, seldom covering more than five kilometres. My pace was still good.

Around that time I noticed a tailing off of Dennis's enthusiasm and speed. It was not surprising. He was several years older than me. I asked him about it but he brushed off my concerns. Eventually he admitted that he suffered arthritis in the hips. He talked to his doctor and an appointment was made for him to have his left hip, the worst, replaced. But the National Health Service would not be troubled by him blocking one of their beds.

While he was waiting for his surgery, we took short treks along the Sussex coast. Dennis felt he could manage these easily enough.

One sunny afternoon we were walking along a chalky cliff path when we came upon a man throwing a ball for his black Labrador. The dog was old and its movements, like those of Dennis, revealed the ravages of time.

The dog dropped the ball at the feet of its master, who picked it up and hurled it carelessly into the air. A gust of wind took it dangerously close to the cliff. As it landed it rolled slowly towards the edge. The Labrador lumbered after it. Just as the dog reached the ball its legs gave way. It teetered a moment before disappearing over the brink.

Its master just stood there, gawping.

Dennis ran forward and peered over. The dog had rolled down to a narrow shelf and was sliding towards a ledge. Beyond that was a drop of several hundred feet. The dog tried in vain to scrabble back up, its frantic actions demolishing what was left of the crumbling ledge. Loose chalk and earth hurtled down, scattering passers-by below.

Dennis clambered down to the shelf.

'What on earth are you doing?' I demanded. I am not one to risk my life unless it is absolutely necessary – which it has been on many occasions. In my opinion it was up to the dog's stupid owner to go down, or else await rescue. But Dennis was never the type to wait. He made it down to the ledge. Loose chunks of chalk broke away from under him, and he struggled to remain upright. The dog, fearful and bewildered, backed away from him and in that moment I thought its life was over.

Dennis lunged forward and grabbed the Labrador's collar while still managing to keep his balance. He hauled the dog bodily up into his arms. He turned and started his ascent. Hard chalk turned to gravel under his boots. He made it to the shelf, then slipped. He regained his balance, dropped to his knees and, with a great effort, shuffled up the last few feet to the shelf.

The dog's owner had, by then, come to his senses. He stepped to the edge of the cliff and reached out. As Dennis struggled to his feet, the owner, a big man in his forties, grabbed the dog from him.

'Sooty! You silly old thing. You'll be the death of me!' He swung around with his big beast in his arms. As he did so, the dog's legs lightly brushed against Dennis.

One moment Dennis was standing there, ready to climb back up onto the clifftop. The next, he was gone.

For a moment I thought he'd stepped back down to the second ledge. He hadn't cried out or made a sound of any kind.

As its owner lowered the dog to the ground I stepped forward and peered over. People were staring up at me. Others were gawping at Dennis's body, not splayed out on the rocks, as one might expect, but looking as if he'd chosen to have a brief lie-down on the beach, legs and feet slightly apart, arms straight down by his sides. Only his head seemed oddly angled, his neck askew. Then I saw blood spreading around him, and I stepped back, unwilling to witness any more.

There is a memorial to the intelligence services in the south cloister at Westminster Abbey. However, as there is no desire that officers, past or present, be identified, no service funerals are held there. Instead a short service took place at the Temple Church, in the rotunda.

Several of Dennis's former students showed up. A couple of them I knew as nodding acquaintances. As we gathered around the effigies of the Templar Knights I caught sight of Ambrose. Dear old Ambrose, always there with a warm and encouraging smile when I needed him. Apart from him, none of those present knew that Dennis and I had continued to see each other, so none of them offered me their condolences. To them I was just another lonely old biddy, come to pay my respects to a fallen colleague and show that I was still alive and kicking, before returning to my rest home.

To my surprise Matthew Fawcett was there too, though he did not join in with the hymns and remained lurking in the shadows. He must have been familiar with Dennis of course. It was good of him to come.

*

Ten days after the funeral I went to the nearest branch of WH Smith and bought a thick roll of duct tape. I cut an eight-foot length from my garden hose, threw it into the boot of my car along with the tape and a pair of strong scissors and drove up onto the Downs.

It was a grey and overcast day. Perfect for what I had in mind. I remembered a poem by Rudyard Kipling.

The Weald is good, the Downs are best
I'll give you the run of 'em, East to West.

Like Kipling, Dennis loved Sussex. Right then, I hated the county, the world, and most of all I hated life.

There are various viewing points along the Downs. Dennis and I were fond of one in particular. That is where I parked.

The area was deserted. On one side I had a view of the sea, on the other I could just make out the shape of the Devil's Dyke. Well, I thought, let the Devil take me now.

I got out of the car, opened the boot and pulled out the length of hose, the duct tape and the kitchen scissors. I rammed the hose into my car's exhaust pipe and wrapped duct tape securely around the end of the pipe to seal it. I fed the other end of the hose in through a small gap in the driver's window, which I had partially opened, and sealed that up with duct tape too.

I got in on the passenger's side, shut the door and climbed across to the driver's seat. I strapped myself in – force of habit I suppose. I sat for a few moments contemplating what I was about to do. This hesitation was not cowardice, nor reluctance on my part. But there is a life force in us all that demands to be heard.

I turned on the car engine. Exhaust fumes, invisible but deadly, began to fill the car. I sat still, staring straight ahead, waiting for the carbon monoxide to take effect.

Out of the corner of my eye I noticed a small car approach. I ignored it. As it got closer I turned my head a little. It was a small Renault, very similar in make and colour to the one Dennis drove.

To my surprise the Renault pulled into the parking area and drew up beside me. The driver, a cheerful-looking man in his fifties, gave me a smile and a wave. From where he sat he could not see the hose nor what I was intending to do. He wound down his window.

'Lovely day.'

At that exact moment the sun broke through the clouds and lit up the valley before us.

I reached forward and surreptitiously switched off my car's engine. I pressed the electric button to wind down the passenger's window.

'Yes. Yes, it is,' I replied.

The two of us sat there, staring straight ahead, as the sunlight played across the grass and the clouds scudded across the sky.

After five minutes or so the man turned and called out to me. 'Well, I'd better be off then.' He started up his car, backed out of his parking place and drove back along the route he had come.

I pushed open my door, tore away the duct tape – making a mess of my flaking paintwork in the process – undid the tape around the exhaust and hurled the hose back into the boot of the car.

I stood outside the car for another five minutes, breathing

in the glorious fresh air as it whipped in from the sea, waiting for the last of the toxic gases to dispel. Then I got back in my car and drove home.

26

London, 2019

After leaving James Saunders I headed up to Queensway, a popular tourist area where you could still find public telephone boxes. A few years earlier there had been many, mostly with their insides plastered with advertisements for escorts and call girls, all euphemistically described as masseuses. It could be hard to use the phone without some pimp bursting in on you, swiping all the advertisements to the floor, and replacing them with similar ones for other girls. I had once witnessed a pimp putting up cards while two elderly ladies clipped a luggage strap around the telephone box, preventing him from leaving. He must have got out eventually, as he wasn't there the next time I looked. I suppose he phoned the number on the card to be released. With the advent of call-girl sites freely available on the internet, most telephone boxes were now mostly disused or vandalised.

I found a phone which worked and called Matthew on one of the numbers he had given me. He answered straight away but said nothing. The unrecognised call-box number gave him reason for caution.

'Matthew. It's me.'

'You mean "it is I", don't you?' Matthew knew I was a stickler for grammar and enjoyed needling me if ever I gave him the opportunity.

'Do you want to know what I've learnt or not?' I said. I was ready to slam down the receiver.

'Fire away, old thing.'

'I've met up with James Saunders.'

'Who?'

'I told you. Saunders. His name wasn't on your list but I managed to track him down. I can't say I got much out of him.' That wasn't entirely true. James had given me a name of someone he believed could provide some relevant information: Emily Charalamboulos, living in London. But he hadn't provided her address or a contact number. These would be forthcoming once he had got her approval for me to contact her.

I wanted to follow up this lead on my own. It would be more interesting and, I had to admit, more rewarding if I were able to unmask the mole myself.

'He's living in Bark Place W2,' I informed Matthew. I gave him the number of the house and details of Saunders' marital arrangements.

'I've got Bella and Ambrose here with me,' Matthew replied. 'Maybe one of them can spare the time to do a follow-up.'

'I don't think he's got much to impart,' I insisted.

'Nevertheless, it's standard procedure. What else do you have for me?'

'That's all for the moment.'

'Disappointing.'

There wasn't an answer to that, so I hung up.

I made my way back up Queensway and took a left at Westbourne Grove all the way to Portobello Road, where I bought some ground coffee beans. Back in my safe house I made myself a pot with the Moka percolator. I drank the first cup as soon as it was cool enough and returned for a refill. The little man pictured on the percolator – short and stubby with a bristling moustache – appeared to be 'giving me the finger' as they say in America. This only fired me with a greater desire to discover the mole myself.

I heard a buzzing sound. It was my burner phone, which I had switched to 'silent' but left on 'vibrate'. I expected it to be Matthew and answered quickly. Instead there was silence.

'Hello? Are you going to say something or shall I hang up?'

I could hear someone clearing their throat at the other end. Then after what seemed at least ten seconds, James Saunders' voice came over the line. 'I remembered something else.'

'Yes?'

'Something Emily said.'

'And what would that be?'

'About the ambassador's car. What was causing the problem.'

'Are you going to tell me? Or am I going to have to come back and winkle it out of you?'

'Er… I think it's best you ask her when you see her. But I should warn her first. Tell her to expect your call.'

'I thought you'd have done that by now.' I was trying to be patient, and failing.

'I've been busy, tidying up,' he whined. I could hear a doorbell ringing in the background. 'Hold on, just let me get this. It'll be the lady lawyer.'

'Wait. Give me Emily's address.'

I heard him put the phone down and shuffle off to answer the door.

'I'm just coming,' I heard him say.

There was the distant sound of a bolt being drawn across

and the door unlocked. I heard James's voice again. 'Do come in.'

'Hello,' I said loudly into the phone.

I heard him walk back to the phone and pick it up. I heard his breathing, slow and regular. Then the phone switched off.

I called back. The phone rang twice and cut off. I was inclined to try again but realised the futility of it. If James had to talk to his lawyer, he didn't want me bothering him. From what little I knew of divorce lawyers, he would be busy for the rest of the day and well into the evening. He would call me back later. Just to be sure I left a text message: *Call me back when you can*, but did not add my name. He would know whom it was from.

I found no mention of any Emily Charalamboulos at the Athens embassy in the paperwork Matthew had sent me. Charalamboulos was a Greek name, so I presumed she had been one of the Greek locals. James had told me she was now in London. I could not just ring up the Foreign Office and ask for a list of employees at our embassy in Athens from 1982–1986. They would think I was a spy. Which, of course, I was. But I knew a man who could.

Bernard listened to my request patiently. While he did not take any notes – he did not need to, he had a marvellous memory – I felt I could hear the cogs whirring in his capacious brain. Then he said something that took me by surprise. 'Could you do me a favour, Mother?'

'Of course.' This was the first time my son, distant, cerebral, aloof, had ever asked me for a favour. I was not going to miss the opportunity at this late stage of my life.

'Could we meet up?' Bernard continued. 'I need your advice.'

27

BERNARD'S IDEA OF A DISCREET place to meet amused me. St James's Park, only a few hundred yards from his office in the Ministry of Defence, has featured in so many spy films that a casual observer might be forgiven for suspecting that everyone strolling in the park – especially if they carry a furled umbrella – must be a spy. Either one of ours or one of theirs. Nevertheless I agreed to meet him on his chosen bench.

He was already sat waiting when I arrived, his attention focused on a copy of the *Daily Telegraph* in his hands. Despite the mild weather he sat stiffly in his brown coat with its velvet collar and his brilliantly polished shoes, looking every inch a minister of the Crown.

'Isn't this a bit obvious?' I asked, as I sat at the far end of the bench.

Bernard raised his newspaper as if he were engrossed in it, so it would have been impossible for anyone watching to read his lips. 'I have a perfect two hundred and fifty degree view from where I sit if I just turn my head a little. If I were to lower my newspaper my voice might travel across the water as far as Buckingham Palace, though I don't suppose any of its occupants would care to listen to what I have to say. I had this bench and the surrounding bushes and trees swept for bugs by two of my people shortly before I arrived. I believe we are both free to speak our minds.'

I raised my hand to my mouth, as if suppressing a yawn or a cough. 'So what exactly is this favour you want of me?'

Bernard took a deep breath and got straight to the point. 'I believe the knives are out for me.' He let this sink in. 'Have you ever had that feeling?'

'Indeed I have. Though in my case the knives were real, not figurative ones.' I waited to hear more. Nothing came, so I prompted him. 'What makes you think so?'

'There have been odd questions in committee meetings. Things that are irrelevant to the matters in hand.'

'Questions which impinge on your character?'

'You could say that. Nothing voiced in so many words. But there are a pair of journalists sniffing about.'

I moved my hand to my nose, as if to scratch an itch. Anyone observing or filming our conversation would find my lips impossible to read.

'Isn't that how it goes in politics? It never ends well. Eventually you're booted out, or booted up to the Lords.' I considered this for a moment. 'That wouldn't be such a bad result, would it?'

I was beginning to feel quite maternal towards the poor man. Even if he was my son.

'Stop picking your nose!' A woman's voice, harsh and indignant. I snatched my hand away, then realised the voice belonged to an old-fashioned nanny pushing a pram. She was admonishing a little boy in his first school uniform, shorts too long and peaked cap too large. 'And stay away from the water. It's full of affluence.'

To my mind, she had confused this lake for the Serpentine in Hyde Park, where rich patrons enjoy an 'open swim' in weed-infested waters, but she had a point. The little boy ignored her. He extracted a large green bogie from his right nostril, rolled it up in a ball and flicked it at a pelican. The large bird waddled away. I studied the nanny. She was wearing the iconic uniform of the Norland Nannies: beige-crested dress, brown-crested felt hat, and white gloves. A good cover for someone sent to watch us.

'Too obvious,' said Bernard, echoing my thoughts. 'I'm not ready to go upstairs yet,' he continued. 'I still have things to do, things that will make a difference.'

I believed him. For all his stiffness and awkwardness, Bernard had a highly developed sense of duty backed up by strong morals. I have no idea where he got it from. Certainly not from either of his parents. My mother perhaps. She had instilled many virtues in my children, though she did so by word, definitely not by example.

An old man in a long beige raincoat shuffled up. He carried a brown paper bag from which he extracted crusts of bread that he threw to the ducks in the water. We waited until he had moved on.

'It all sounds a bit vague,' I said.

'Of course. Insinuation, that's all it is. Nothing specific which I can refute.'

'Who do you think is behind it?'

'I have no idea.'

'A person in your position must have enemies.'

'Easy to spot and root out. One can deal with people like that. No, this is someone working behind the scenes, hidden way back in the shadows.'

'Your "Moriarty".'

Bernard laughed, though it came out as a dismissive snort.

'So what are you going to do about it?'

'There's not much I can do until he, or she, reveals themselves. But it's the family I'm concerned for. Bridget and the boys.' Bernard had two handsome sons of twelve and fourteen. I hardly ever saw them. It occurred to me that I would very much like to see more of them.

'And then there's Eva and Silvana, and baby Alice…'

At the thought that Alice might somehow be at risk, the little girl I had rescued, my heart jumped. 'You think they might be harmed?'

'If there's a scandal.'

'What kind of scandal?'

'There is no scandal. That doesn't mean they can't create one.'

At that moment one of the pigeons, chasing a crust of bread, got too close to a hungry pelican. Before its prey could flap away, the larger beast had darted forward its great beak and engulfed the pigeon. I could see the clumsy bird flapping inside the pelican's throat pouch. The pelican raised its crested head, jerked its neck upwards a couple of times to improve the angle of its victim's position, then swallowed the pigeon whole. Satisfied, the pelican waddled into the water to digest. It reminded me of Matthew, devouring the entire contents of my fridge before waddling off down the road. Should I mention Bernard's problem to him? Matthew had a lot of influence. No, I thought. That would only complicate matters.

'If you want my advice…' I said.

'Yes?' Bernard turned to me. Although he hid it well, I could see the worry in his eyes.

'Do nothing, for now at least. Don't let them see you're concerned. They will interpret this as weakness. Carry on as normal.'

'And if they strike?'

'Then they will have revealed themselves, and you will know what to do.'

We sat silently a few moments, as Bernard mulled this over.

'Thank you for listening.' Another few moments passed, then he spoke again. 'I like the colour of your hair. So much better than that awful red job you had at John Sandoe.'

'You recognised me?'

'Of course.'

'I thought my disguise would fool anyone.'

'Not your own son, Mother.'

'Obviously not.'

Bernard lowered his paper and offered it to me. 'Would you like to read my paper, madam?' he asked, as if he had just become aware of me. 'I've finished with it. You may find the letters to the editor of interest.' He stood up without using his hands – he liked to keep himself fit, as did I – and strode off back to the ministry. As he walked I saw two men, who up until now had kept themselves out of sight, fall in about a dozen paces behind him, matching him step for step. I recognised the two Ministry of Defence policemen who, just a few weeks ago, had been on the point of arresting me. At least Bernard had those two to watch his back.

28

I WAITED UNTIL I WAS on a moving Circle Line train back to Notting Hill Gate – I had checked that I had not been followed – before opening the copy of the *Telegraph*. I had asked Bernard to find the address of Emily Charalamboulos, a person who had worked with James Saunders at the British embassy and was almost certainly now living in London.

In between the lines of the letters page I found Bernard's writing – so neat it could almost have been missed as part of the published letter itself – giving me the name, address, telephone number and email address of Emily Charalamboulos, spinster and cat lover. Typical of Bernard to be so thorough. It had been a long day and I committed the information to memory and, as backup, took a surreptitious photograph with my burner phone. I would contact Emily in the morning.

When I got home I googled Emily Charalamboulos, but found nothing. She had not made much of a mark on the world at large. I went to bed early and tried to struggle through more of Matthew's bloody receipts and documents without discovering anything of interest. They soon put me to sleep.

The following morning I cooked myself a boiled egg with 'soldiers'. I am particular about how I like my eggs cooked:

the whites firm, the yolks runny. Dennis didn't care if the white was as 'runny as snot', as he liked to say to annoy me. This egg was a Burford Brown with a wonderful golden yolk. I had taken it out of the fridge and left it, with the fat end pierced, to warm up in a small bowl of hot water. By the time I was ready to boil it the water was lukewarm. I popped it into boiling water as I made my toast: *pain de campagne* from Paul bakery by Holland Park tube station. The toast was buttered and cooling by the time the egg was ready. I switched on the television to watch the news and sat down to enjoy my egg and a cup of hot coffee.

I dipped my soldier into my perfect yolk, raised it to my mouth and froze. A minor item in the news had caught my attention. A woman was 'helping police with their inquiries' (a wonderful euphemism) in connection with the suspicious death of her husband, from whom she was separated, in Bayswater. That is not what stopped me enjoying my breakfast. There are suspicious deaths in London every day. What shocked me was the photograph of James Saunders. He looked some fifteen years younger than he had when I visited him. But the threat of divorce can age a person terribly.

I jumped up and hurried to the phone. I am good at remembering numbers, especially mobile phone numbers, with their five-digit prefix and six-digit coda. I dialled Emily Charalamboulos's number without hesitation. There was no answer. I tried again, and again there was no response.

I took the tube from Ladbroke Grove to Hampstead and marched briskly down Hampstead High Street to Rosslyn Hill. I turned left into Downshire Hill and almost immediately ducked into a small yard backing the shops. I waited behind a van, watching the street through its windows. When I was sure that I had not been followed

I carried on along the quiet street until I found the right number. The Georgian houses were set well back from the road, with deep front gardens separating the houses from the street. The particular house I wanted was fronted by a four-foot brick wall surmounted by tall metal railings. Shrubs and bushes had been allowed to grow so thickly through the railings that it was all but impossible to make out the house, except for the very top floor. The gate to the front garden was set between heavily constructed brick pillars and was at least six and a half feet high. It had once been a more modest four foot, and the step and a half of York stone up to the gate would have made this seem less unwelcoming, but someone had had the height increased recently – I could see a couple of loose screws and some wood shavings on the step – and had then had the gate freshly painted in some Farrow and Ball variant of what I would call moss green. The place gave every indication of being inhabited by someone who did not wish to be found.

I rang the doorbell, which was set into the brick gate post. There was no answer. I pressed the bell again, holding it for at least fifteen seconds. A voice came on the loudspeaker beside the bell.

'Hello?' It was a woman's voice. Weak, tremulous. It held no trace of a Greek accent.

I took a chance. 'Emily Charalamboulos?'

'Who is that?' She had not denied her name. Now I had a few choices. Telling the truth would get me nowhere. Usually I would say that I had a package that needed to be signed for. Failing that, an urgent communication from her previous place of work relating to her pension increase. That normally produced a swift response. But the large Georgian house in a prime location suggested that Emily was not in desperate need of a pension increase. I went for the simplest option and mentally held my breath. 'Amazon.'

The intercom crackled. 'Can you pop it in the box?'

There was a large wooden box attached to the front of the gate. Annoying.

'It won't fit.' The box was spacious, made to fit even the most awkward packages.

'Just leave it by the door, and I'll come and fetch it.'

'If it's stolen before you fetch it I shall lose my job. I'm on probation with Amazon as it is. Neither of you will be happy with a stupid photograph.'

An impatient sigh. 'All right, I'll be there in a minute.'

I was glad there was no camera on the doorbell. My voice is strong and clear, and on the phone I can pass for a much younger woman. If she had been able to see me, she might have had second thoughts. As it was, the moment I heard the door of the house open and the slap, slap of loose sandals on York paving approaching the gate, I stood aside and pressed myself up against the railing. The door opened a crack. She spoke, 'Hello?' She stepped out, saw me and jumped back. But as she tried to slam the gate I grabbed her arm and held it tight.

'Who are you? What do you want?' There was panic in her voice.

'I'm not here to harm you.'

'Go away. Leave me alone!' She was trying to pull away from me, but she ended up dragging me in through the gate. I kicked it shut behind me and she suddenly realised that there was no escape. Like a small mammal in a predator's jaws, she stopped struggling and went limp.

I didn't let go of her. She might run off the moment I freed her from my grasp. But I did give her a reassuring smile, and used words I always feel break the hardest ice.

'I'm dying for a cup of tea.'

Emily's hands were still shaking as she poured me the tea. Both the cup and the spoon rattled as she set the saucer down. I took hold of her arm, gently this time, to reassure her.

'I won't bite.'

She smiled thinly, not convinced.

'Aren't you joining me?'

In answer, she poured herself a cup and sat on the sofa facing mine, keeping a low coffee table between us, as if she felt it would keep me at bay. A cat, a huge Maine Coon, leapt up onto her knees. She stroked it and held it close as if it were her emotional support.

I had explained who I was and that James Saunders had mentioned her name.

'Poor James. Did you see the news?'

'Yes I did,' I replied.

'That wife of his. Awful woman.'

'Do you think she's responsible?'

She didn't answer. She played with the purring cat, which stretched out so she could tickle it under its front legs. The cat was so large, it seemed to be appraising her less as a provider of its supper and more as if she were an ingredient.

'But how did you find me? James doesn't have my new address. Nobody does. All my old mail goes to a post-office box. It's not forwarded here.'

'It's not hard to find someone if you really want to.' Her expression changed. Her eyes, large and blue, showed growing panic.

'You're hiding from someone.'

She nodded, avoiding my eyes.

'Someone you worked with in the embassy? You have a Greek name, but you don't look Greek at all.'

'I get my colouring from my mother. She was English. My brother took after my father, who was Greek. We were both brought up bilingual.'

'So that's why you were working in the British embassy in Athens in 1984.'

'Just for a few months.' She was on the defensive.

'Why was that?'

She looked up at me. 'Why do you want to know these things? What good does going over them now serve anybody? I've done my best to forget all that. And I tried to forget all about him.'

'Him? Who?'

'Freddie.'

'Freddie de Lazlo?'

'Yes. I was in love with him.'

So we were back to Athens.

29

Athens, 1984

Ambrose and I met up again the day after my dinner with Matthew. Ambrose had rented me a small set of rooms with a phone and warned me that, when I was off duty, I was going to get thoroughly bored. He had been calling me every morning between nine and ten to inform me whether I would be needed. I never was. But that morning he suggested we meet up for a bite of lunch.

Our lunch was very different from the dinner I had 'shared' with Matthew the previous night, before our evening stroll in the park had been sharply curtailed. Ambrose took me to a little stall he knew where they made the best souvlaki – little cubes of pork fillet marinaded and grilled on a skewer, then inserted into pitta pockets with a mixed salad of shredded carrot, cabbage, a little feta cheese and a special sauce of the owner's own invention.

We strolled down to the park – the very same one that Matthew and I had strolled through the evening before. Ambrose headed straight for a bench under the shade of some trees: the same trees Matthew had disappeared into the night before. I half expected him to come staggering out, trousers around his ankles, screaming that he'd been assaulted, but the park at midday was now a very different place, a haven for birds and butterflies. Though I did see a rat emerge from the woods, take one look at our souvlaki and make a dash back into the undergrowth.

As we ate Ambrose did the talking. He was careful to take a bite, chew and swallow and then keep the souvlaki held up in front of his mouth, so that no lipreader or long-distance microphone could pick up what he was saying.

'Sir Roland is quite... er... concerned. Apparently the cruise did not go entirely as planned, or hoped for. And there are rumours that the, er, surprise guest was not happy with the outcome. So I'm going to ask you to step up and join the surveillance team. If that's all right with you?'

This, I learned, was typical Ambrose. A diffidence, a shyness, as if every request was a terrible imposition for which he would apologise in advance. Tall, slim, bent a little at the neck, like a younger Prince Philip, with his hands often clasped behind his back as he spoke, Ambrose seemed like an overgrown schoolboy. And like an enthusiastic schoolboy, he kept up his buoyant attitude during many of our adventures together. Yet, as I was also to learn, there was an iron will and determination at his core. He never asked anything of anyone he wouldn't cheerily have done himself.

'It could be dangerous. For you I mean. Sir Roland's been made aware of the risk, and he's considering sending Lady Mary back to England until this is over.'

'I thought I was supposed to be keeping a low profile.' I had followed his lead in chewing and talking, making it hard to read my lips.

'You were, but Sir Roland asked for you himself.'

'But he thinks I'm an idiot.' I kept my hand in front of my mouth, as if I were coughing up a piece of pork that had blocked my oesophagus.

'Well, he's had time to reconsider. I know he admonished

you at Cape Sounion. Mavros wasn't supposed to guess that Sir Roland had any bodyguards, but you rather gave yourself away.'

Ambrose swallowed the last of his souvlaki and put his lips to the straw inserted in his can of Coca-Cola. 'I always enjoy these souvlaki. Perhaps next time I'll get us two each. One's never quite enough.' There was a pause. 'By the way, how much did Matthew stiff you for dinner?'

'I kept the receipt. I'll have to check. A lot of drachmas.'

'Oh, I'm sure. Get it to me and I'll divert some funds from somewhere to cover it.'

He stood up and brushed the crumbs off his shirt. He turned away from the park and faced the wood. 'There's a young chap, new, whom you should meet. I think the two of you will get on, and you can teach him some of the ropes.' He looked at his watch. 'Time to get back to the office. I shall be in touch shortly.' He strode off back north towards the embassy.

I stood and brushed any crumbs off my blouse. A small spot of grease had stained it. Should I hurry home and wash it out, or could I bear to live with it until evening? I was about to move off when I heard a sharp snap. Someone had trodden on a broken twig. I turned and peered into the shaded darkness of the wood. I stood there waiting for two long minutes, but nothing moved.

I backed away slowly, half expecting… what, someone spying on us, or some elderly Greek gent hoping for a pickup? Then I heard a second twig breaking. I turned and hurried away.

30

THE 'NEW' CHAP AMBROSE WANTED me to team up with was not new to the service. But he was new to the Athens desk and, whatever he had been doing elsewhere, he was remarkably unskilled at surveillance and pretty well all the things I excelled in. From his pallor I guessed that his had been a desk job, possibly in some basement research department, and that he had requested a transfer to some brighter location where both he and the sun could shine.

There was something else about him. Some of his mannerisms seemed to echo those of Ambrose: his tall stoop, his hands clasped behind his back; the open, optimistic expression that stayed with him even in times of crisis; the clipped, old-fashioned way he had of speaking. His name was Freddie de Lazlo, but if I guessed correctly, it could just as easily have been Freddie Flynn. He and Ambrose might have been first cousins, or uncle and nephew, or simply not connected at all. Whatever the truth of their relationship, I was happy to help Ambrose and repay his kindness and courtesy by taking the younger man on.

Freddie was a fast learner, but that wasn't the only reason I liked him. He had an infectious sense of humour which made light work of even the dullest jobs. Some days we were assigned to shadow Sir Roland's security detail while our ambassador attended foreign embassy functions or met with the Greek prime minister. Other times we were sent in advance to check out security at locations Sir Roland was to visit: an English-speaking school, for example, or a museum to which Britain had lent some of its treasures. We were supposed to be working undercover, but the regular appearance of two English people in casual clothes in advance of the ambassador's every visit was bound to give us away. I would have preferred to work differently, and more secretly, but security was not run the way either Ambrose or I would have liked. This was a hangover from the junta's regime. In those days the draconian police and the eternal presence of the army had kept most dissidents out of sight (or in prison), so diplomatic security had never been a major issue. Athens was considered a cushy posting, with its cultural history, its nightlife and its sunny beaches. Everyone at the embassy, except Ambrose and his small team, felt everything was running smoothly, so why make changes?

I kept well away from Sir Roland. He might have requested me on his security detail, but that could just have been Ambrose's way of making me feel accepted. Ambrose was a wily bird, and not above telling blatant lies if he thought they would ease the situation.

One trip sticks in my memory. It would be impossible to forget. Lady Mary and some friends – embassy wives – had been invited to lunch at a charity event organised by the Belgian ambassador's wife. It was to be held at the Astir Palace Hotel, at the southern tip of Vouliagmeni, an increasingly smart and fashionable beachside suburb of Athens.

Freddie and I checked out the hotel a couple of hours before the event and gave the team the okay. The motorcade of embassy cars swept past the guards at the gate and up the long drive to the hotel. The lunch went without incident. Afterwards, Lady Mary and some of the diplomatic wives wanted to go swimming. The problem was that the Astir Palace is built on a rocky outcrop and does not enjoy a beach. It has a couple of swimming pools, but the ladies wanted to swim in the sea. The manager suggested they go to the privately run beach nearby where, for a fee, they could get some loungers and a cabin, change into their swimming costumes, and enjoy the sands which sloped gently into the shallow sea. So the embassy cars drove them all down to the private beach. The procession made quite a stir.

All was well until Lady Mary and her friends went for a dip. I had followed them to the shore and watched them playing with a beach-ball in the shallows and swimming baby breaststrokes while working hard to keep their perfectly coiffed hairstyles above water. Freddie lay on a nearby lounger to keep an eye on their bags, clothes and towels.

After some forty minutes I noticed a large, bronzed woman standing over Freddie while making a big show of towelling herself dry. Freddie didn't move and I could tell, from the regular rise and fall of his chest, that he was fast asleep. I could also see that he was enjoying an erotic dream. How could I tell? Freddie was sporting an enormous erection which had risen beyond the waistband of his trunks. The Amazonian woman eyed it with what I could only assume was aroused interest.

At that point the diplomatic wives returned for their towels and clothes, left draped over several loungers. As they approached, the bronzed woman started yelling at them. Lady Mary attempted to placate her. Thinking the remarkably muscular woman wanted money, she held out a large denomination drachma banknote. The angry woman snatched the banknote, threw it on the ground and stamped on it. She proceeded to hurl the diplomatic wives' clothes onto the damp sand around the loungers while they stood dripping. It looked as if her next move might be more threatening.

I ran forward to help but Freddie, now wide awake, said, 'I'll deal with this.' He placed himself between Lady Mary and the muscular woman and began to reason with her in Greek. I had no idea he was fluent in the language. It turned out that he wasn't. He was addressing her in Ancient Greek – the sort we learned at school.

Even though the Ancient Greeks did not have a word for 'please', and even though she clearly didn't understand a word of anything that came out of Freddie's mouth, the mighty Amazonian was placated by Freddie's enthusiastic charm. She looked delighted. Lady Mary looked concerned. The French ambassador's wife stared at Freddie's erection – dwindling but still prominent through his trunks – and exchanged a knowing look with the Belgian ambassador's wife.

At that point a beach attendant arrived and explained in broken English that there had been a mix-up and that this was the Amazonian's usual set of loungers. He hadn't expected her to show up today. Being Greek, he took no responsibility for the drama he had inadvertently caused.

The Amazonian wasn't entirely satisfied so, while I escorted the ladies to their official cars, parked on the street outside, Freddie escorted her along the beach to soothe her and reassure her that her honour had not been besmirched.

The diplomatic cars moved off at a stately pace. Freddie was nowhere to be seen, so I gave instructions to Lady Mary's driver to follow the other cars until they reached Athens city centre, while I waited behind.

At last Freddie reappeared, his cheeks flushed the sort of pink that gives a blond Englishman away when he's been exerting himself pleasurably.

'What kept you?' I asked. I tried to hide the sarcastic note that threatened to creep in.

'She said she would like to see more of me.'

'And did she?'

'Well, it would have been ungentlemanly to refuse.' And that's all we had to say on the matter. I should have given him a telling off for falling asleep on duty, but I was impressed by Freddie's willingness to oblige a lady in the interests of diplomacy. It did not put me off him in the slightest. If anything, it drew us closer.

The following day was a Sunday, and we both had the day off. Freddie asked if we could meet up and go over some matters of protocol. He wanted to improve his knowledge and asked if I might help. That, of course, is exactly what Ambrose had asked of me, so I suggested we meet in the park and hoped the souvlaki stall would be open. Freddie had very different ideas. The previous day he had noted a smart restaurant in Vouliagmeni and suggested it as our venue. As my credit card had only recently recovered from Matthew's onslaught, I was all for finding something lighter on the purse. But Freddie was adamant. 'My treat,' he insisted, 'and bring a bikini.'

We met at one o'clock the next day. Most wealthy Greeks – shipping tycoons, property developers and the odd exporter of prohibited antiquities – never seemed to eat lunch before three in the afternoon, so there was only a handful of people, mostly spring tourists, eating in the restaurant.

Freddie arrived at the same time I did. I suspected he had been waiting nearby until I showed. He had booked a table in the shade but with a view of the public beach and families sunbathing and swimming. That March was already unseasonably warm, with the temperature rising to more than thirty degrees centigrade in the shade.

Freddie took the corner chair on my right, so we both had a view of the sea and the boats sailing in the bay. Unlike Matthew, he let me choose from the menu. I selected grilled *barbounia*, or red mullet, caught the night before, and took a chance on a Cretan dakos salad. That was a mistake. The Cretans make some wonderful dishes, but a tomato and herb salad undermined with dry cheeses and even drier husks of stale bread isn't one of them. Freddie went for a simple steak, rare, and a Greek salad which he gallantly shared with me after noting my disappointment with the dakos.

We shared half a bottle of white wine, Freddie bowing to my choice of fish. We finished the meal with Greek yoghurt and honey, sprinkled with crumbled pistachios, followed by Greek coffees 'metrio'.

'You told me to bring my bikini. I only have a one-piece.'

'No matter, we're going for a swim.' He paid the bill and walked with me to the entrance to the Astir private beach.

'You did the lunch, let me do this,' I offered. The entry fee was extortionate, even back then.

'Wouldn't dream of it,' he laughed. 'I've come into a bit of an inheritance. You wouldn't want me to spend it all on myself, would you? Wouldn't be any fun.'

Once on the beach he stripped off – he was wearing his beach trunks, a less revealing pair this time, underneath his trousers – then waited while I changed into my one-piece. When I emerged I noticed the Amazonian woman had left her lounger and was approaching Freddie. He must have seen her too, for he suddenly took my hand and we strode down to the water and plunged in together. He swam strongly, but I kept up with him until we were about a hundred yards out. He had such an infectious grin, splashed with salt water as it was, that I couldn't help smiling.

He performed a perfect duck dive – hands and head down, tipping his chest forward, throwing his legs high so he disappeared into the deep with hardly a splash. Laughing, I waited for him to come up. I waited another thirty seconds, then I started to worry. I bobbed my head under the water, but there was no sign of him. I swam deeper. Still no sign.

I surfaced and called out his name.

Still nothing. I was really worried now. How was I going to explain this to Ambrose? Besides, I was becoming very fond of Freddie.

I called out his name again. People on the beach were looking, gathering at the shore.

Then I heard my name shouted from the rocks to the north of the bay. I turned and there he was, his lithe, fine-muscled form clambering over the rocks and diving back into the sea. He must have swum almost two hundred feet underwater on one breath.

Freddie surfaced beside me, gasping, then splashed water in my face. Relieved, I swam back to the beach, easily outstripping him. We lay on the hot sand, our feet in the tiny ripples of the sea, the sun warming our bodies.

Afterwards I took him back to my place and we made love. For an Englishman, Freddie was remarkably accomplished, and I understood why the Amazonian had been jealous to see me with him.

Later, I asked him where he had picked up his skills.

'Long story. You sure you want to hear it?' I nodded. 'A few years ago I went to Club Med for a week. I had just broken up with a girlfriend and I was licking my wounds. They have a funny rule. If you're a guy on your own, they make you share a room with another single guy on his own. Or maybe they only had that bed spare. Anyway, one evening my roommate, a French chap, tells me he's met the woman of his dreams. His problem is that he wants to take her to bed, but he needs me to find somewhere else for the night. He already has a solution. His new girlfriend has a sister. So why don't I join them for a dinner? He'll slope off with his new woman and I can have the sister. "What if she doesn't like me?" I ask. "She will," he says.'

Freddie took a deep breath. 'Well, he was right. The only trouble was she only spoke French, and my French was a little rusty. So we mostly communicated with body language. Well, sex really.'

He sighed. 'She flew off the next morning and I thought that was the end of it. But a few days later she showed up at my flat and said she was going to leave her husband. He hadn't made love to her in a year. I was about to start my job in the service, so this was all a bit awkward. Anyway, I taught her a little English, and she taught me… well, what I know.'

I pulled him towards me and we made love again. Then, like the gentleman he was, he got up, showered, put on his clothes, kissed me and left.

Back at work we gave nothing away of our affair. Most evenings we met up, sometimes grabbing a quick bite before hungrily going back to my place and spending longer and longer together into the night, until we talked of his moving in with me. I recommended caution. Agents were not supposed to get involved with each other. I was pretty certain Ambrose would disapprove, and I did not want to let him down.

31

After we made love Freddie and I would lie on my tiny balcony, away from prying eyes, he with his head on my stomach, I running my fingers through his luxurious hair, chestnut brown with copper streaks, bleached by seawater and sun.

It was soon after our swim at the Astir beach that I noticed a change. Something was bothering Freddie. Thinking it might be guilt about some girlfriend left behind in England, I ventured to tease it out of him.

'It's nothing like that,' he answered. 'It's something… to do with work. But I don't want to stir the wasps' nest if it's all in my imagination.'

I let it rest there. But over the next few days he looked increasingly worried. I tried again to prise it out of him. His tetchy answer, 'I can't talk about it now. But if I get proof, you and Ambrose will know straight away,' shut me up. I was going to have to be patient.

The following week we had three call-outs in three days. Sir Roland's diary was filling up. There was a conference involving several European heads of state, though this looked more like a trip on the gravy train, as we called it. The giveaway was that it only lasted one day and gave the heads of states' partners enough time to go shopping and make it back to their home cities to show off their purchases the following evening. Sir Roland attended a couple of other events, but they were of no great consequence. After the last of these, as we were heading back to the ambassador's residence, his official Daimler's engine started to make an ominous knocking. His driver slowed down, but Freddie and I, in the following car, told him to get Sir Roland back to his residence and we'd sort the problem out the following day.

As the British embassy was a prestigious client, the garage sent a mechanic to take a look at the Daimler. After tinkering with it for a few minutes, he declared that they would need to have it at the workshop to give it a thorough overhaul. They had no pickup vehicle available that day – Thursday – but if the Daimler were to be driven to the workshop in Monastiraki the first thing on Friday morning, they might be able to have it back that evening.

Early on the Friday I offered to follow the Daimler in my car, so I could give the driver a lift back to the residence. Freddie said he'd like to come along too. He wanted to pick up a friend on the way back. We were looking forward to a long weekend together, as Sir Roland and Lady Mary were due to take a break back in England for Easter. Freddie asked if he could sit in the back of the Daimler, in Sir Roland's usual seat, and the driver, an old Greek fellow, agreed.

We set off before the traffic had really got going – in those days there was less traffic in the city – and headed up to the workshop.

As we approached Monastiraki Square, where the old flea market was located, an official-looking man stepped out into the road and directed us towards a side street. Our driver wound down his window and asked what the problem was. An overturned truck full of goats ready for market, he was told. He shrugged, wound up his window and headed into the narrow street.

I was in half a mind to park up and wait while the Daimler was delivered to the garage, but then had second thoughts and drove after it. Normally tables and chairs set for restaurants would line this street, making it impossible to drive through, but the tables had yet to be set up, and the Daimler was able to edge through slowly.

That was when I saw them: two young women of middle-eastern appearance, stepping out in front of the Daimler, which came to a sudden stop. At the same moment two men strode out of a restaurant. They carried AK-47s – submachine guns with which I had a close acquaintance. The younger of the two men aimed into the back seat of the Daimler and fired. His gun jammed.

In those remaining seconds I managed to slam on my brakes, leap out of the car and run towards the older man just as he fired, raking the side of the Daimler, the bullets smashing its side window and finding their mark in poor Freddie. In that moment I recognised the man firing. He was the greasy-haired character who had come aboard the MY *Fantasy*, the man who had argued with Sir Roland and had left the yacht in an almighty rage.

I bowled straight into him, knocking aside his weapon, but the younger man hit me with the butt of his AK-47 and I went down, stunned.

As I struggled to regain my feet the two men ran to a waiting car. Their driver was the man who had directed us into the alley and set up the ambush. Our own driver, his face white, steadied me, clasping me to his chest. He was doing his best to stop me looking into the back of the Daimler. I pushed him aside and threw open the door.

Freddie was slumped in the back of the car, his white shirt bloodied and riddled with bullet holes. Shards of glass glittered in his thick, rich hair, the hair I had so often run my fingers through. He reached out for me with one hand, while the other arm lay useless, its bones shattered. He opened his mouth to say something, and I saw the pleading in his eyes as a thick stream of black blood rose in his gorge and he fell back.

I threw myself at him, cradling his body in my arms.

I did not cry then. That was later, when I was alone. I held his hand, the one he had reached out to me, and rocked back and forward as I felt his life leave his body.

The driver got on his radio and alerted the embassy. Half an hour later Ambrose arrived. He and the driver had to prise my stiff fingers off Freddie's body. While paramedics took Freddie away, Ambrose led me to my car. I sat in the back seat, while Ambrose sat in front and turned around in his seat to debrief me.

Stunned as I was, I managed to keep my voice steady as I related to him, in as much detail as possible, the events of the morning right up to Freddie's murder. I mentioned that Freddie had been worried about something at work, but that I had no idea what it was about.

Ambrose, who up until now had shown masterly calm and patience, showed a flash of anger. His mouth tightened, and his question came from between clenched teeth. 'You must have had some inkling?'

'None. I pressed Freddie, but he didn't want to cause alarm without proof. I was sure I would have another chance to get him to share his concerns.'

'Dammit.' Ambrose's knuckles went white as he clenched his fists. 'The Greek police will want to talk to you. It's a formality. Don't expect them to act on any information you give them. And you should, for the time being, omit mentioning that person you identified as the assassin. We have him in our sights, and we would like to be the ones to pay him back. Meanwhile, I'm going to have to tell my sister about her son.' So I was right, Freddie was Ambrose's nephew. 'I don't know how I can even begin to do it.'

'But you know who shot Freddie.'

'If he's the same person who met Sir Roland on Mavros' yacht, then yes, I do. His name is Sabri Khalil al-Banna.'

I had heard that name before, but I was more familiar with his *nom de guerre*. He was the Palestinian militant and proscribed terrorist Abu Nidal.

32

Ambrose drove me to his own flat in the city, where the police interviewed me. He left me with them while he went to telephone his sister. I could hear him in the other room, stumbling over his words as he tried to soften the blow.

The Greek police were not helpful. After what Ambrose had said I did not expect them to be. Shortly after their soft 'interrogation', two Greek counterterrorist agents arrived and ushered the police out. But these two were hardly more thorough. I had avoided naming Freddie's killer. As Abu Nidal was on the US terrorist list, he was certain to have fled Greece, possibly by private plane or boat to Turkey and beyond, before the police even arrived on the scene.

The counterterrorist agents were anxious to avoid an escalation of what they saw as a diplomatic incident. They explained to me, as if to a child, that all evidence pointed to a serious error on the part of the assassins. They must have intended to take Sir Roland's life, for reasons of their own. (I, of course, was convinced that it was as payback for Sir Roland's rejection of his request – though I wasn't supposed to know that.) Abu Nidal had killed poor innocent Freddie by mistake, presuming Sir Roland would be the Daimler's passenger.

Greece had had its problems with Palestinian factions before. Back in August 1973 the Black September Group had opened fire in the Athens Hellinikon International Airport when security had asked to check their bags. They had intended to hijack a plane and hold its passengers hostage in return for the release of some of their imprisoned members. In the event, they killed three people and injured fifty-five civilians before taking thirty-five hostages. There was a standoff and the killers eventually surrendered. But that wasn't the end of it. Later that year there was an airport attack and airplane hijacking in Rome. The hijackers demanded the Greek government release the two terrorists guilty of the Athens airport attack. Even though the Rome hijackers eventually reduced their demands to getting their plane refuelled and being allowed to depart, the Greek authorities were keen to avoid a repetition of escalating events. After all, they had their own home-grown terrorists to deal with.

Once the counterterrorist agents had left, Ambrose reappeared. He looked drained. He fell into an armchair without saying a word. I found some gin and a bottle of tonic water and poured us both strong measures.

Ambrose's hands shook so much he could hardly hold his glass. I held it steady for him. He gulped the whole lot down in one, then held the glass out for a refill.

'It's not the first time I've had to pass on news about a death. But this was one I can never do again. My own sister.' He choked up. 'I loved Freddie as if he were my own son.'

Suddenly he was sobbing, deep harsh sobs. I held him in my arms and we stayed like that a long time together. In all the time I knew him, that was the only time I saw Ambrose lose control.

I kept my position as 'undercover' security for another year, until Sir Roland retired as ambassador in 1985. His official security detail was stepped up and I felt myself sidelined. Freddie's death was a blot on my career, even though nobody said as much, and when Sir Roland became Chairman of the Anglo-Hellenic League a year or so later, he retained one driver/bodyguard, who stuck with him. In my mind, and that of Ambrose, Sir Roland was taking a risk. But there were no subsequent attempts on his life, and the general feeling at the embassy was that Abu Nidal and his thugs had made their point, and were unlikely to risk their own lives without a fair chance of success.

Ambrose felt differently. He did not blame me at all. His venom was aimed solely at Abu Nidal. He spent as much of his spare time trying to trace the man's hideout as the Americans did after 9/11 tracking Osama bin Laden. Abu Nidal sought sanctuary with all the Middle East's dictators: the only places where he was safe from Ambrose's revenge. He was in Syria until it got too hot for him and Hafez al-Assad threw him out, just three days before two young SAS men, organised by Ambrose, planned to eliminate him. Then Ambrose traced him to Libya. He put together a team to arrange a hit, but Libya was harder to enter unnoticed and the hit was postponed twice. Then came the Lockerbie bombing of Pan Am Flight 103 in December 1988. With Gaddafi in the spotlight as the most likely perpetrator, the Libyan dictator threw Abu Nidal out of his country. He already had enough problems of his own.

Iraqi dictator Saddam Hussein granted Abu Nidal asylum in Baghdad. But he soon tired of this troublesome thorn in his side. About a week before Ambrose's team were to cross the border from Turkey into Iraq, Hussein sent his secret service men to arrest Nidal. Reports differ at that point. Some say Abu Nidal died resisting arrest, others that he shot himself rather than surrender and spend the rest of his life in Saddam's torture chamber. Either way, Ambrose was deprived of his revenge.

Ambrose never let his obsession get in the way of his daily work. Our mutual loss brought us close, and we would often spend evenings together, watching the sun go down over a drink or two. Sometimes we were joined by Matthew Fawcett. While Ambrose and I had been tainted by Freddie's death, Matthew, who had been north in Meteora on that terrible day, went entirely unscathed. It had no adverse effect on his rapid ascent in the service, which led to him heading up the Middle East desk. Whenever he visited, he was sympathetic and tactful. The three of us drank in silence – Matthew enjoying Bismarck's favourite tipple of Black Velvet – Champagne and Guinness – though in his case Ambrose secretly swapped the Dom Perignon for a much cheaper Spanish Cava. If Matthew noticed the difference, he never said so. I suspected his visits to Ambrose, which became more frequent towards the end, coincided with the opening of a gay nightclub just round the corner from Ambrose's apartment. From the balcony we could hear throbbing music start up, and see men of all ages heading towards its source. Matthew would glance at his watch, exclaim, 'Is that the time?' and head off with a peck on the cheek for me and a pat on the back for Ambrose. On a couple of the early visits he brought embassy staff along with him. These men were shy types, and I do not recall their names. They stood around awkwardly and after two or three such visits Matthew came alone. He had known Freddie well, whereas the faceless young men who trailed along behind him seemed strangers.

When Sir Roland retired Ambrose stayed on in Athens, while I returned to London. I was never held responsible for what befell, but I bore it badly. I was given new assignments, but the internal wounds and scars remained. I realised that, of all the men I had known, Freddie was one of the very few I truly loved.

33

Hampstead, 2019

I WAS INTRIGUED, BUT NOT dismayed, by Emily Charalamboulos's declaration of her love for Freddie.

'So, did you and Freddie have an affair?'

'Oh no, nothing like that. I never told him how I felt. I just loved him from afar.'

So she had never been my love rival. That was surprisingly comforting to know, even after all this time.

'Besides,' she continued, 'Matthew was always hovering around him, making sure nobody got close.'

'Matthew Fawcett?'

'Yes. He adored Freddie.'

'So did a lot of people.' Had Matthew been a love rival? I hoped not.

'And Iorgos.' She quickly corrected herself, 'George.'

'George?'

'My brother. He'd recently joined the embassy staff.'

Freddie and George. They sounded like some music hall comedy routine.

'They went around with Raymond.'

'Raymond Turnberry?'

'Yes. The three of them were obsessed with Greek history. Always visiting museums together. Raymond kept a tortoise.'

He still does, I thought, but refrained from mentioning it.

'George was billeted in the north of Athens. He always had trouble getting into work on time. So Freddie said he'd meet George in Monastiraki, as they both knew a bit about cars. George was in the square when the shooting broke out. He ran for safety, along with hundreds of others. He had no idea Freddie was involved.'

'He wasn't involved. He was the victim.'

'That's what I meant.' Her lips trembled. She tried to put the cat on the floor but it sprung back into her lap. 'When George found out what had happened, he asked around. He discovered someone had put something in the fuel tank. That's why the engine was knocking. And he remembered seeing someone from the embassy in Monastiraki that morning.'

'Was it Bella Walsingham?'

'I'm sorry, I don't know that name. All I know is that George suspected that the incident with the car and the shooting were connected. You see, the car was kept in the embassy garage. Only someone with access to the garage could have tampered with the car. George wanted to know if the person he'd seen in Monastiraki had seen anything suspicious.'

'He'd seen someone he knew? Who was it?' I leant forward. At last I was going to get a name.

'I never found out.'

'What do you mean?'

'George went missing and I never heard from him again. Not until a month or so ago.'

'Where has he been all this time?'

'In a prison in Siberia.'

'Good grief.' I sat back. 'How on earth did that happen?'

Emily took a deep breath. She dug her fingers into the cat's thick fur. I expected it to twist around and take a swipe at her with its claws but it just lay there purring as she massaged it nervously.

'Someone at the embassy needed some important documents to be taken urgently to Moscow. George obliged and flew out that evening. He bought his own ticket, as he was promised he would be reimbursed in full on his return. When he reached Moscow his belongings were searched, the documents were found on him and he was accused of handling Soviet state secrets, given an immediate trial and sentenced to thirty-five years detention.'

I had listened to her story with scarcely a question. Now they all tumbled out.

'Why didn't the British government protest and try to get him out?'

'Nobody knew where he'd gone. He'd travelled on his Greek passport, under the name Iorgos, so the British were never notified, nor were the Greek authorities. He had no diplomatic protection.'

'What did you do?'

'I filed a "missing persons" report with the police, but after just a few days they gave up. They thought he'd eloped with some girl.'

'Wasn't there anyone at the embassy who could help?'

'Apparently some documents had gone missing, and they thought George had something to do with it. There was a terrible kerfuffle and eventually I felt it best to resign.'

'Poor you.' It seemed the right response. 'How did you learn all this? The arrest, the prison in Siberia?'

'About four or five weeks ago I suddenly heard from George. Out of the blue. He had completed his sentence and the Russians didn't know what to do with him. It seems the notes of his trial and sentence had been lost sometime between the collapse of the Soviet Union and the end of the Yeltsin era. They put him on a plane back to Athens and he was found wandering around the airport in a confused state. After a couple of days in hospital he got in touch with me – on my old landline, which I have on divert – and told me his story. Well, what I've told you. Nothing more.'

'Not the name of the person in Monastiraki?'

'No. But George said he was going to get his revenge. He wanted his life back and he was going to make that person pay, one way or the other. I offered to put him up, but he said that might be dangerous, for both of us, and I was to stay out of sight until he contacted me again. I don't know where he is and I've heard nothing from him since.'

34

I TOOK A TUBE TRAIN from Hampstead down to King's Cross station, where I changed onto the City Line towards Hammersmith. It wasn't until I reached Royal Oak – a blighted, semi-industrial area without an oak tree in sight – that my phone pinged to tell me I had a message.

I studied the message. *Must meet*, it read. I didn't recognise the number. I hesitated to answer, as it could have come from anyone: Matthew, Percy, Ambrose, even Bernard. It could also have come from some scammer pretending to be an offspring of mine and hoping that, after a brief exchange of messages, I would send them £1,000 towards the cost of a new phone. By the time I reached Westbourne Grove I decided to answer.

Who is this? I wrote.

At first there was no reply. Perhaps I, or they, were out of signal. Then I got another ping. *B.*

Who? I wrote.

The answer came back instantly. *Bella.*

Bella Walsingham.

As I desperately needed the loo – too much tea at Emily Charalamboulos's – and wanted to check a few things at the safe house, I wrote back: *Need half an hour. Shall contract you then.* I had meant to write '*contact*' but bloody predictive text has its own agenda.

The reply came just as I reached Ladbroke Grove station. *Need to meet asap.*

OK, I replied. Predictive text couldn't fuck that one up.

I hurried back into the safe house, flicked on the radio, tuned it to BBC Radio 4 and hurried into the loo for relief. By the time the news came on I was on the computer.

There were several online items about James Saunders' death together with a report that his wife had been taken in for questioning. An item labelled 'Breaking news' appeared on the BBC site. It said that police had released James's wife. She had been in Scotland the whole of the previous day and could not have been involved in her husband's death. Not directly, I thought, but there were other ways, and there were people who might oblige for the right amount of hard cash. A minute or so later the same information was relayed by the BBC radio newsreader. I turned the radio off.

Then I remembered what Matthew had said when I had called him about my meeting with James Saunders. He had told me that both Bella and Ambrose were with him. That meant that both of them would have heard that I'd spoken to James, and would know his address. So either of them could have gone there and... Well, in Ambrose's case that was highly unlikely. He was quite capable of killing James, if it was necessary, but I couldn't imagine him doing so in cold blood without good reason. Bella on the other hand... She was a large and powerful woman. What did I really know about Bella? Apart from what was in the public domain, which was precious little, I knew nothing. I googled her. There were a few brief mentions, but nothing about her career in the service, of course. She was simply listed as 'Civil Servant'. More forthcoming was thepeerage.com. It listed Bella as the daughter of Colonel Thomas Pasley Walsingham and the

Honourable Sarah Ludlow, younger daughter of Viscount Ludlow. Bella had an elder brother who had joined the army but been killed in Brunei at the age of twenty-four. Apart from that, nothing. I was about to try a more general search when my phone pinged again. Another message from Bella's number, this time on WhatsApp, insisting we meet up asap. Well, I wasn't going to have her round to my safe house for a cosy cuppa. Far too risky. We would have to meet on neutral territory, out in the open, with plenty of people around.

I sent her a reply: *Little Wormwood Scrubs in one hour.* Predictive text did not mess up that one for me. But I had not been specific enough. *Circular path, north end*, I added. A few moments passed, then I got her reply. *Aggrieved*. Then the message was deleted and replaced with *Agreed*. I wasn't the only one at the mercy of the machines.

I entered Little Wormwood Scrubs through the south-east entrance, passing Fitou's Thai restaurant on my right as I did so. I had eaten there a couple of times and found it good.

It had taken me fifteen minutes to reach the Little Scrubs. Unless Bella was in a car and had started from Notting Hill or closer, there was no way she could have got there before me. It is essential when arranging such meetings to get there well before the other party. If you let them choose the location, they will suggest a place they know well. Indeed, they may already be there, waiting for you with a nasty surprise.

I had changed my clothes, and now wore a dark-green patterned top over brown slacks and dark brown trainers. They would give me some sort of camouflage from prying eyes.

I headed straight for the thicket in the centre of the scrubs. Sometime in the past, perhaps during the last world war, the area had been planted with fruit trees. Or maybe they had simply sprouted from discarded fruit. Now apples, cherry plums and mirabelles grew in profusion. I strode through the narrow paths, forged by fruit pickers and dog walkers. Brambles loaded with blackberries and blackthorn with sloes tore at my slacks. I pressed on, taking first a left-hand path, then a right, glancing back over my shoulder every so often, ensuring I was not being watched or pursued.

Eventually the trees gave way to an open grassy area edged by an asphalt track that ran around the whole of the Little Scrubs. Bella was most likely to take the circular, open route to meet me, and I would be able to see her approach well before she saw me. She would probably stop at the wooden bench with the simple but touching inscription on its brass plaque: 'I love you'.

I stepped back into the thicket, moving slowly from tree to tree, as if engaged in picking late blackberries. All the while I was keeping one eye on the asphalt track and glancing back to the narrow paths behind me.

I had been there about fifteen minutes – some forty minutes in all since I had arranged our rendezvous – when a voice spoke behind me.

'Hello, Felicity.'

I whipped around. Bella Walsingham was standing under a plum tree just a few feet away. How had such a large woman managed to get so close without my hearing her? Well, she had had the same sort of training I had, and almost certainly from dear old Dennis, so I shouldn't have been surprised. But I was cross with myself for not anticipating that she would match me, trick for trick.

'Bella,' I said. 'Good to see you.'

'Is it?' Her expression gave nothing away. She just stood

there, eyes darting from one tree or thicket to another, as if expecting an ambush.

'What was so urgent that you had to meet me?'

She studied me for a while before speaking. 'You are the only one of us in hiding.'

'That's true. But there was a reason for that.'

'Perhaps. Your reason satisfied Matthew, at any rate. But you are the only one I don't recall from Athens.'

Why was she questioning me? What was her concern? 'That's easy to explain,' I said. 'I was mostly working undercover, on security detail for Ambassador Bingham. Come to that, I don't remember you there either.'

'This is not about me. You are the only one of us I don't know. I trust the others, Matthew, Ambrose…' She tailed off.

'What about Raikes?'

'Raikes is dead.'

'What?' This came as a shock. 'What happened?'

'They're trying to figure that out. Police say it was a hit and run, but his injuries… well, they don't stack up. Ambrose says it looks like he was struck repeatedly about the head with a blunt instrument. Something wooden.'

'Do they have any idea who did it, or why?'

Bella studied me with a look of impatience. 'How about making an intelligent guess?'

I deserved that. It was the sort of comment I would have made. I was beginning to like this woman.

'He was getting too close.'

'Yes. But to what?'

'To whatever it is we're looking for.' I knew I sounded hopelessly vague.

'Don't you know?'

'Do you?'

'Are you serious?'

There was a snap of a twig breaking. We both turned and saw a woman, about our own age, on the earthy path, picking ripe apples from a tree. She saw us and smiled.

'Lovely day.'

'Yes, isn't it?' replied Bella. Neither of us moved. The woman picked three more apples which she placed in a small trug. She stepped past Bella, who gave her a frosty smile. I smiled too, as she passed me. I think my smile was the winner. The woman reached the asphalt track and gave us one more look. Our smiles were gone. She moved on fast.

'Well?' demanded Bella.

'All I've had from Matthew is a pile of old documents, bills, receipts, going back years. I don't know what he's told you, but he's kept me out of the loop.'

'With good reason.'

'What do you mean?'

In answer Bella reached into her handbag. When she drew it out, it was holding a handgun. I hardly had time to make out the model – a SIG-Sauer P226 – when she raised it and fired.

35

BELLA'S BULLET WHIZZED PAST MY ear, so close that for a moment I thought she had drawn blood, and found its target behind me. I heard a grunt and spun round to see Aleksi, gun in hand, stagger backwards and slump into a briar patch. A trickle of blood pumped from the wound in his chest. I stood over him.

'I thought you had learnt your lesson.' His throat was covered with a large sticking plaster where I had pierced it with his knife.

'I don't give up,' he gurgled.

'Neither do I.'

His heart must have been hit, for he lost consciousness almost immediately. Bella stepped forward, knelt and felt his pulse.

'He's gone.' She stood up. 'Friend of yours?'

'I knew his cousin,' which was true. I hoped that was the last I would see of his family.

'Help me shift him,' Bella said. Fortunately there was hardly any blood. This can happen when the heart stops suddenly. A few seconds of consciousness, then it's over. What little blood there had been had sprinkled the brambles then passed straight into the dark earth below. Many of the bramble's thorny stems were of a reddish hue, so the wet blood, as it congealed and dried, would soon be indistinguishable from the rest.

Together we rolled his body up over the bush, so that it fell on the far side, away from view. I don't think I could have ever managed it on my own, but with Bella's sturdy weight behind it, we achieved the job quickly. Afterwards I gathered up handfuls of blackberries which I crushed and wiped over any obvious streaks of blood. By the time I'd finished it looked like some wilful and clumsy child, overindulging in blackberries, had got tangled in the thorns.

While I did the cover-up, Bella held her iPhone high to find a strong signal.

'Occurs, Lows, Broad,' she said out loud, then did a screen grab and sent it via WhatsApp to a number logged in her phone.

'What3words,' I said, to show I knew what she was doing.

'Someone will be round tonight to dispose of the body.'

'I don't envy them their job,' I said.

'They're used to it.' She took a look around, kicked a stray bramble off the path, and turned to me. 'Fancy a coffee?'

Our first choice of venue was Mug, a coffee and toastie bar almost next to Fitou's. But it was small and full of dog walkers with their pets, and we risked being overheard, so we strode down to Adrianna's café in St Helen's Gardens, a few blocks south. There, the clientele was made up of locals, who arrived in twos and threes and were welcomed by staff and fellow customers. There was nobody sitting alone, so we felt safe talking at a table outside, concealed by the remains of a dead olive tree in a tub.

Bella went into the café to order a flat white for me and a

double espresso with hot milk on the side for herself, then came out to join me.

'I'm sorry about that.'

'The suspicions?'

'No, that was understandable. I mean the fellow trying to kill you. Getting a little rusty, not as good at spotting a tail as I once was.'

'You think he was following you?'

'It's a possibility. What happened to his gun?'

'I have it.' I thought I had managed to snatch it up without her seeing it, but the wily look in her eyes told me I was wrong.

'You'd better hold onto it. You will probably need it.'

I instinctively felt for it in my handbag. The hard metal was reassuring. I had found something else in Aleksi's pocket, but I wasn't going to tell Bella.

'What did you mean when you said "With good reason" when I told you I felt Matthew was keeping me out of the loop?'

'We are all under suspicion. That's why Matthew chose us.'

'That's what Raikes said.'

'When?'

'After our first meeting. He followed me.'

'Did he?' She studied me carefully. 'And now he's gone.'

Our coffees arrived. Hers was accompanied by a small jug of hot water.

'I asked for hot milk,' she said, firmly but kindly. The young woman took away the hot water and reappeared a few moments later with hot milk.

'You are a dear, thank you,' said Bella, with another warm smile. It disappeared the moment the young woman was gone.

'We are all under suspicion and all potential targets. Who knew where you were hiding?'

Percy, who had taken me there, and Matthew. And Matthew's team.

'Matthew knew. And his people.'

'That's interesting. Matthew's people are top-notch. And discreet. What about the man I killed?'

'Aleksi?' Of course he knew the street where I lived. He must have been watching and followed me here. I was mortified that I had allowed myself to drop my guard. Embarrassed, I remained silent.

Bella poured her milk into her coffee and took a sip. It was a little too hot for her. 'I heard about your safe house from Ambrose. Not the exact location, but the general whereabouts. Ladbroke Grove.'

Ambrose! I couldn't believe it.

'But we're old friends,' I said. 'He would never betray me.'

'Never can be a surprisingly short time in our line of business. But don't see it as a betrayal. See it as insurance.'

I had no idea what she meant.

'I think Ambrose wanted me to help you if something went wrong.'

'What do you mean, "go wrong"?'

'Not all people are what they seem.'

'I know that,' I replied tetchily. 'We learn that lesson on our first day.'

Bella stared, her grey eyes boring into me. She tried her coffee again. This time it was drinkable. She took a small sip, then downed the rest in one gulp.

'Just watch your back. That's all I can say.' She stood to go.

'Watch my back? Against whom?'

'Trust no one.' A black taxi with its light on came by. She hailed it and was gone before I had a chance to say more.

I waited a few minutes, sipping my coffee and listening to the banter of the young men and women all around me. When I was absolutely sure that Bella was long gone and that nobody was watching, I felt inside my handbag and pulled out the object I had extracted from Aleksi's pocket. It was the polaroid photograph of me in my 'new' look with red hair. The one the make-up artist, Sarah Azizi-Ryan, had told me had been ruined.

36

I CALLED AMBROSE ON HIS burner phone.

'Tell me about Raikes.'

'You know he's dead.' Ambrose, sometimes diffident, never beat about a bush in moments of crisis. I stayed silent.

'Official report says he died in a hit-and-run,' he continued.

'I heard that.'

'The reality is that he was beaten about the head and died some time before being hit and run over by a car. I've seen both the forensic pathologists' reports.'

'Two pathologists?'

'Two reports. The first was done hastily. Matthew needed confirmation of cause as a hit-and-run. The pathologist then took the body home, where she has her own laboratory. Unfortunately there was a delay.'

I already knew about the 'hit-and-run', so I let Ambrose continue.

'As she reached home she found a police operation in progress. They had raided a cannabis farm in the house opposite. They stopped her and asked what she had in the boot of her car. When she replied "a dead body" they thought she was being sarcastic, then insisted she open up the car. You can imagine what I had to do to prevent this going any further.'

I certainly could. Ambrose always kept a very low profile, and hated raising his head above the parapet. But he had the ear of the people who counted, so I did not suppose he had encountered as much difficulty as he was making out.

'It was on more detailed exploration that she discovered that Raikes had been bashed from behind with a wooden croquet mallet. It came from a set his late wife had given him on his retirement. It had never been used.'

'It has now.'

'By someone with a good striking action.'

'I believe it's called a "stop-shot".'

'It certainly stopped poor old Jonathan.'

'Never keep a potential murder weapon in the home.'

'Like Trotsky's ice-pick. Good for making iced margaritas, or tequila and tonic, or for driving into the back of your head.'

When faced with the bleakest news, Ambrose and I always made light of it.

'That's what I used to think,' I countered. 'That it was a sharp metal spike for use with an ice bucket. But I've seen the actual thing: an ice axe, the sort used by mountain climbers. Ramón Mercader had sawn down the handle and concealed it in his raincoat.'

Pleasantries over, it was time to exchange information. 'I received some intelligence concerning the death of your nephew.'

'Freddie?' I heard a small quaver in Ambrose's voice.

'He was going to meet someone in Monastiraki that morning.' I stayed practical, to the point. I did not want Ambrose getting emotional. I need not have worried. The quaver was over in an instant.

'It would be interesting to know whom that might be.'

'Young chap by the name of George – or Iorgos – Charalamboulos.'

'The one who disappeared.'

'You've got a good memory.'

'Should have. I was the one trying to find out where he'd gone.'

'I met his sister.'

'Emily. She was quite distressed about it.'

'And the missing secrets.'

'There were no missing secrets.'

I did not respond for a moment. Someone had suspected documents had gone missing, but Ambrose was denying it.

'Ah, I know what you mean,' he continued. 'There were some documents that had been mis-filed, but they were found again pretty quickly.'

'Before or after Emily resigned?'

'Hmm, just after, I believe.'

'You didn't find that suspicious?'

'The missing papers were insignificant. We were all devastated by Freddie's death. George Charalamboulos going missing was a minor inconvenience. The rumour was that he'd eloped with some Greek girl.'

'Any idea who started the rumour?'

'If rumours could be traced to their sources there would be fewer misunderstandings, fewer wars. One person says one thing, another says another, two and two are put together to make thirteen, and before you know it, what started as a vague rumour is being reported as fact.'

I shifted gear. 'Tell me something. When I met up with you all in the Marylebone mews house, none of you seemed that surprised by my appearance. Had anyone shown you a recent photograph of me?'

'No. But we are all used to giving nothing away. You could have turned up looking like a Wagner Valkyrie, or one of Macbeth's witches, and none of us would have blinked an eye.' That was true. If I wanted to find out how Aleksi had acquired that polaroid, I was going to have to delve elsewhere.

'I meant to say,' added Ambrose, 'the pathologist found a fleck of blue paint in Raikes' hair. Very diligent of her, considering the car had scalped him.'

'Do we know if Raikes had unearthed anything of interest?'

'He reported to Matthew Fawcett, as do all of us. I expect we shall have an update from Matthew when he's digested everything.'

'The information or his dinner?'

'Both,' replied Ambrose with a light chuckle. '*À bientôt.*' He cut me off.

I went to my desk and made a list. I did it on paper, not on the computer. It wasn't beyond the realms of possibility that someone had hacked into it and was reading everything I wrote. I remembered that nice girl who coloured my hair and took my photograph going out of the bathroom more than once while the colour was setting. She could easily have infected the machine before I had located it myself.

I wrote down the names of Matthew's team: Ambrose, Raikes, Bella Walsingham and myself. I put Matthew at the centre of a circle, with four lines radiating out from it. At the end of the lines I put one of each of us.

Then I put a line through Raikes, poor fellow. Who had killed him? Why had he been killed? What had he discovered?

Radiating from my name were three others: Raymond Turnberry, James Saunders, and Emily Charalamboulos. I had interviewed all three. Matthew had both Ambrose and

Bella with him when I had told him about James. I put circles around each of them. I found it hard to believe that Ambrose would have turned on Raikes, unless he had very good reason. Which he might have done. I could well imagine Bella Walsingham wrapping her meaty hands around James Saunders' scrawny neck and choking him to death, especially after what I had witnessed in Little Wormwood Scrubs. And what about Matthew himself? Who really knew what went on in that devious mind of his? But he would have had to ditch the other two first. And the same went for Ambrose and Bella. They could all three provide each others' alibis.

What was it Freddie had said, that fateful day? He was going up to Monastiraki in the ambassador's Daimler and would pick up a friend on the way back. Had that friend been George Charalamboulos? Or was there somebody else from the embassy? The person George Charalamboulos had seen? And what bearing did this have on what Matthew was having us do? Up until now I had felt as if I had been working in a thick fog. What at one moment I took to be hard facts proved to be nothing more than shadows, and what seemed like nothing more than thin wisps of mist turned out to be impenetrable barriers.

37

THAT AFTERNOON I WASHED THE colour out of my hair; or some of it at least. With Aleksi dead, his body hidden and soon to be disposed of by experienced professionals, I was no longer in fear of my life.

I showered in hot water and rubbed my hair thoroughly with soap. Plenty of brown dye ran out through the plughole, and just a little red. I took a quick look in the mirror and saw that most of the dye still held. I got back in the shower and tried shampooing my hair, but it made little difference to the colour.

I sat in the bedroom and used the hairdryer. Perhaps my hair would look better when dry. It didn't. The red shade, put on by the expert, was beginning to show through the dark brown, applied by an amateur – me. Then I had a better idea. In a cupboard under the kitchen sink was some bleach. I took it into the bathroom. I was not entirely sure what effect pure bleach would have on my hair and scalp. I also found a bottle of hydrogen peroxide under the bathroom basin. I mentally tossed a coin and opted for the latter.

I stepped back into the shower and lathered my hair with the peroxide. After about five minutes I stepped out of the shower and looked in the mirror. My hair appeared to be getting lighter. I stepped back in the shower. Pretty soon I noticed a tingling in my scalp. Good, I thought, it's starting to work. Then the tingling changed to irritation and almost instantly to pain. I turned on the shower and washed the peroxide out as fast as I could. Then I rubbed in the conditioner that the colourist had left me.

I waited a while.

Was I supposed to wash the conditioner out or dry my hair with it in? It was so long since I had paid any attention to my appearance, especially my dry and wiry hair with its myriad split ends, that I could not remember.

Then I looked at the instructions on the tube, which is what I should have done in the first place. They told me to leave the conditioner in for no more than two to three minutes, then wash it out with warm water. The conditioner had already been in for more than five minutes, but I didn't think that would pose a problem. I dutifully washed it out with warm water, then applied the hairdryer. I combed my hair as it dried, ensuring I kept the original style.

After fifteen minutes I stopped and had a good look at it in the bedside mirror. The result I found quite pleasing. The brown had lightened considerably, without revealing too much of the red dye beneath. I think the overall effect, uneven as it was, gave a rather natural impression that I had been sunbathing and swimming in the sea. Sun-streaked highlights is, I think, how they describe it. The only thing to spoil that impression was the rim of red scalp along my forehead, where the peroxide had left its marks. But at least it had removed the last of the brown dye patches around my neck.

A message flashed up on WhatsApp: *St James's Park, same place, now.* I wasn't used to being addressed in such terms by my own son. Mind you, I wasn't used to being addressed by my son at all. Fortunately my hair was now quite dry. I slipped a headscarf over it, dressed quickly and put on a pair of wide sunglasses. I scuttled out of the house and hopped onto a tube train bound for Hammersmith. I got out at the last stop, crossed the road at Hammersmith Broadway and got onto a District Line train heading for St James's Park.

I found Bernard on the same bench as before, but this time there was no pretence of us being strangers. He addressed me directly.

'What took you so long?'

'I came as soon as I got your message.' I was surprised to find myself on the defensive. I suppose it is often like that between mother and child.

'Sit down,' he snapped.

'Where are your protectors? Better hidden than usual?'

'Bugger that. I'm not trusting anyone on this one.'

'What's the problem?'

'What do you make of this?'

He flicked across a note the size of a postcard. It lay face down. I picked it up and read it.

I have heard the expression 'her blood ran cold' many times. It always sounded a ridiculous exaggeration. But that was the feeling I now experienced.

Just seven words, but they put fear into me.

Ask your mother who your father is. The words were typed in an unnecessarily fancy font, as if the writer intended to tease as they typed them.

'Well?' demanded Bernard.

'What do you mean, "well"?'

'What does this note mean? That's what I'm asking.'

'You've never worried about your parentage before. I am your mother. Isn't that enough?'

'For Chrissakes, Ma! I've never worried about it before because it's never come up before. Not in a way that mattered. But if the knowledge can harm my career, when I'm under fire from all sides, then I bloody well need the truth now!'

'Don't raise your voice, dear. People will think we're married.' That quietened him, for the moment at least.

'I'm sorry. It's just that… well, things are coming to a head and I still don't know who it is who is gunning for me.' He lapsed into silence.

My phone pinged a WhatsApp message. I ignored it. Whatever it was, it could wait.

'Who do you think it might be?'

Bernard laughed. 'In politics, just about everyone carries a knife. But few of them have the guts to wield it.'

'Then who is your Brutus? The friend who waits for Caesar to falter, then stabs and twists the final blade?' My phone pinged again.

'Don't you want to answer that?'

I opened my phone and then the app. It came from a number I did not recognise. There were two messages. The first read: *We're watching you*. I looked up, scanned the area, but I could see no one who might be watching. The second message caused me to shiver. *Cease your investigation or we shall tell the world who your son's late father was.*

'Anything important?' Bernard asked.

'No, dear, just a reminder that I've got a meeting first thing tomorrow.'

'Well?'

'Well what?'

'Are you going to tell me?'

'About the meeting? No. It's private.' I could stall forever if I had to.

'Not about the meeting!' Bernard had raised his voice. He suddenly remembered where he was and that people might be listening, even though there were very few people about. He put his hand over his mouth and faked a cough. 'About my father. Who was he?'

'Somebody I had a fling with a long time ago.'

'What was his name?'

'You know, I was never really certain.' Well, that much was true, at any rate.

'Very helpful.' Bernard must have inherited his sarcastic flair from me.

I was never going to tell Bernard that his father was an accomplished spy working for the Soviet Union. Nor that he had become one of the richest men in Belarus. Though if Bernard were to suffer disgrace, lose his position as a government minister and fail to get a peerage, any potential inheritance might come in useful. I put such flippant thoughts out of my mind.

'So it wasn't Dennis?'

'Would you have liked it to be?'

'That wouldn't be so bad. Eva and I were fond of him.'

'You and your sister used to tease him remorselessly.'

'I suppose we were testing him. Seeing if he came up to scratch.'

'Up to scratch?'

'If he was worthy of you.'

It was my turn to be silent. The twins had shown me almost as little affection as I had to them when they were growing up. We had been distant, both figuratively and in reality. I had spent far too much time away, to the detriment of our relationship. It was sobering to know that they, in their own manner, had been looking out for me.

38

BY THE TIME I REACHED St James' Park station I was seething. How DARE they attack me through my own son. What had Bernard ever done to warrant it? He was a man of probity and honour, and they were… well, I had no idea who they were, of course. But when I found out I was going to make them pay. Of that I was certain.

I was also certain that if they thought they could stop my investigation by means of blackmail they were very wrong. They were panicking, which meant I was getting close to discovering the identity of the mole. Their dirty tricks only served to make me more determined to push on and uncover the truth. But how could I do that without risking Bernard harm? And how had they discovered the truth about his father? Dear old Dennis must have guessed, but I had told no one. Not even Ambrose. Not Percy, not Matthew. Nobody.

Well, I had told one person. Bernard's father. But only in his dying moments. And even then it was barely a whisper. How could anyone else possibly know?

As I waited on the platform – why are there so few Circle Line trains running these days? – I thought about it long and hard. Then I realised there was another person who might have known the truth about Bernard's parentage. The late Patrick Dallaway, my old friend and colleague from our time in Bonn. Had Patrick shared my most guarded secret with Ambrose? Or had Patrick long ago told someone else, someone in high office, perhaps Matthew's mole? And had that person stashed the information away to use when it would have the most devastating effect? I thought back to what Bella had said, echoing my basic training. Trust no one. Not even those closest to you.

At last the indicator board informed me that a Circle Line train was due in one minute. My phone pinged again. I intended to ignore it until I got home. I could see the train a couple of hundred yards up the track, barrelling towards the station. I stepped up to the safety line. My phone pinged two more times, insistently. I pulled it out of my bag and opened it. As I did so a WhatsApp message was deleted. So were the two I had read in the park. At the same time the waiting passengers surged forward, many of them tourists ignoring the tannoy warning to step back to allow the passengers off the train first. The incoming train was only yards away when I felt a sharp shove in the small of my back, which sent me stumbling towards the edge of the platform. I was on the point of toppling onto the line, where I would be run over or electrocuted, when a strong hand grabbed my arm and hauled me back from the brink of death.

'Whoops, that was a near one,' said the young man who had saved my life. 'Are you all right? Do you want to sit down?'

Those people who had been waiting for passengers to get off the train were now swarming aboard. I tried to work out which of them might have been responsible for shoving me, but the sonalert had already sounded its warning. My rescuer leapt aboard and the doors closed. As the train moved off he gave me a cheerful wave.

I sat on a bench and waited for my nerves to settle. Had someone really tried to kill me, or had it merely been a show of impatience from someone in a hurry to get home? Or was it a warning, and the perpetrator none other than my young rescuer?

I took the next Circle Line train. I had intended to get out at Notting Hill and walk back to the flat, but then I remembered that I had decided to confide in Matthew about the threats to Bernard. Perhaps he could suggest a solution.

I stayed on the train until it reached Baker Street where I got out, crossed the Marylebone Road and strode down Chiltern Street until I reached Paddington Street. From there I walked east, turned down Marylebone High Street and carried on along Weymouth Street until I reached Devonshire Mews South. Matthew was known to work late – catching up, since he always rose late – and I had to speak to him alone. If whoever was threatening me and Bernard had my phone number, then perhaps I should get it changed.

As I turned into the mews – it was dark now – I saw a tall man leaving Matthew's office. For a moment I thought it might be Ambrose, but he didn't have Ambrose's telltale stoop. His collar was turned up, as if he did not want to be recognised. He turned and headed towards me. That is, he marched briskly towards the southern entrance of the mews.

Rather than hesitate and give myself away, I kept walking north, towards the far end of the mews. As we passed I shot a glance at him. The face was familiar. But where had I seen him before? In what context?

Suddenly unsure of my mission, I carried on up to the top of the mews and walked to Great Portland Street station. I took a train bound for Hammersmith and got out at Ladbroke Grove. I passed an uneasy night.

*

I finally fell asleep at around five in the morning, just as the noisiest motorcycles started off to work. I presumed their owners were bankers, keen to get to the City or Canary Wharf before their competitors. Why they don't have quiet, electric vehicles – the sort of things private equity likes to invest in – is beyond me. They seem to revel in waking everyone up with their barely silenced classic Harley-Davidsons, vaunting their ability to rise early and make more money in an hour than most people will see in a lifetime.

In my day we admired the American paean to individual freedom suggested in the film *Easy Rider*. Now our only reward is a sudden screech of brakes followed by a metallic crash as a motorbike jumps a red light and writes itself off against an early morning rubbish truck. At my age, I like to go to bed early and get a good night's rest. Then I wake early. There's still a lot of life in me and I intend to make the most of it before time's arrow finally strikes me down. Yet I do on occasion, when worn down by tiredness, suffer a bout of melancholy. It is so easy to wallow in self-pity, to feel, as the Irish poet Thomas More did:

When true hearts lie withered,
And fond ones are flown,
Oh! Who would inhabit
This bleak world alone?

Many true hearts – Dennis, Freddie, even Jonathan Raikes and so many more colleagues in the service – do indeed lie withered. But I have a duty to honour them and, in some cases, ensure that their memories live on and that their killers are brought to justice. Perhaps that is what drove me now.

It was with a sense of renewed hope and purpose that I sprang out of bed at the first ring of Matthew's call. 'Come in, I have some information to impart. Bella and Ambrose are on their way. See you at ten.' As usual, he sounded a little out of breath. But that was beginning to sound normal for Matthew.

This was encouraging. Perhaps the man I had seen the previous night had given Matthew the information he needed. Perhaps Bella and Ambrose had provided Matthew with enough facts for him to reach a conclusion. And perhaps at last we would know the identity of the mole. We had been working in a murky fog. Now, I hoped, that fog was about to lift and I would be able to make some real contribution to the group.

Once I had showered and dressed I realised I had enough time to take a bus in, rather than the tube. I usually arrive early for meetings, but the thought of being stuck with Matthew for half an hour, while he teased me with clues and at the same time stuffed himself with an enormous breakfast while leaving me hungry, did not appeal. I grabbed a croissant in a café and took the number seven bus at Ladbroke Grove, estimating, rightly, that I would arrive just before ten o'clock. Ambrose was invariably punctual, arriving exactly on the dot of the appointed hour. Bella, I guessed, would be the same.

39

I FOUND MY BUS RIDE relaxing. I enjoyed crossing Portobello Road and watching the market traders set up their stands. The rest of my journey, past St Mary's Hospital (where I was born), along Praed Street and into Edgware Road, where I had briefly lodged above a bank at the corner of Church Street, all held fond memories.

As it was after nine I swiped my Freedom Pass across the reader then climbed the stairs to the top floor. At Westbourne Grove I was able to claim a seat at the very front – 'the tourist's position' – and enjoy a first-class view of London's West End. I considered this one of the pleasures of London life, and it was something I missed after I moved to the country. I hopped off at John Lewis and made my way up Harley Street.

When I first joined the service they made me take a thorough medical in Harley Street with an old-fashioned and overly intrusive private doctor who wore an increasingly crumpled pinstriped suit. Harley Street was quite different in those days. Each property had its own live-in housekeeper who would double as a receptionist. As you walked up the street these ladies, many already in their starched white uniforms, would be polishing the brass plaques on the front doors and gossiping with their next-door receptionists.

The visits continued annually until the late 1990s, when the doctor retired and my mandatory medicals became biennial. Cutbacks I suppose. These later assessments were more perfunctory than the earlier ones, and were carried out by an NHS doctor in a variety of hospitals.

When I officially retired (unofficially we never fully retire and continue to be available for service), I was sent back to Harley Street for a thorough going-over. By now the era of starched uniforms had long gone. Behind the smart modern desk and switchboard was a young Polish receptionist, giving the consulting rooms a more efficient and up-to-date appearance. Once past the threshold, however, I found myself in the same fusty consulting room, now occupied by an almost identical doctor in an almost identical pinstriped suit. I guessed he was the original doctor's son. Harley Street consulting rooms are hard to acquire and, I suspect, are jealously passed down from father to son.

This consultation was by far the most extensive and intrusive I had ever endured. There was a reason for this. Both the Soviets and, more lately, the Chinese had been known to use low-level polonium-210 and deep resonance sound-waves to disorientate and disable British and American operatives in their respective embassies around the world. This doctor's job was to check whether I had been subjected to infrasound or, indeed, any sort of poisoning. Well I had been poisoned, but that was a long time ago, and I had survived with little or no lasting damage.

It took me ten minutes to reach Devonshire Mews South. I was five minutes early, so I lingered at the entrance to the mews in Weymouth Street. Matthew had a 'Ring' video doorbell with which he could spy on anyone approaching his door, so I kept well back. At exactly one minute to ten I saw

Ambrose get out of a taxi at the north entrance of the mews and pay the driver. He walked south towards me and we met at Matthew's door together. I pressed the bell.

Matthew took a long time to let us in. Considering he could see perfectly well on his videophone that it was us waiting and that we had both arrived exactly on time, there was nothing to explain the delay. The two mews houses that were his offices were not large, so he couldn't have been more than a few yards from the door when we arrived. When he at last opened the door he looked flushed and tired, and yet at the same time he seemed triumphant, as if he had overcome a problem and was bubbling to tell us when the right moment arose.

'Welcome, welcome, my dears, do enter.' He stepped aside to let us in. I noticed Ambrose stiffen a little at being called 'dear', but he let it pass.

'Can I offer either of you a coffee?' Matthew had one of those machines where you insert a capsule and it heats up before squirting a syrupy liquid. Not bad, but not as good as having a proper espresso machine. At least it was better than those nasty cafetières that give you thin coffee-flavoured water.

Ambrose and I both declined the coffee. We stood around expectantly.

'Pity,' said Matthew, 'I was just about to make myself one. We're still waiting on Bella, but she should be here any minute.'

He did not offer us seats. The secret door that led to his inner sanctum remained firmly closed. Ambrose and I exchanged looks.

Matthew made himself a coffee and sat down at a long desk which was scattered with papers and handwritten notes. He had always been untidy.

'Where are my manners?' he exclaimed. 'Do sit down.' He glanced at his watch. 'Shouldn't be long now.' We sat at the table at right angles to him.

There was a large clock stuck on the kitchen wall. I watched the seconds tick off. I saw that Ambrose was counting them too.

Matthew had started fidgeting. He straightened a couple of pens and some papers on his desk, as if suddenly realising how messy it looked. He dunked a chocolate biscuit in his coffee, but he held it in too long, distracted. As he withdrew it the biscuit collapsed over his papers, leaving a big splash of coffee and chocolate. It did not seem to bother him. He was preoccupied with some much more important problem.

'This is not good,' he said. 'Bella is never late. Early yes, but never late.' He glanced at the wall clock. It was fifteen minutes past ten. Even with the best planning there are all sorts of reasons people are late in London: traffic jams, broken-down tube trains and buses. Most of us make allowances for tardiness. But Matthew glanced at the watch on his fat wrist and said, 'I'm giving her five more minutes.'

As the second hand of the wall clock ticked around to twenty past the hour Matthew became more and more tense. As the hand reached the top of its arc he struggled up out of his chair. 'That's it, time for action.' He dialled a number, which was answered promptly. 'She hasn't shown. I authorise you to go in.' He cut off the call and put his phone on the table.

'Now what?' asked Ambrose.

'Now we wait,' said Matthew. 'Won't take long.'

Any beneficial effect I had received from my slow and relaxing bus ride into town was long gone. The three of us sat there in silence, with just the ticking of the big clock as our theme tune accompaniment.

After around ten minutes Matthew's phone rang. He snatched it up as if he were a cobra striking a mouse. 'Yes,' he snapped. He listened for what seemed like a long time but was only twenty-two seconds – I counted them off on the clock. 'Very well, alert all ports, airports, and private airfields. She is not to leave the country!' He switched off his phone and turned to us. 'There is no sign of Bella Walsingham in her flat. It appears the bird has flown.'

'How could you get confirmation in so short a time?' I asked.

'I've had people watching her flat on a twenty-four hour rota.'

'So Bella's always been top of your list of suspects?' asked Ambrose.

'Not at all,' replied Matthew. 'I've had you all under surveillance from the start.'

40

'I WAS NEVER SURE THAT it was one of you four,' said Matthew. 'I'm including our late colleague Jonathan Raikes in the mix here. It could just as easily have been someone else, but I was convinced it had to be one of our personnel from our times in Athens. Perhaps one of those long-retired and long-forgotten people you've managed to track down.' He was looking straight at me.

'Bella was only in the embassy a few months,' said Ambrose. 'She was hardly there long enough to make an impact.'

'But she had an extended posting in Cyprus.' That was me speaking. I had, of course, done my research.

'Well done,' said Matthew.

I shifted uncomfortably in my seat. The moment Matthew gave you a compliment, you knew there was something nasty coming.

'Now, I suppose, is the time I should level with you both.' He turned to Ambrose. 'This is going to be painful for you, old boy.'

Ambrose nodded, permitting Matthew to continue, no matter.

'That terrible day in 1984, the day that has remained with us all, when poor young Freddie died in a hail of bullets…'

I glanced over at Ambrose. His lips were tight, his face set, but he could not hide his eyes. A faint mist clouded them. He blinked it away.

'We always believed that this was an attempt on the life of our ambassador, Sir Roland Bingham.' Matthew remained standing, the wattle under his chin quivering with emotion as he recalled the events.

'Two women, two men, one of them the notorious Abu Nidal. Both men armed with Kalashnikovs, able to fire six hundred rounds a minute.'

All right, I thought, checking Ambrose. *No need to spell out the gory details.*

'And then making their escape and getting away with it!'

Yes, we know all that, I thought. *Just get to the point.*

'Now new information has been uncovered. Sir Roland was never the intended target.'

'Then who was?' I asked. I was dreading the answer.

'It was Freddie himself.'

'Freddie?' Ambrose's voice came out as a strangled croak.

'How on earth do you arrive at that conclusion?' I wanted to hit Matthew, but there was no stopping him now.

'Freddie knew something. He thought of telling others but he always kept it to himself.'

'Until he had definitive proof.' That was Ambrose.

'And what was this information?' I wanted hard facts.

'That he had discovered the identity of a mole in the embassy. Someone who was passing secrets to the Soviets and the Black September group, fronted by Abu Nidal. That was why he had to be killed.'

'If he suspected someone of something so major, why not come straight out and say it?' Ambrose was shaking his head in disbelief. 'He knew the risks. If you delay exposing a mole, even by a day, an hour, who knows what secrets will get out, what lives will be lost.'

'His mistake was to trust Bella.'

I had always had my suspicions about Bella. Her exalted history of famous spies in the family. It was almost too perfect a cover.

'She was either the mole or under the mole's control.' Matthew sat down, as if the terrible weight of his knowledge was too much for him to bear.

'We have to stop her.' That was both Ambrose and me speaking in unison.

'I have people on the case. Efficient people. I don't believe she will get far. But even if she does, there is a second party still at large.' He looked straight at me. Ambrose turned to follow his gaze. His eyes bored into mine.

What did Matthew mean? Did he think I could possibly have had something to do with Freddie's death? I turned from Ambrose to him and waited.

'Vasilis Mavros,' continued Matthew. 'The Greek shipowner.'

It was all becoming clear.

'Mavros, Abu Nidal and our mole were all in it together. Bella was supplying British secrets to the Soviets through Mavros. Mavros was facilitating Abu Nidal's acceptance in the world community. Nidal needed the terrorist proscription lifted. In return Mavros was to get exclusive rights to transport oil from Libya, Syria and any other proscribed state supported by the Soviets. The financial rewards would have been enormous.'

'But he failed to get the United Kingdom to grant Abu Nidal permission to operate on sovereign territory,' I added. 'Sir Roland saw to that.'

'Correct.' Matthew seemed surprised I knew so much. Of course, he had no idea that I had rifled through Sir Roland's confidential papers. Only Ambrose knew that.

'Giving the Soviets our secrets I could understand,' I said. 'Getting involved with a slimy terrorist like Abu Nidal was risky and could lead to Bella being compromised and exposed. No mole would do that.'

'Think of her less as a mole,' replied Matthew, 'more of a deathwatch beetle: for years burrowing through the foundations of liberty, undermining the service from within, until the whole edifice is in danger of collapse. Bella, through Mavros, was in an excellent position to persuade Sir Roland that Abu Nidal's case was acceptable to the Crown. The plan was simple. Satisfy Sir Roland, then Sir Roland would persuade Whitehall, and Whitehall would convince the Foreign Secretary and thus the British government. Abu Nidal and his cohorts would be able to live and operate in the UK, without risk of arrest.'

'It would never fly.' Ambrose had recovered his composure.

'But they weren't to know that. The Greeks are persistent. It's one of their more enduring characteristics. And persistence usually wins out in the end. So Mavros helped our mole by arranging young Freddie's death.'

Matthew looked from Ambrose to me, then back to Ambrose again. A twisted grimace appeared on Matthew's face.

'I think we've talked enough. Now is the time for action.'

41

Athens, 2019

I arrived at Heathrow airport with plenty of time to spare. This was just as well, because there were major delays in checking in. The airport authorities were trying out their new eye-scanning system that was supposed to speed things up. It had the opposite effect, of course, and I, along with fifty or so other travellers, barely managed to board our plane in time.

At the new Athens airport, which had been completed in advance of the Olympic games of 2004, I was met by the team Ambrose had put together. Their leader, Rory Moncrieff, had been a part of the SAS group that had attempted to kill Abu Nidal in Syria. Now he was commanding two much younger men, Bill and Mike, giant broad-shouldered hunks who treated him with awed respect and obeyed his every command.

They had a large SUV waiting in the car park. A number of long sports bags were stowed in its trunk. I could imagine what they contained. I only had a small carry-on suitcase, and a carrier for a long dress. When immigration asked me why I had come to Greece, I told them it was for my daughter's wedding. She was marrying a handsome Greek boy.

'Every Greek boy is handsome,' the immigration officer laughed. He scanned my passport and sent me through.

Rory and his two heavies drove me straight to Flisvos Marina, where I found Ambrose waiting in a hired Bentley outside the gates. He was dressed in the regulation uniform of an elderly British gentleman on holiday: three-piece lightweight linen suit, not the shapeless beige job we used to call a 'teabag', but a beautifully cut creation in a linen and cotton mix, with a waistcoat, Panama hat, expensive sunglasses and deck shoes partially concealing bright red socks.

'Nice socks,' I said.

'Paul Smith.'

'Expensive.'

'Quite reasonable, really, and one has to dress the part. You look pretty… spiffy yourself.'

He was right. In my guise as 'Lady Jessica' I had splashed out and bought a wardrobe – in a charity shop in Marylebone, where the discards were of top quality – and was wearing a superb one-piece mid-length belted shirtdress of mixed silk and cotton by Dior. It had a high collar, which hid the wrinkles around my neck. On my feet were a pair of 'gold' leather pumps, and I carried a small matching handbag. I wore tights, despite the warm weather. My legs are not as alluring as they once were, and I had no intention of displaying their well-marbled blue veins that would put a Colston Bassett Stilton cheese to shame.

'Ready?' asked Ambrose.

'I am,' I answered.

One of Rory's heavies – Bill – took the wheel and we drove in through the gate. He uttered the name 'Lord Lexington', and the guard lifted the barrier. We were expected. We drove a couple of hundred yards to where the very largest motor yachts were berthed. I saw a massive hulk, some three-hundred feet long. This was a Saudi-owned vessel, not the boat we were to board. Beyond it was a more modest yacht, but still huge at around fifty metres. Its stern bore the name MY *Fantasy 5* and its ensign, which fluttered in the light breeze, announced that it was registered in Valletta, Malta. Presumably for tax purposes. We pulled up alongside the elegant yacht and were helped out.

Ambrose had abandoned his customary stoop. For the first time in years he stood ramrod straight.

'How do you manage that?' I asked.

'Don't ask.' Then, after a pause, 'Corset. Bit tight, to be honest.'

One of the crew disappeared inside. A moment later he reappeared with the yacht's owner. I recognised the fat and bloated figure that had once been slim and athletic. His hair was thin and balding but he wore it in a ponytail, as if he was still young and virile enough to attract any woman who took his fancy. Which, with the even vaster fortune he had accrued since I had last set eyes on him, he probably could.

Vasilis Mavros walked along the gangplank and stepped down to welcome us. He shook Ambrose's hand.

'Lord Lexington,' he said, '*kalos orisate!*'

Mavros turned to me, raised my hand to his mouth and kissed it. 'Lady Lexington, please let me welcome you aboard.' He turned and ushered us aboard his yacht. The crew – captain, bosun, stewards and deckhands – were all lined up in a row to greet us. I recognised just one man among them: Lefteris, the bosun. He was chunkier, coarser and more grizzled than I remembered, but still the same man, and still just as mean looking. They saluted as we acknowledged them and stepped past them into the large salon. Neither Mavros nor Lefteris had seen through my disguise.

Bill and Mike carried our luggage aboard. Mavros had been told we would be bringing our own 'bodyguards'. Mavros' people had insisted they could provide more than adequate security, but Lord Lexington's people (i.e. Ambrose) had informed them that the presence of his Lordship's personally selected bodyguards was not negotiable. Bill and Mike were assigned a shared cabin at the stern of the yacht.

It had not been hard for Ambrose to get one of his young tech wizards to create a backstory for 'Lord and Lady Lexington'. He had posted extracts of information about them in copies of 'Dempster's diary' in the *Daily Mail*, backdating them to the 1980s when Lexington was starting to make his 'legendary fortune'.

Snippets of the couple's fictional biographies could also be discovered, if you looked hard enough, scattered across the internet. There was a whole Wikipedia page detailing Lord Alexander Lexington's private, and highly secretive, investment fund. The site stated that, through intermediaries and overseas holding companies, the fund had got in at the early stages of just about every major US-based tech company, as well as getting into Bitcoin when you could pick them up for under five dollars apiece. There were numerous references at the bottom of the page with links to several sites and articles backing up the information provided. Hardly anybody ever has the time to check the links. They are happy enough to go with whatever Wikipedia provides as if it is gospel truth, and Mavros was no different.

If you googled me you would find me down as Lady Jessica, daughter of the last of a long line of Lincolnshire landowners.

Ambrose's tech wiz had managed to find and alter an online copy of *Country Life* dated July 1972, where a young woman, looking not unlike the way I did in those days, poses by a country stile in tweeds, Barbour and green wellingtons. You know the sort of thing: 'girls with pearls,' we called them.

This edition stated that my name was Jessica Langthorne, and that I was interested in horses, had won several rosettes for my riding and dressage skills, and had embarked on a secretarial course at the Lucy Clayton school of deportment. I had 'come out' that year and had every expectation of snaring one of the many wealthy heirs who were swarming over me like bees around an English rose – though *Country Life* didn't put it quite as blatantly as that.

More recent online articles mentioned my charitable enterprises, details of which were kept private for political or security reasons. I knew that Mavros loved to mix with titled aristocracy. Lord and Lady Lexington exactly fitted the bill.

Our visit was, ostensibly, to inspect the yacht. Mavros had quietly put it on the market. It wasn't that he needed the money. He was about to take delivery of something even larger, but all Greeks like a deal and, if there's a slightly dodgy element about it, then so much the better.

In this case 'Lord Alexander' was considering buying it through one of his offshore companies. Mavros would be selling the yacht through one of his own offshore entities, so the transaction would never appear in any Greek business's accounts, and so there would not be any tax liability. There probably wouldn't in any case. From what little I knew of accounting, the yacht's depreciation would be enhanced to mitigate any profits in other parts of the Greek shipowner's business.

Mavros was prepared to demonstrate the yacht and its capabilities himself. After a show of hesitation from Ambrose (or Alex, as I had to remember to call him), who claimed to be far too busy developing investment algorithms with his team, Ambrose had bowed to pressure from 'Lady Jessica' and agreed to Mavros' offer of a three-day trip around the Aegean and its islands. That way we could really appreciate the beauty of the yacht and the possibilities of keeping its mooring at Flisvos, where berths were hard to find.

42

MAVROS INTRODUCED US TO HIS temporary captain, an Englishman. Tom had been engaged specially for the voyage. The regular captain, Nicos, was currently occupied in Viareggio. I knew what that meant. Captain Nicos would be taking delivery of Mavros' brand new yacht from the Sanlorenzo shipyard, and gently running in the engines as he made his way back to Piraeus. That was why Mavros was not concerned about giving up his berth. He would already have secured a considerably larger one close to where that Saudi Arabian superyacht was squatting. As his new yacht would be of an Italian design, it would certainly be sleeker and more beautiful than that ugly Arab monstrosity.

Tom was in his thirties – young for a captain – but he had a confident and relaxed manner about him as he edged the MY *Fantasy 5* out of its berth. It is a lot easier to leave port than it is to dock, but all the same you have to keep your wits about you. Even a small scrape against your neighbour can cost the owner half a million or more to fix.

Mavros invited Ambrose onto the bridge to watch as Tom manoeuvred the yacht into deeper waters. Two deckhands signalled that the anchors were up and housed. Tom opened the throttle gently and the engines powered the yacht forward. We sped past the myriad oil tankers, reefers and bulk carriers waiting out at sea to come in and offload their valuable cargos.

I watched from the top deck as we headed south-west towards the island of Hydra. Just a year earlier, Hydra had lost all its electrical power for a couple of days. A large Russian-owned yacht had dragged its anchor and damaged the cable which carried power from the mainland. The water filtration broke down, food rotted, and people got sick. Tourists, I mean. The locals shrugged off the inconvenience. They had experienced losses of power for decades, long before Leonard Cohen had settled on the island in the early 1960s and made it his home. I just hoped Mavros and Tom were more careful with their anchors.

Hydra is a pretty island. The main port is formed of a natural horseshoe-shaped bay enhanced with berthing docks for yachts. Bars and restaurants have been set up over the red-veined marble paving which glows more impressively at night than by day, when the port is crowded with tourists off the ferries.

Mavros led us to a bar's outdoor seating where we could watch the sun go down. He ordered for us: two Aperol spritzers – never something we drank back in the 1980s – and an ouzo for himself. His drink arrived with a small carafe of water. We three sat in a row, facing the sun as it sank over the sea and hit the water. After that he took us for dinner in a little taverna a hundred metres or so inland, in an open square where he ordered pork on a spit, which was delicious, together with a wonderful white wine, which his chef had brought from the boat. We finished with Metaxa brandies. As the alcohol warmed him, Mavros recounted some of his life stories. I was disappointed that, forty years on, they were still the same old tales he had told when I was playing second stewardess on his first yacht. I guessed his more recent anecdotes were so debauched he could not recount them in mixed company.

After nearly an hour of this Ambrose checked his watch, a 1929 Cartier 'tank' model that had belonged to his uncle, and declared that it was past his bedtime.

'Ah,' said Mavros, 'you mean somewhere in the world they are waking up and you are wanting to check the stock prices.' He tapped his nose. Ambrose turned to me, as if to say 'you can't get anything past this clever bugger', laughed and shrugged. 'Well,' he said, 'some people you never can fool.' He rose. 'Come on, darling, time to get back to the boat.' He turned to Mavros. 'This has been a wonderful day. Your yacht is everything you said it was.'

Mavros stood and shook Ambrose's hand. For a second Ambrose flinched, but he overcame his reaction. 'Sorry,' he said, 'bit of back pain. I need to do my exercises to get over it.'

Mavros nodded. 'I, too, suffer from back pain. Too much sitting hunched over a computer, and not enough exercise. This summer I plan to remedy that.' He smiled. 'Tomorrow, we see the island of Spetses. You will love it.'

Ambrose and I headed back to the yacht, shadowed by Bill and Mike. The four of us crossed the dock onto the yacht. Ambrose and I went down to our cabin. Bill and Mike followed.

'All good, sir?' asked Bill. 'Will you be needing us any more tonight?'

Ambrose shook his head. 'I wish you a good night's sleep, gentlemen.' He turned the door handle and we entered our cabin.

Ambrose went straight into the shower room, turned on the basin taps and scrubbed his hands furiously. He came out a couple of minutes later. I knew he was feeling a powerful revulsion, but Ambrose was good at concealing his emotions.

'Which side of the bed do you prefer?'

I usually took the side closest to the door. This was old practice, in the event of intruders. But I knew Ambrose preferred that side too, so I deferred to him. We had only slept in the same room once before. Though on that occasion neither of us had managed to get any sleep. The expectation of being riddled with submachine-gun bullets at any moment had forced us to grab only a few minutes sleep in turns. Eventually we had given in, fluffed up our pillows and laid them under the blankets to pretend we were asleep in the bed. For the rest of that long night we had sat upright in chairs, guns in hands, waiting for the dawn to break.

This was a very different situation. The double bed was wide, comfortable and neither too soft nor too hard. 'I'll let you go first,' said Ambrose.

While I went to the bathroom, scraped off my 'Lady Jessica' make-up, brushed my teeth and changed into my lightweight pyjamas, Ambrose sat at the desk and scribbled some notes. From force of habit Ambrose, a classics scholar in his youth and a cryptographer at heart, would write his notes in Ancient Greek. Except here, on a Greek boat, Greek of any sort wasn't appropriate. Even the lowliest deckhand might be able to read and understand it. So Ambrose switched to even more ancient Sumerian: cuneiform wedge strokes that even I could not decipher. Leaving him deep in thought, I got into bed on the porthole side. I began to read a novel acquired, like my clothes, in Oxfam. It was the sort of book I thought Lady Jessica might have chosen to re-read: Evelyn Waugh's *Brideshead Revisited*.

After a few minutes of listening to Ambrose's scratchings

– his writing had always been hard to decipher, even when he wrote in English – I put the book aside.

'Aren't you coming to bed?'

Ambrose was startled. 'Sorry, I was lost in thought.'

'What sort of thought?'

'Just working out our speed and currents.'

'We're in port. We're not moving.'

'I was thinking about something else.'

I switched off my bedside lamp. This was Ambrose's mission entirely, all the way from planning through to execution, so I did not press him.

Ambrose got up, went into the bathroom and I heard the shower running. A few minutes later he reappeared, dried and refreshed. He wore old-fashioned heavy-duty paisley pyjamas.

'Where did you get those?'

'What's wrong with them?'

'Nothing.'

'Shall I turn up the air conditioning? It's a little warm in here.' I was not surprised, in those pyjamas. He twisted the dial and the air conditioning roared on with a whoosh of cold air.

'I won't be able to sleep with all that racket.'

He turned the dial most of the way back, so there was just a hum. 'I was wondering…' he said, as he climbed into bed on his side.

'Yes?'

'Do you think we should bicker a bit?'

'Bicker?'

'You know, like husbands and wives do. Make us look more convincing as a couple.'

'I'm not going to spend the rest of my time aboard this boat bickering,' I grumbled.

'Yes, just like that, very convincing,' he said. I shut up. 'Anyway,' he continued, 'it will only have to be until tomorrow evening.'

'So we'll do it then?'

'I think that's best.' He reached over and took my hand in his. 'We've come this far. All he has to do is follow our lead.'

43

THE NEXT MORNING, AFTER A leisurely breakfast of Greek yoghurt and honey, followed by freshly baked croissants with apricot jam and Greek coffees, we upped anchors and cruised to the neighbouring island of Spetses. Since the journey was short, we went at a relatively slow pace, around fifteen knots.

As we passed the little island of Dokos, inhabited by a handful of monks in a monastery, Mavros regaled us with a story about a dog he had rescued. As with all his stories, he came out of it a hero.

'We were sailing past Dokos a few years ago. Some of the youngsters wanted to go for a swim, so we anchored in a bay. They dived off the boat, and two of them swam to the shore where they found a little dog, its fur matted with salt water and burrs, shivering. It trotted up to them and they called out for the tender to come and fetch them. We took that little dog with us and after the cruise I passed it to my gardener so he could take care of it.'

'What a charming story,' I said. A favourable comment had been expected.

'We called the dog "Lucky". The gardener cleaned its fur, and it was fed the best fillet steak the rest of his life.'

'You are a very kind and caring man.' I was laying it on

a bit thick, so much so that Ambrose rolled his eyes, but Mavros lapped it up.

'You English, you love your dogs more than your children, no?'

'That's an exaggeration,' I said. A few months ago, before I rescued baby Alice, he might have been right. 'But we are a nation of animal lovers, that's true.' Hoping to move the conversation on, I added, 'So Lucky had a long and happy life in the lap of luxury?'

'Not at all,' Mavros answered, delighting in contradicting me. 'A month later an eagle flew down out of the sky and snatched him. Now his spirit flies with the eagles.' Mavros chuckled. 'You see, Lucky was not meant to enjoy a long life. I had interfered with the plans of the gods, and they restored the… how you say… the equilibrium.'

When we arrived at Spetses we avoided the port and anchored instead in a bay to the south. Mavros disappeared into his room and reappeared fifteen minutes later in swimming trunks so brief they were hard to spot under his pendulous paunch. He was carrying a spear gun and a net.

'Today,' he announced, 'I shall catch lunch. Would you care to join me?' Ambrose and I shook our heads. 'No problem.' Mavros jumped off the back of the yacht. A deckhand threw him a pair of goggles with a snorkel attached. Mavros put them on and disappeared beneath the water. He reappeared thirty seconds later, snorkelling under the rock cliff that lined the bay. With a cheery wave he disappeared again. This carried on for two or three more submersions, then Mavros failed to surface. The deckhands, whose job it was to keep an eye on anybody in the water, especially their boss, exchanged worried glances. After about a minute one of them called up to Captain Tom, who came running down the steps to the swim deck. He had just started to strip off when Mavros surfaced by the stern of the yacht, spluttering. In his right hand he waved the spear gun, in his left he held a writhing octopus.

'You see!' He coughed, spitting seawater. 'I told you I would catch lunch.' He called for a container. A deckhand scooped up seawater in a yellow bucket. Mavros roughly tore the suckered tentacles from his arm and deposited the octopus in the bucket. The deckhand placed it in the sun and reached down to help Mavros scale the ladder onto the deck.

'Malaka!' Mavros cried. The octopus had climbed out and was heading fast across the hot deck towards freedom. 'Catch it!'

The deckhand let go of Mavros, who fell back into the water. The octopus was snatched up and dropped back into its prison. The deckhand returned to help Mavros up onto the swim deck. The octopus made one more effort to escape, hauling itself out with its grasping suckers. This time it moved more sluggishly. The deckhand grabbed it again and slammed it back in. This time, the octopus stayed put.

'Sir Alex, Lady Jessica, come and see what you're having for lunch!'

Ambrose and I peered into the bucket. The octopus flattened itself against its flat bottom, its tentacles stretched outwards from its body.

'You see,' said Mavros, shaking saltwater over us, 'she tries to make herself look big. Fearsome.' He waved his hand over the water.

Bands of colour radiated from the cephalopod's head: pulsing purple, yellow, black and red. It reminded me of the warning yellow and black stripes of a wasp. As a defence mechanism, it worked. Anyone would instinctively hesitate to touch it. The bite of a blue-ringed octopus was inevitably fatal. But this was an Aegean octopus. Its saliva may have contained paralysing toxins, but they were not powerful enough to harm a human. The creature inflated itself with water, making itself look as large as possible.

Mavros elbowed me aside. 'Watch.' He reached one hand into the bucket. The terrified octopus cringed, its eyes widening like a startled cat's. It flattened itself against the bottom, desperate to get as far away from Mavros as it could.

'I see you didn't use your harpoon,' said Ambrose.

'No need. It was hiding in a hole in the rocks. I just reach in and pull it out.'

'It needs fresh water,' I said. I snatched up the bucket and stepped towards the edge of the swim deck, tilting it as I did so. The creature seized its chance. It suckered itself up the side of the bucket. 'Oh my goodness!' I faked a stumble and the octopus flopped out onto the hot wooden deck. This time its movements were feeble. It appeared disorientated, unsure which way to go. I could not bear to see it suffer. As Mavros lunged towards me I held the creature over the water and let it drop. As it fell I sensed its suckers running down my fingers. It splashed into the sea and floated there, siphoning water into its body.

'A net! Get me a net!' Mavros shouted to nobody in particular.

The octopus squirted a thin jet of ink. A second squirt sent it shooting to the bottom of the sea.

'You… you…' Mavros checked the insult that was forming on his lips. 'You let it go.' He glared at me, like a furious little boy.

'I'm so sorry,' I said. 'It slipped.'

Ambrose stepped up behind Mavros. He winked at me.

44

THAT NIGHT LEFTERIS TOOK US in the yacht's tender to Spetses town. Shadowed from a safe distance by Bill and Mike, we strolled around the town and looked in at the Bouboulina Museum. It usually closed at two o'clock but opened that evening specially for Mavros and his honoured guests. Mavros, already banking 'Lord Lexington's' payment for the yacht in his head, gave us the tour himself.

The much-widowed female shipowner Laskarina Bouboulina had, in 1821, launched the 'Agamemnon', a thirty-three-metre corvette armed with eighteen heavy cannon. With that ship she had spearheaded the revolution against the occupying Ottoman Empire. Although she was killed soon afterwards she had been awarded the title of admiral, the only woman to achieve such an honour until recent times.

Mavros hinted that he was descended from Bouboulina (as well as the gods!). He might well have been but, as he hailed from Chios, the island more than three hundred kilometres away, I considered it unlikely.

Mavros led us along the seafront, down to where restaurants lined what would have been the old fishing harbour. Bill and Mike, still following us, were accompanied by Lefteris. He had struck up something of a friendship with them.

Mavros chose a small taverna, where he was welcomed effusively – he was known to be a generous tipper. We were shown a table with a good view of the sea and sat down to peruse the menu. For once, Mavros let us choose for ourselves. When the owner came to ask what he wanted to eat, Mavros pointedly avoided ordering the octopus, which he could have enjoyed in a salad with oil and vinegar as a starter or grilled as a main course. He ordered *barbounia* and chips, then tossed the menu onto the table like a grumpy child and stared out to sea. He was clearly losing patience with his guests. This was a business deal, after all. When his baklava arrived at the end of the meal, he swiftly came to the point.

'Well, Lord Alex, you've seen all over the boat. Do you have any questions?'

'I don't know that I do,' replied Ambrose, adopting the sort of smile that signified he was about to drive a hard bargain.

'Then perhaps, after dinner, we can agree on a price?'

'Oh, but we haven't been to Mykonos!' I exclaimed.

Mavros frowned. 'I had no idea you wanted to go to Mykonos. It's way across the Aegean.'

'Darling,' Ambrose said to me, 'give us a few minutes together.'

I obediently got up and wandered off along the semicircular bay. There was a slight breeze which carried Mavros' and Ambrose's voices across the water to me. Ambrose suggested that, if we were to make the detour to Mykonos so that Lady Jessica could do a bit of shopping, he would be happy to stump up Mavros' full asking price. I could see Mavros having to restrain himself from jumping at the offer. When you're offered your asking price without a quibble, there's an inclination to think you've underpriced an asset and that there may be a better deal around the corner.

'I have an important meeting arranged in Athens. I was planning to be there tomorrow afternoon,' Mavros replied. 'Let me see if I can postpone it. If you will excuse me?'

Mavros got up and walked off towards the bar. He made a phone call. He spoke briefly, then listened for quite a while. He glanced over at 'Lord Alex', then looked over at me. He returned to the table and beckoned me back. As I joined them Mavros had a big smile on his face, though his eyes were dark and cold.

'It's all fixed, said Ambrose. 'We're going to Mykonos.'

'Oh, that is so sweet of you,' I beamed. Mavros spread his arms wide as if to say, how can I refuse such a delightful guest?

Mavros called Lefteris over and whispered a few words in his ear. Lefteris nodded and, without looking up, rejoined Bill and Mike and led them into a small taverna for a final drink.

Eventually we made our way back to the boat. Our two bodyguards said goodnight and headed down to their cabin. I caught Bill giving Ambrose a knowing look but Mavros, as far as I could tell, missed it.

I felt relief. The novelty of playing Lady Jessica, endlessly compliant and agreeable, was beginning to grate. One can only play a character diametrically opposed to one's own for a short time. And that time was fast running out.

After a nightcap of brandy (I disposed of mine without swallowing more than a sip – I needed to keep a clear head) we retired to bed. Mavros would soon turn in, as he wanted to be up early. We said our goodnights and went down to our cabin. Ambrose fell asleep almost immediately, while I remained restless, pondering on the night ahead.

At around one in the morning I heard the engines start and felt the yacht moving gently out of the harbour. The chains rattled as the anchors were winched up and stowed, and then the engines powered up. We were on our way to Mykonos.

Somehow the motion of the boat through the water rocked me to sleep. I dreamed of being Admiral Bouboulina waging war on the Ottoman fleet. But in my dream the Greek cannons fired blanks while the Ottoman admiral bore down on us and rammed us amidships. That wasn't supposed to happen.

I was woken by a knocking on the door. I checked my phone. It was three in the morning and the yacht's engines had stopped. Our plan had begun.

We had a plan, of course. For it to work it needed just two things: Mavros had to have let his guard down, and we needed to be in open water, preferably under cover of night. So far so good.

The idea was for Bill and Mike to overpower their new chum Lefteris, the bosun – who would have stayed awake to steer the yacht to Mykonos – take over the bridge and stop the engines while the rest of the crew, including the captain, were asleep. This should be at the halfway point between Spetses and Mykonos, somewhere between the islands of Kea and Kythnos. We would be joined by Rory Moncrieff, who had been preparing in Kea. He would have tracked our progress and would join us in a large speedboat. We would kidnap Mavros, drugging him if necessary to keep him silent, then take him back to Kea where Rory had arranged a safe house where we would be able to interrogate Mavros at our leisure.

Some plans work perfectly. Some, even with diligent planning of every detail, fail spectacularly. It helps to be philosophical in such moments of failure. Sadly, that sort of philosophy is something I've never been able to achieve.

I shook the drowsiness out of my head. That brandy must have been more powerful than I thought.

I opened the door, expecting to see Bill and Mike. Instead, standing in the doorway was Mavros. Behind him stood Lefteris with a handgun pointed directly at my heart.

45

'How can I help you, gentlemen?' I asked in my calmest 'Lady Jessica' voice.

'Get the old man up,' snapped Mavros. 'Bring him to the swim deck.'

Ambrose was struggling to wake. Mavros must have slipped a strong sedative into that last brandy. No wonder Ambrose had fallen asleep so quickly. 'Come on, Alex,' I said. 'Put on your dressing gown.'

'And you can drop the Lord Alexander and Lady Jessica nonsense.'

While Lefteris kept his gun trained on me, Mavros growled something in Greek.

Ambrose may have been drowsy, but he was fully aware that the tables had turned. As I helped him into his gown he stumbled against his side table. He managed to keep himself upright and allowed me to help him get his arms into the dressing gown. As his right hand emerged from the sleeve he pushed something into my hand: a steel nail file, with a blunted point. I dropped it into the breast pocket of my pyjamas. Ambrose's left hand dropped something into his own pocket.

'*Viassou*,' grunted Lefteris, telling Ambrose to hurry up.

As we stepped out into the corridor, I glanced at the door of Bill and Mike's cabin.

'Don't worry about them,' said Mavros. 'They will be asleep for a very long time.'

Did that mean he had killed them, I worried, or simply given them a heavy dose of sedative? Lefteris could have administered a slow-acting poison while they had been drinking in the taverna. I helped Ambrose up the stairs and out onto the stern deck.

'Down to the swim deck,' insisted Mavros.

Perhaps I expected to see Rory and whatever rescue party Ambrose and he had put together, but I was disappointed. As we made our way down the curving teak steps to the swim deck, I saw nothing but a bleak expanse of dark sea.

'Get in the water.' Mavros' voice was eerily calm.

'He's an old man.' I held onto Ambrose, deciding what to do next. A blunt nail file wasn't much of a weapon against a loaded pistol.

'Get in or you'll be pushed in.'

The chrome stepladder had been slotted into place, ready for use. It led down into the black water that lapped around the rocking yacht. I took a step down onto one tread, and then another. I stopped. 'You can't seriously want me to get in?'

'Both of you.' Mavros pushed Ambrose forward. Ambrose stumbled over a bucket and toppled forward into the water. He was still under the influence of the sedative. I let go of the ladder and dived in after him. My hands felt for his dressing gown in the dark, closing on a sleeve. I dragged him back to the surface. Ambrose thrashed helplessly for a moment or two, then calmed down. The shock of the cold water had dispelled most of the effects of the sedative in both of us. It was lucky I had only sipped the laced brandy. I reached up to grab the ladder. My hands closed on… nothing. The ladder had been withdrawn from its sockets. I held Ambrose tight with one hand and lunged upwards to reach the floor of the swim deck. The hull of the boat, made of painted steel or fibreglass – I could not tell which – was far too smooth and slippery for me to get any but the weakest purchase. Of course, I might have done better had I had all my fingers. But one finger had been partially severed not that long ago. I knew I had to hold on tight, or Ambrose and I would drift away from the boat and be lost in the darkness.

'Help us up,' I said.

'Or what?' asked Mavros. 'You had something like this in mind for me, no?

'We're here to purchase your yacht.' This was Ambrose. 'What the hell do you think you're doing? You're risking a diplomatic incident.'

'I don't think so.' Mavros squatted down so he could see our faces. 'You have no diplomatic protection, and you are not who you claim to be.' I noticed that his English vocabulary had suddenly improved. His projected image of a simple Greek had always been a front. 'I don't know who you are, but I have a pretty good idea.'

'What are you going to do with us?' My fingers were slipping, losing their grip. I needed Ambrose to carry his own weight, but he was tangled up in the cords and soggy weight of his infernal dressing gown.

'First I shall ask some questions. And if I do not hear the right answers, then tomorrow the authorities will discover the neatly packed bags of Lord Alex and Lady Jessica abandoned in Athens airport, but there will be no sign of the bags' owners. And all their enquiries will be useless, because, as we all know, Lord Alexander and Lady Jessica never existed.'

Mavros reached into the bucket – the one Ambrose had stumbled over. Above the lapping of the waves and the putter of the auxiliary engine, which powered the lighting and the air conditioning, I heard a squelching sound. Mavros withdrew his hand from the bucket and threw what he was holding into the sea.

'What are you doing?' I was getting more anxious by the second. I could not hold on for much longer.

Mavros grabbed another handful of whatever was inside the bucket. As he pulled his hand out I saw something red and glistening. He threw it into the water. 'These are the heads and guts of the fish we ate on our first night together,' he said. 'Also leftovers, rotten seafood, things I told Lefteris to keep back. I knew they would come in useful.'

I heard a splash behind me. I turned my head, but not fast enough to see what had caused it.

'They're coming,' said Mavros. There was a gleeful glint in his voice. 'We have many sharks here in the Aegean. They have been around for millions of years. But now we have new species coming through the Suez Canal. There have even been sightings of Great Whites.' He paused to let this sink in. I heard another splash behind me. 'You don't have much time left.'

'What do you want?' This was Ambrose. I could feel him flagging. We were both treading water, but Ambrose was weighing heavily on my left arm. The weakening fingers of my right hand slipped further and I dropped deeper into the sea, taking Ambrose with me. He kicked manfully to keep his head above water, but we could not remain in this position much longer.

'What was your plan? Are there others working with you?' Mavros slammed his fist on the swim deck. 'Tell me!'

Well, if he did not know, then I was not going to tell him.

Ambrose spat out seawater and answered. 'This was my mission entirely. My friend here came along to support me, but she had no knowledge of my true purpose.'

'I am not stupid,' Mavros replied. 'I have seen this woman before. I don't remember where, but I know her.'

'Freddie,' groaned Ambrose. He sounded weak, but I saw by the light from the saloon that he had managed to rid himself of the dressing gown which had been weighing him down.

'What's that, old man?' asked Mavros. He had to lean down to hear Ambrose's voice above the exhaust's watery putter.

Ambrose lunged out of the water with surprising agility. In his hand he held a pair of scissors which he had secreted in his pocket. The blades glinted as he thrust at Mavros' throat. But the Greek was faster. He jerked out of reach before the blades could touch him. He grabbed Ambrose's wrist and wrenched it backwards, forcing him to drop his weapon. There was a clatter as the scissors hit the deck and a small splash as they dropped into the sea.

'Lefteris,' called Mavros. The bosun, holding his gun ready, stepped forward. '*Skotoste ton!*'

I didn't know that much Greek, but I knew that Mavros was ordering Lefteris to kill Ambrose. 'No!' I shouted. 'I'll tell you everything.'

The pistol shot when it came was simply a loud crack, lost on the sea. At that very moment a wave washed into my eyes, and I was certain Ambrose was dead.

46

As my eyes cleared I saw Lefteris stagger forward and topple into the water. Mavros was as shocked as I was. He spun around as Tom, his new captain, raised his smoking gun and pointed it at him.

'Set up the ladder,' Tom commanded.

'Are you crazy?' Mavros shouted. 'You work for *me*.'

'No, he works for me,' said Ambrose. The effort to stab Mavros' throat had drained his remaining strength and he was slipping away.

'Set it up and stand back,' Tom ordered Mavros, who stood up, slotted the ladder into its brackets, and moved to the back of the swim deck. 'If you try anything I won't kill you,' warned Tom. 'But a bullet in the crotch can be very painful.' His aim settled on the shipowner's groin.

I could see Mavros considering his options. He could try to rush Tom and disarm him, but Tom's aim was steady. I reached for the ladder rail. At that moment I felt Ambrose slip away and sink beneath the water. I grabbed the sleeve of his pyjamas and hauled him towards me. The wet sleeve ripped, but I got Ambrose's hand onto the rail and a foot on the bottom tread.

'Help him up,' barked Tom, his gun still aimed at Mavros' groin. Mavros stepped forward, bent down and grabbed Ambrose's flailing hand. My old companion seemed barely conscious as Mavros hauled him upwards and I pushed from below. Ambrose collapsed face down on the swim deck.

'Now help her,' Tom said. Mavros turned to me, halfway up the ladder. As he bent forward, Tom gave him a hefty kick in the backside that propelled him off the deck. His yell of surprise was cut off as he splashed head first into the water and submerged. Before Mavros had time to surface Tom had hauled me up and disengaged the ladder, which he hurled onto the deck. I knelt over Ambrose, who lay face down, white and motionless. I pumped his lungs, trying to expel the seawater, hoping to get him breathing. Suddenly a great gush of water spewed from his nose and mouth across the deck. Ambrose coughed and spluttered. I kept on pumping.

'You can stop doing that now, Waspy,' he groaned. 'I'm still in the land of the living.' He rolled over on his back and sat up, gasping to catch his breath.

I stood up and joined Tom, who was staring down into the water. Mavros was struggling to get a grip on the boat's hull, with less success than I had.

'Give me the ladder. Get me out of the water!' he yelled.

'Like you did with us?' I heard a loud splash behind him. Mavros spun around in the water, trying to see what was there. He spun back to me, treading water furiously.

'Stop fooling around. Get me out!'

'Not until you tell us what we want to know. Why did you have Freddie killed?'

'Who?' Mavros, terrified by the splashing sounds behind him, seemed genuinely confused.

'Freddie de Lazlo, the young man at the British embassy.'

'I don't know who you mean. Get me up, and give me time to think.'

I reached into the slimy mess in the bucket, grabbed a

handful of stinking fish heads and guts and tossed them into the sea. 'You can think while you're waiting for that Great White.'

'I was joking. There aren't any Great Whites in the Aegean.'

'Then you won't mind staying where you are.' There was a loud splash as two large fish fought over the floating offal. Mavros spun around, took one look at their tall fins breaking the surface and spun back to me.

'I remember. I remember! That unfortunate boy at the embassy. I had nothing to do with it. It was all that crazy man, Abu Nidal.'

Mavros lunged upwards, but he was too fat and out of shape to reach the deck. His fingers scrabbled helplessly at the hull, tearing his fingernails.

'What was he to you?'

'This Freddie? Nothing. I didn't know him.'

'But you knew Abu Nidal. And you two were conspiring together.'

The water around him had gone still. Ominously still. Mavros' eyes darted around him. The waters were too dark to make out anything but vague shapes. Tom opened a side hatch in the back of the yacht and turned on a switch. Immediately underwater lights came on in the hull, lighting the area beneath Mavros. He saw what we could see: long dark shapes swirling through the deep.

'Get me out of here!' he screamed.

'You were in league with Abu Nidal.' This was Ambrose. He had recovered his breath and now crawled to the edge of the swim deck.

'Never.'

'He was a guest on your yacht,' I said. 'You set him up with Sir Roland Bingham.'

Realisation hit Mavros hard. 'I knew I had seen you before, you bitch! Second stewardess on my first boat, forty years ago. You can dye your hair, you can wear different clothes, make-up, but without contact lenses you cannot disguise your eyes. And your figure is not so different. Not bad, for an old woman.'

I let this pass. 'What was your relationship with Abu Nidal?'

'I shipped arms for him.'

'And what did you get in return?' I saw a smile break through his fear. It was a smile of greed.

'He used his contacts to help me break sanctions, shipping oil for blacklisted countries. Libya, Iran… but he's been dead a long time. You can't prove anything.'

'We are not interested in that. What we want to know is why Abu Nidal killed Freddie. Was he aiming for Ambassador Bingham?'

'Bingham? No. Abu Nidal had no quarrel with him.'

'That's a lie. I heard them arguing.'

'Bingham refused to help him. But so did every nation. We had to shut the young man up.'

'Why? What harm could he do you?'

A big wave suddenly struck Mavros, leaving him gasping. He drifted away from the boat. 'Help me!' he spluttered.

'Why? Tell me why he was killed,' said Ambrose.

'There was a rat in the embassy.'

'A rat?' Ambrose and I exchanged looks.

'A mole?' I said.

'Rat, mole, stupid English names for a traitor.'

'He means Bella Walsingham,' I said. 'We know about her.'

Mavros laughed. 'No. Somebody else. If you want me to tell you, get me out of here.'

'Who?' said Ambrose. 'I was in the embassy. I knew everyone.'

Something else was preying on my mind. 'You made a phone call last night. Who warned you about us? Was it the same person?'

There was a sudden splash in the dark, but no reply.

'Flashlight!' barked Ambrose.

Tom found a flashlight in the side hatch. He switched it on and turned its harsh beam onto the water. There was no sign of Mavros. I thought I could make out a dark stain in the depths, and the swirl of a fin and tail, but then they were gone.

47

I HEARD THE PUTTER OF its motor long before I saw the outline of the speedboat in the moonlight. Rory Moncrieff cut the engines and allowed the boat to glide towards the swim deck. It came to a neat stop just inches from us. Rory threw a line to Tom, who tied up on a cleat. Rory leapt onto the swim deck with a second line and tied the stern of his boat. 'Sorry I'm late, you gave me different coordinates, and I was nearly an hour away.'

'Perhaps it's as well you didn't get here any earlier,' said Ambrose. 'We might all have been killed.' He turned to me. 'We should pack up our stuff and go with Rory. We're not going to learn anything more.'

'You haven't explained Tom's part in this.'

'Of course. Tom is my sister's grandson. Freddie would have been his uncle. It's always best to have people you trust on a mission like this. Tom will stay on board and report Mavros missing when he docks in Mykonos.'

'What happened to Mavros?' asked Rory.

'That's a story for the journey home,' I said.

We packed quickly and efficiently. Ambrose and Rory checked on Bill and Mike. To our relief we found they had been drugged by Lefteris, who had plied them with Metaxa brandies before they retired. The plan had been to embarrass them, and whoever had authorised their mission, when they awoke to find 'Lord Alexander and Lady Jessica' missing. Fortunately they were resilient types, and a coffee provided by Rory from a flask – we did not use the galley for fear of disturbing the crew - perked them up. As Tom put away the swim-deck ladder, all four of us boarded Rory's launch. Tom would tell the crew that Lord Alexander and Lady Jessica had been put ashore earlier with Bill and Mike. And that Mavros had been heard arguing on the deck with Lefteris late at night.

Rory started the engine and edged away from the MY *Fantasy* as quietly as possible. When we were a few hundred metres off, he throttled back and we sped towards the mainland. At the same time Tom started up his engines and headed onwards to Mykonos. We would both reach our destinations early in the morning.

Rory's speedboat entered the harbour at Porto Rafti on the mainland. He had a car waiting for us which sped us to Athens airport in time to catch a late morning flight back to London. Ambrose and I took seats well apart from each other, as if we were strangers. Bill and Mike, using passports in their real names, travelled together. At Heathrow we went our separate ways.

I returned to my safe house in Notting Hill. Before I went to bed I listened to the news on the radio. There was a brief item about a Greek shipping tycoon being lost at sea. Apparently he had seen off a couple of guests – names withheld – and had gone missing after getting into a fight with his bosun. Boats had been out looking for them all day but the vast area of sea between Spetses and Mykonos was considered too wide an area to search effectively. Mavros had never been popular in the Greek shipping community, and already his rivals were sizing up bids for his fleet of reefers, bulk carriers and tankers. The account brought up the story of Robert Maxwell, the disgraced tycoon who had, depending on which version you believed, accidentally fallen off his yacht, committed suicide to avoid disgrace, or been thrown overboard by agents of the Israeli secret service Mossad. I hoped that this story would lean towards the 'accident'. It was so much easier to swallow.

48

MEMORY IS A COGNITIVE FACILITY which does not always perform on cue. Why is it that things you would rather forget pop into your head at the most inconvenient times, while the things you really need to remember require a bloody good jolt to set them free?

I woke late in the morning. The strain of playing 'Lady Jessica Lexington' day in, day out, together with our ordeal in the sea, had taken its toll on both Ambrose and me. Ambrose had been coughing all through the flight back to London. His cough had become so persistent that the person beside him had asked to change seats. I had been concerned that Ambrose was developing pneumonia. At baggage reclaim I passed close by him. 'Are you going to be all right?' I hovered, as if waiting for my case, though I had travelled with a light carry-on.

'I'll stay with my sister in town.'

'I'll be in touch.' I marched off towards passport control.

Once I had made myself a coffee, relaxed and enjoyed it, I switched on my phone. I'd left it off all the time I was in Greece, but kept it on charge. I know you are not supposed to do this, but I sneer at people who let their batteries run down. In my line, that is something you just cannot afford to do.

There were eight messages, which had all been subsequently deleted from, of all people, Bella Walsingham. Why was she trying to contact me? People were searching for her. She must have known that. What was she thinking? What did she want?

There were also two messages from Bernard, two days apart. The first asked me to meet him urgently. The second message informed me that he had identified several possible orchestrators of his problem, but he wanted to discuss their names with me before he acted. I was the only person he felt he could trust.

Perhaps I was somehow to blame for that. Bernard had never been good at making friends. But then politics is a dirty business at best, and most politicians, who once worked for the common good – which inevitably led to collateral damage of innocent individuals – now operate solely for their own benefit and financial gain, believing that rules and regulations are not for them. This leads to the collateral damage of our entire nation.

I phoned Bernard. He answered on the second ring.

'Thank God. Where have you been?'

'I do have a life, you know. I was visiting an old friend in the country. Forgot my phone and it ran out of battery.' As if.

'I have three names I would like you to consider.'

That was a relief. I could do without another outing to St James's Park.

'Fire away,' I said.

'The first is Sir Esmond Canover.'

'The head of MI5?' I considered it unlikely. But it was a possibility.

'I believe he and his aides have been briefing against

me. Little hints to the press and the PM.' Bernard's voice had a tinge of defeat in it. That did not sound like him at all.

'I thought you had the prime minister's confidence.'

'So did I.'

'Just as long as you don't have his *full* confidence. That's a sure sign he's ready to ditch you.' I immediately regretted my brutal assessment.

'Bridget's starting to notice.' Bernard's marriage had had its ups and downs. He wanted to keep it on the up.

'Give me the other names.'

'You're not going to like this.' It sounded ominous.

'An old colleague of yours. From your time in Athens.'

I stiffened. 'Go on.'

'Ambrose Flynn.' Ambrose! That could not be possible. Could it?

'I know you two haven't been in touch since you left the service.' Well, if that's what he knew, he was not as all-knowing as I thought.

I was on the point of informing him that Ambrose and I had just returned from a trip and that Ambrose was currently recuperating at his sister's home in St John's Wood, when I stopped myself. 'What makes you suspect Ambrose could possibly be involved?'

'His name has come up. You won't know this, but he's still kept in active reserve. And there are few secrets that he doesn't hold in that big head of his.'

Well of course I bloody well knew. But I could not believe it of Ambrose. Or could I? It had already occurred to me that Patrick Dallaway, in a final flash of clarity and revenge, might have told Ambrose who was the father of my twins. Once the earworm of doubt enters your brain, it is impossible to extract it. It remains there, like a looped recording, until it dominates your every thought.

'And the third name?' I wanted to drown out Ambrose's earworm.

'You won't like this either.' Bernard drew breath. Come on, I wanted to shout, out with it. 'Percy Bishop.'

Percy Bishop! He and Ambrose were the two people I trusted most in the world. How could either of them be involved in plotting Bernard's downfall? What if they were both in it together? But why? I felt like those young girls who scream OMG! out loud in public, as if the tiniest dramas in their lives are of vital interest to the rest of us.

'Why on earth would you bring his name into this?'

'Just a rumour. Like all rumours, it's impossible to know where it started. Bishop has powerful friends, and equally powerful enemies. As do I. He and I have always enjoyed a good relationship. So I am inclined to discount all I've heard. But I thought I should share it with you.'

Percy Bishop? Could he have engineered everything from the very start? Could he have set up my 'assassination' in the Chestnut Tree tea rooms simply to get me out of the way? That red laser dot on my chest could have been aimed by anyone in the tea rooms, or anyone standing out in the street. I had never heard a gunshot, not even a suppressed one. Had the bullet Percy 'extracted' from the wall been in his pocket all along, ready as evidence to get me to go to ground? Surely not? It was all too preposterous. Wasn't it?

What would his motive have been? Even if he had made me go into hiding, he had got me out with the help of that young woman, Azizi-Ryan. But then her photograph had ended up in Aleksi's pocket and almost got me killed. Was that Percy's doing? Had I been given my freedom simply to make me an easier target? Just thinking about it made my head spin.

'Ma, are you still there?' It was Bernard.

Suddenly my memory came unstuck. 'Bernard,' I asked, 'who was that man you were with in John Sandoe's bookshop?'

'My permanent under-secretary of state, Grant Byford.'

'How would he benefit if you were to lose your position?'

'He wouldn't. He's a civil servant. His job, as it says on the tin, is permanent.'

'How long does a permanent under-secretary of state for Defence usually last?'

'About five or six years.'

'So not *that* permanent?'

'Not when you put it like that.'

'But he does have influence on policy?' I knew the answer to that one, but needed to get it from the horse's mouth.

'Of course he does. Influencing defence policy, and ensuring that our strategies are cost-effective and achievable are his prime responsibilities.'

'To whom does he report?'

'To me of course.' Bernard hesitated a moment, then corrected himself. 'To me and the prime minister.'

'Because the under-secretary is a prime ministerial appointee?'

'Yes, of course.' Bernard was beginning to sound his usual tetchy self, which was an improvement. A few minutes ago he had been feeling sorry for himself. Now he was getting irritated by his interfering mother. He was almost back to his old self.

'Bernard,' I said softly. 'When the knives come out they are almost always held by those closest to us. Remember what I said about Julius Caesar and Marcus Brutus.'

'You mean I should be looking closer to home?'

'Just a suggestion.' I ended the phone call. I had more immediate matters to attend to.

49

WHILE I HAD BEEN SPEAKING to Bernard, Bella Walsingham had been calling me. I had not answered because I would have had to call Bernard back, and I did not want to be to-ing and fro-ing between Bernard and Bella. I needed all my wits about me.

The moment I cut Bernard off I called Bella. She answered straight away.

'Felicity! I've been trying to reach you for days.'

'So I see. I heard you were on the run.'

'Not at all,' she insisted. There was a brief pause, then, 'I'm lying low, if you must know.'

'I won't ask where.' I was avoiding confrontation. She had saved my life, after all. But was that just a tactic to get me to drop my guard? Would I be her next victim?

'Can we meet?'

'Where?'

'Somewhere out in the open.'

'No,' I said. I had had enough of meetings in parks and gardens. Too quiet, too isolating. Too easy a place to kill someone. 'Somewhere busy, with lots of people.'

Bella went quiet for a moment. 'All right,' she said. 'How about the Chelsea Arts Club?'

'You have to be a member.'

'I'm a member of several London clubs. The CAC is by far my favourite. I'll see you there in an hour. Oh, and I'll sign you in. You can be Patricia Christie.'

'Who's Patricia Christie?'

'Someone I was at school with. Hearty girl, good at hockey.'

'I am neither.' If Bella, who was pretty beefy herself, could describe another girl as hearty, then this Patricia must have been enormous.

'I'll tell the ladies on reception. I'll be in the billiards room. Probably not alone.' She ended the call.

What did she mean by 'not alone'?

The Chelsea Arts Club, rather like John Sandoe Books, is made up of three cottages which have been knocked together and extended. The club was established in the Kings Road in 1890 by James McNeill Whistler, whose painting of his mother, or 'Arrangement in Grey and Black No.1', as he named it, many of us know well. The club moved to 143 Old Church Street in 1901 and has been there ever since.

I took the 52 bus from Ladbroke Grove all the way down to Knightsbridge, where I jumped off and waited for the 452. It would have been hard to follow me undetected, unless they had several people on the job. This seemed unlikely. I changed at Sloane Square onto the number 11 heading for World's End and got off at the Old Church Street stop and made my way north.

The Chelsea Arts Club entrance is a small Gothic arch set in a white nondescript building. I rang the doorbell. A moment later I heard a buzz and the door opened a crack. I pushed through and found myself in a small dark hall. Two young ladies sat behind a desk.

'Hello, who are you here to see?' said one.

'Patricia Christie, to see Bella Walsingham.'

'Bella's in the billiard room. You can go straight through. Just make sure your phone is off.'

I had been to the club before, under very different circumstances. It hadn't changed since my last visit. The billiard table itself was covered and not in use, but the tables set around the large room were occupied by groups of threes and fours. I heard Bella's roar of laughter coming from a bunch at the back of the room, close to the garden.

'There she is!' waved Bella. I relaxed. There was little she could do to harm me in this crowd. Someone stood up to get another chair, and I found myself with a friendly gang of ageing artists. The one nearest to me, tall and thin with a patrician nose, smiled and said, 'Bella's told us all about you.'

'Has she?' I glanced at Bella.

'You're Patricia Christie, great granddaughter of James Christie, one of the club's founders. Do you paint?'

'Well, I dabble a bit.' Yes, but not in art, I omitted to mention. Perhaps I could start.

'You must join the club! Won't you propose her, Bella?'

'Not a bad idea. Patricia's up from the country, so membership won't cost much. We're all on tight pensions these days. Now let me get Patricia a drink.'

'I can get it myself,' I offered. I was not going to give Bella the opportunity to slip something toxic in my glass.

'Nonsense. Only members are permitted to buy drinks. Club rule. Come with me.' She marched across to the bar. 'What are you having?' Before I could answer, she continued, 'They make an excellent Bloody Mary. You've got to try it.' She turned to the young barman, 'Rex, a Bloody Mary, with all the trimmings.' She turned back to me, 'Do you want to grab that table? She indicated an empty table by the stairs leading up to a gallery, but I wasn't going to leave her unsupervised with my drink. As I said, it could have been poisoned. I took one sip and was convinced it had been. The spicy strength of Bloody Mary mix almost blew my head off. My eyes watering, I stumbled over to the table and sat down. Bella joined me.

'Were you followed?'

'Pretty sure I wasn't, but a team could have managed it.'

'They don't have a team. It's just one or two men.'

'Do you know who they are?'

'No idea. But one of them – or it may have been two – broke into my flat a few nights ago. I'm a very light sleeper and I have my escape route. We all do, don't we?'

I nodded. Well, I do and I don't.

'I made it to King's Cross and bought a sleeper ticket for Gleneagles. I got off the train moments before it departed. But I left my other phone on under my mattress. They will have tracked me to Scotland.'

'How long have you been here?'

'Pretty much the whole time. The first few days I told the staff I had the 'flu, so the kitchen sent my meals up to me. I came down for the first time today. The club's been very good about it.'

'But why all the subterfuge?'

'Polyakin.'

'The Soviet double agent?'

'He was never a double agent. I've been delving through the archives. The information was misfiled, purposefully I suspect. It showed that when we sent Polyakin back to Moscow he was tortured, put up against a wall and shot.'

'Does Matthew know?'

'He does now. And he's devastated. He blames himself, poor fellow. I knew I had to tell him eventually.'

'Who else did you tell?'

'Ambrose Flynn. He and I go back a long way.'

'So do we.' Ambrose again. What had I been missing? 'Anybody else?' I asked.

'Just one person.' I waited with a deep sense of foreboding. Then she said the name. 'Our old head of security, Percy Bishop.'

50

Bella stood up. 'Now you know where I've been hiding, I'd better move on. Nothing personal of course, but best to be safe. As my guest, you will have to leave now.' She went over to her drinking companions, retrieved her overnight bag from the floor and headed out into the garden. I waited a few seconds. Then, curious, I went over to the French doors and looked out. There was no sign of Bella.

I turned to her friends. 'Is there a way out through the garden?'

'Only if you want to climb a ten-foot wall,' one wag replied. I could imagine Bella doing a lot of things, but vaulting a high wall in a skirt wasn't one of them. I stepped out into the garden. To my left was a paved area dotted with teak tables and chairs, straight ahead was an expanse of fake lawn. Bella had vanished.

Then I noticed a couple of kitchen staff in aprons. They lit up cigarettes and leant either side of a door to chat. I wandered over to them.

'Is there a way I can get to the street this way?' I asked.

'There's a service passage, if that's what you mean?' said one.

'Did a lady carrying a small suitcase just come by here?'

'Maybe, we're not watching all the time, we're working.'

'Have you thought of the fire escape?' asked his friend.

'What fire escape?'

'Door in the garden wall. Leads to the back of Elm Park Gardens.'

'Thank you.' So there were two escape routes Bella could have taken. I squeezed past the men and hurried along the corridor, passing the kitchen on my left. A door opened onto the street. I looked out. There was no sign of Bella.

I had no reason other than curiosity for following Bella. Tradecraft is no good against someone younger than yourself who knows the same tricks as you, and most probably knows some newer and better ones.

I headed home, taking the 49 bus from South Kensington. The wonderful thing about London buses is that they do most of your spying for you. I took a seat downstairs, which gave me a good view of the screen which flashed images from five cameras set around the bus. These are intended as a warning to miscreants, fare dodgers and abusers. They are also perfect for keeping an eye on your fellow passengers.

I was pretty certain I had not been followed to the Chelsea Arts Club. But now I was heading home I had the distinct feeling that I was being watched.

I studied the screen carefully. People who had taken the bus at South Kensington gradually got off as they reached their destinations. There was a young woman who had got on at the stop after mine. It was a well-tried trick. Most people, concerned about pursuit, only check people getting on at the same time as themselves. I watched this young woman closely, but she dismounted just four stops later, at Cornwall Gardens. She could easily have walked the distance in the time it took to wait for a bus. Laziness gets you in the end.

If she ever reached my age she would be shuffling along on wasted muscles and shrivelled limbs.

Experienced pursuers, such as I, prefer a more subtle tactic. You get on at the stop before that of your prey and take a seat towards the back of the bus. There you can observe the monitors without giving yourself away. When I boarded the bus I noticed a young man in a hoodie sitting two rows from the back. He kept his head down and looked engrossed in his phone. Perhaps he was. Then again, perhaps he was relaying information on my progress to somebody further along the bus route.

When we reached Upper Addison Gardens I waited while fresh passengers boarded. As the driver was about to close the doors, I stood up with a cry of 'sorry!' and hopped off the bus. It moved off towards Shepherd's Bush station, taking the man in the hoodie with it.

In my day the Routemaster buses had open platforms at the back. This meant passengers could board and alight whenever the bus slowed to a safe pace. It made shadowing the enemy much more exciting, and just that little bit harder. The Routemaster's phasing out in the early years of the millennium was mourned by all agents, our side and enemy alike.

I crossed Holland Park Avenue and walked into Royal Crescent, passing the first-floor flat where I had been on stakeout for more than a month in the mid 1980s.

I had to wait six minutes for a 295 bus. The moment I stepped aboard I saw the young man in the hoodie seated at the back. Or it could have been another young man altogether. It was hard to tell. But if it was the same one he was clearly a professional. He still had his head down, studying his phone as if he were playing 'Angry Birds' or whatever that game is that David Cameron used to play when he was supposed to be running the country. I should not single out Mr Cameron. Many waste their time on video games when they should be working. Later politicians learnt from Cameron's mistake and were cautious enough not to demonstrate their foibles. But that's as far as their caution went.

I got out at St Mark's Road, walked to the Sainsbury's under the flyover for ingredients for a chicken salad, then strolled home. There was little point in trying to throw pursuers off my scent. If they had been following me all morning then they must know where I lived.

The moment I got inside I made a call to Aaron. He's the man you phone when you need something sorted. It was Ambrose who had first given me his number.

I told him my boiler needed fixing, then, when he had given me the all-clear to speak, I told him what I had in mind.

'Nothing simple then, yeah?' he said with a hint of irony as I reeled off the list of equipment he would have to install. 'That lot's going to cost you, right.'

'Not a problem,' I said. With luck I would claim most of it back from Matthew. 'Just one thing. I would rather you did not mention this to Ambrose. Not yet anyway. It's supposed to be a surprise.'

'I'll have to invoice you for the materials.'

'Naturally.'

'But I'm happy to do the labour for free.'

'That's very generous of you.'

'Two reasons, right. One, I'm about to take a long break in Grenada, thinking about retiring.'

'Oh, I hope not. And the other?'

'I want to see if it works as well as you think it will.'

51

AARON ARRIVED AFTER FIVE O'CLOCK. I had almost given up on him.

'Sorry about the delay. Some of those parts you wanted were hard to get at short notice, so I had to make them myself.' He hauled two metal boxes from his van which had the slogan 'Jiffy Plumbers we'll be with you in a jiffy' stencilled on either side, along with a mobile phone number.

'Don't bother calling it,' he said. 'It's there to make it look authentic, but all calls go to an inbox. After a couple of tries customers ring someone else.'

I shut and locked the door, then offered Aaron a cup of tea while he got to work.

'Nah thanks, I'll have something when I'm finished, yeah.' I had forgotten he always worked straight through to completion without a break.

Over the next two hours there was so much banging and sawing that I was glad I had no neighbours above or below me. At least none I was aware of. At around eight o'clock the TV presenter next door thumped on the wall in protest. Aaron kept on working.

'Another twenty minutes should do it.'

Ten minutes later I heard a fist pounding on the front door and frantic ringing. I peered through the net curtain. It was my neighbour, apoplectic with rage. I opened the door a couple of inches.

'How long's that bloody banging going on for? Any more of that and I shall phone the Noise and Nuisance Team at the Kensington and Chelsea Council.'

As Aaron had stopped banging to install my new appliance, the house was quiet. 'The only person making a noise and nuisance of themselves,' I snapped back, 'is you. I am fully entitled to make as much noise as I like until eleven o'clock, and to start up again at seven in the morning, if it pleases me.' In truth, I abhor noise: the roar of motorcycles delivering drugs at four in the morning, the SUVs thumping music from oversized loudspeakers as they struggle to squeeze into spaces built for smaller cars, the thundering of police helicopters overhead. Give me a silent street, where my failing hearing can still make out the stealthy tread of a prowler, and I'm at peace.

'How much longer is this going on for?' my neighbour demanded.

'Another two or three hours should do it.'

'Three hours!'

'And then the homeless mothers and babes can move in. Good luck getting them to keep the noise down.'

His mouth opened and shut a couple of times. Then he turned on his heels and stormed back to his house, slamming the door so hard that he damaged the lock. I could hear him opening and shutting the door a couple more times, then slamming it again, as he tried to free it.

I took one last look outside. Parked across the road was a small Nissan car. I could just make out the occupant sitting in the driver's seat: a young man wearing a hoodie. I was less concerned than I would have been a day or two earlier. If all went to plan, I would soon be out of here. But would it be on foot, or in a coffin?

Aaron finished well within the twenty minutes he had promised. We spent the best part of an hour testing the system and checking that I fully understood the controls. I needed the element of surprise, and by the time the hour was over I felt I had mastered enough to achieve this.

It was remarkable how Aaron had managed to conceal all the electronics in the wood panelling. I had guessed, rightly, that his father had constructed the flat's secret rooms and dividers, with Aaron as apprentice, so he was familiar with the wiring and hidden compartments where he could position tiny cameras, invisible unless one was searching for them. All that could be seen were their tiny lenses, so small that they all but disappeared into the shadows.

Once Aaron had packed up and left the house I spent time alone, again familiarising myself with the equipment. For one awful moment a part of the mechanism jammed. I almost resorted to calling Aaron back to fix it, but was pleased when I discovered what had caused the problem, fixed it myself, and reset the whole apparatus.

I called Emily Charalamboulos.

'By this time tomorrow I should have phoned you with good news,' I told her. 'But if you don't hear from me by then, you must tell your brother to leave the country unobserved by whatever means possible.'

'Thank you,' she replied, in that quavery voice of hers. 'I'll phone him right away.'

'So you *do* know where he's hiding?' Emily gasped and went silent. 'Don't worry, your secret's safe with me. Just tell him to be prepared.' I cut her off before she could respond.

Before I went to sleep I called both Matthew and Ambrose. I had considered calling Percy too, but I felt it would be simpler to talk to the other two first. I asked them to come round to my flat at ten in the morning, as I had some very interesting news to impart, which I could not risk by phone or email. Matthew agreed immediately. Ambrose hesitated. He sounded terrible, his lungs congested. He must have been in the early stages of double pneumonia. Nevertheless, I insisted. It was, after all, a matter of life and death.

52

AT NINE FORTY-FIVE THE NEXT morning I sat and waited by the bay window, positioned well back from the net curtain. Although I could not be seen from the street or the buildings opposite, anyone with infrared sights might make out my movements from my body heat and take a shot. I had hung a sheet of aluminium foil between myself and thc window, with a letterbox-shaped hole cut into the foil so that I could watch the street. Any heat radiation from this narrow rectangle should baffle a would-be sniper.

The man in the hoodie was no longer parked across the road, but he could have re-parked anywhere else in the street, or been replaced by a colleague.

I still had both of Aleksi's handguns. I placed one under a cushion on the sofa, where I would sit. The other lay in a drawer in the bedroom.

At two minutes to the hour I observed Matthew waddling up the street towards the house. Trailing him was Ambrose, gasping as he propelled his body, exhausted by prolonged fits of coughing, as fast as he was able. I had expected them to come separately. That way I might have had a brief private conversation with whoever arrived first. I regretted that I would have to forgo that advantage.

As Matthew waited for poor old Ambrose to catch up with

him, I placed my phone face down on the coffee table and covered it with the crime thriller I had read both forwards and backwards. I had set the phone to record on QuickVoice Pro. Whatever the outcome of this meeting, I needed to leave behind a record.

I dismantled my foil screen and stashed it out of sight behind a sofa. Now these two had arrived, I no longer anticipated an assassin's bullet.

As Ambrose caught up with Matthew and prepared to mount the steps to the front door they linked arms, like old friends. It was hard, though, to assess who was supporting whom. Ambrose, helplessly out of breath, needed all the assistance he could get. Matthew, his paunch straining at his belt, studied the steep steps with dismay and hesitated. Then he took a deep breath and suddenly launched himself forward and up the first step, pulling Ambrose up after him. Now it was Ambrose's turn to go first. Each step seemed a minor triumph, overcoming the entire flight a reason to pause and celebrate. They stood together at the top, still linked together, trying to catch their breaths. On the stroke of ten Matthew pressed my doorbell.

I buzzed them in and retreated to the kitchen, where I had brewed coffee in the percolator. I turned on the gas to reheat it.

Matthew plonked himself down on the sofa nearest to me, where I had intended to sit. Ambrose virtually collapsed into the sofa facing him, his back to the bay window. I had wanted them both to sit together, where I could keep my eye on them. Getting either of them to move now would be near impossible.

'Who wants coffee?' I asked, as cheerily as if this was a mothers' knitting group and we were all here to do nothing more strenuous than crocheting.

'Not for me, dear,' said Matthew. Ambrose tried wheezing a reply, then gave up and simply shook his head. I switched the gas off and pulled my chair up so that I sat with them to the left and right of me.

'Now tell us,' said Matthew. 'What is it you've discovered?' He leant forward, eager to hear. Ambrose barely moved, his breath rasping.

I also leant forward. On the small coffee table sat my report which I had printed in triplicate. Each page dealt with one single point, written as a short paragraph. I had, for security's sake, taken my computer offline to type the pages. There was every possibility that it had been hacked and that someone, somewhere, had been reading every item I looked up, every note I wrote.

'If you could both turn to page one…' I passed them each the top page. 'You will see that initially, back in 1984, we believed that the shooting of Freddie de Lazlo had simply been a tragic mistake.'

Matthew and Ambrose barely glanced at their first page. There wasn't much to read, and nothing they didn't already know.

'More recently,' I continued, 'we reached the conclusion that Freddie was, in fact, the intended victim, and that he was killed to stop him voicing his suspicions. Suspicions that we had a mole in our Athens embassy.'

'Yes, Bella,' interrupted Matthew. 'We know all that. She's gone to ground. Though how anyone that large can disappear defeats me. But we're pretty sure she's still in the UK, most probably in Scotland, somewhere in the Highlands. But she can't disappear forever. At some stage she's going to have to surface, and then we'll have her.'

He sat back, looking as if he had the situation well in hand.

'There's just one problem about that. This mole was working closely with Vasilis Mavros.'

Ambrose coughed violently. He wiped the sputum with his handkerchief, which he folded carefully and put away in his trouser pocket.

'Yes,' confirmed Matthew. 'Again, we know all this. That is why you and Ambrose went to Greece.' He straightened up. 'By the way, I haven't had the chance to congratulate you on… well, putting Mavros out of action.'

'It's a pity we did,' croaked Ambrose. 'He might have told us a lot more.'

'Oh, but he did.' I studied Ambrose. 'He told us that the mole was not Bella.'

'But he failed to tell us who it was.'

'We know it was someone close to Freddie. Someone very close.'

Ambrose stared back at me. There was something akin to panic in his eyes.

'Go and sit beside Matthew, will you?'

'But… but I'm not well.'

'Go on.' I said it firmly, meanly even. Ambrose struggled to rise but before he could move Matthew had somehow managed to haul himself up.

'Don't trouble yourself, old boy. If she wants us together, I'm happy to move.' He shuffled around the coffee table and plonked himself beside Ambrose. They both now had their backs to the bay window, exactly where I wanted them.

'As I said,' I continued, 'it was someone very close to Freddie.'

'You can't believe… can't suspect that I had a part in his death?' Ambrose looked aghast. 'My own nephew!'

Matthew shifted uncomfortably away from him, as if

propelled by his own disgust. 'Unbelievable, your own nephew,' he repeated. Ambrose hung his head in despair. 'And I was so certain it was Bella,' continued Matthew, 'when she gave us the slip.'

'Mavros might have told us more,' I said, 'if he had survived. But that was the plan, wasn't it? Mavros would kill me, or himself be killed. Either way, the mole would remain undiscovered.'

A low moaning escaped Ambrose. Matthew shook his head in sorrow for the old man's shame.

I got up and stood behind the sofa facing them. 'There was something else I've learned from Bella.'

Matthew jerked his head up. 'Bella! Have you heard from her? Do you know where she is?'

'I saw her only yesterday. But I've no idea where she is now.'

Ambrose coughed painfully and slumped against Matthew. The fat man, pressed up against the sofa's arm, found himself blocked.

'She told me something that changed everything. Something that nobody in the Service was ever supposed to discover. That Polyakin, the supposed fake Soviet defector, whom we sent back to Moscow, had been tortured for two weeks and then put up against a wall and shot.'

'Where did she get that from?' Matthew snapped.

Ambrose straightened up. 'Polyakin was exposed by you! You had him sent back to Moscow.'

Matthew remained silent, his eyes darting fiercely from Ambrose to me and back again.

'And you were the one who was close to Freddie, weren't you, Matthew?' I leant against the back of the sofa. 'You fancied him, invited him back to your flat, and that is where he stumbled across something that tied you to the Soviets. Or maybe just something that aroused his suspicions.' I leant forward and reached for the gun under the cushion. I felt nothing. The gun had gone.

'And you had him killed for it!' This was Ambrose. He stood, his pretence of sickness suddenly gone. He had kept it up far longer than I had expected. Ambrose lashed out at Matthew, his fists striking soft flesh. Matthew reached into his left-hand jacket pocket, produced an electric stun gun, jammed it against Ambrose's ribs and fired. Ambrose went down like a steer in a slaughterhouse.

Matthew reached into his right pocket and pulled out Aleksi's gun. He must have found it under the cushion where I had hidden it. It was a Makarov. I had been shot in the belly by one before and I did not wish to repeat the experience. I backed away. Matthew struggled to his feet with difficulty.

'I suppose you're pleased with yourself,' he said. 'Finally unmasking the mole. But it's a little too late for congratulations, isn't it?'

'Before you kill us both, tell me something. Why did you do it? Was it blackmail? Because you liked young men?'

Matthew threw back his head and laughed.

'Hardly that, my dear. Everybody in the embassy knew my predilections. It was never a guilty secret. We're talking about the 1980s, not the 1950s. Nobody cared, for fuck's sake.'

'Then why?'

Matthew sighed, as if trying to puzzle it out for himself. 'Well, the money was wonderful, of course. The Soviets were notoriously stingy, but they paid well for the sort of information I could provide. And they panicked when Polyakin went over to the West. They provided the evidence

I needed to "expose" him. They were delighted when I got him forcibly returned to Moscow. Gave me a special award, secretly of course, and a generous pension. But it wasn't really the money. It was the power. The knowledge that I was smarter than all of you.' He stepped forward. The Makarov was aimed directly at my stomach. I took a step back as my abdominal muscles tensed in anticipation. 'But then someone surfaced from the past, someone I thought was long dead.'

'George Charalamboulos.'

'Cost me a fortune to keep him and his sister quiet. And then she went and told someone else.'

'James Saunders.'

'He had to go.'

'That's where you slipped up.'

'Slipped up? How?'

'When I phoned to tell you about him, you said you had Ambrose and Bella with you. Bella told me that was a lie, so I checked with Ambrose last night, and he said the same thing.'

'So the old bastard's been faking it all along.'

'Seems only right and fair, as that's what you've been doing to us.' I wondered how far I could push him before he pulled that trigger. 'The clues were there from the start. Even that first day in 1984 when I met Ambrose in Athens.' I glanced around, hoping I could find something to put between myself and his gun. There was nothing.

'When I asked about you, Ambrose told me you were on leave of absence for your mother's funeral. I looked your mother up. She died in July 2010. If I'd checked earlier perhaps I could have saved a few lives. Jonathan Raikes, for one. What was it he said to me? "Matthew's taking a very big risk. It could all backfire horribly." He nailed it exactly.

After you made the first payment to George Charamboulos, he disappeared. You were desperate to find him. And your masterstroke was setting us, the best spy-catchers in the business, to hunt him down. All this stuff about "orders from on high" was complete fabrication. You were running the show with, I take it, the help of your Russian friends.'

Matthew shrugged in acceptance. 'Go on.'

'But I was the one who had been closest to Freddie. I remembered he had gone up to Monastiraki to fetch a friend. I thought he meant George Charamboulos, but it was you he went to pick up. You set him up for the hit. When George returned from Russia, you knew I would pose the greatest danger, so you arranged for me to be killed by the Bulgarian hit man, Aleksi. When that went wrong you found a way to keep me busy, wasting my time with old and meaningless documents. Getting me to sign the Official Secrets Act was a smart move. Made it all feel so much more official.

'And keeping us apart, telling us to report only to you, and not to discuss what we'd discovered. That way you'd know if any of us had come close to guessing your secret. Raikes worked it out and that's why you had him killed. And then James Saunders, whom you pretended you'd never heard of.' I paused to catch my breath.

'You'd hoped I'd be stuck inside for good. "Your incarceration may prove a boon," you said. But once I was out and free you knew I was a danger to you. So Aleksi was activated again. And when that didn't work, you tried to stop me by blackmailing my own son. Through his under-secretary, Grant Byford. Another of your stooges, I take it? I saw him leaving your mews house, but it took me a while to make the connection. And you created noise, false rumours, implicating Percy Bishop and Ambrose, so I wouldn't know whom to trust.' I was building up to a pitch, pacing about the room, but Matthew kept his gun on me all the time. I considered making a dash for the safe room, but that would mean leaving Ambrose to his mercies. Out of the question.

'You must have been desperate. When all else failed you pinned everything on Bella, then sent Ambrose and me down to Greece. Mavros knew what you were, and had always posed a danger. So you sent us down to kill him, or be killed. Either way would be a win for you, and you could mop up survivors later. At some point your nerve failed, and you warned Mavros who we really were. But it was a mistake to let Bella escape, and when she found out about Polyakin, she told me. Even if you dispose of us, Bella will come after you.' I had run out of steam.

'Well done, my dear. I think you've covered just about everything. I would applaud, but my hands are full.'

Ambrose groaned. He was beginning to recover from his short, but intense, three-thousand-volt shock. Matthew turned and pointed the Makarov at Ambrose's head.

'Wait,' I said. 'There's something you need to see.'

'What?'

'I've had CCTV installed all over this flat. It's been recording you ever since you walked up the street. You kill us, the recording goes straight to the authorities.'

'You seem to forget that, in this instance,' said Matthew, 'I am the authorities.' But I could see he was rattled. 'Show me.'

I picked up the remote control from a side table. I was so concerned about selecting the right button that I almost fumbled it, which could have been disastrous. I found the button and pressed it firmly. A section of panelling slid aside and revealed the large monitor installed by Aaron and set into the wall between us.

'Give that to me.'

I handed him the remote.

'How does it work?'

'Press the green button. Green for Play.'

With his left hand Matthew depressed the green button while keeping the Makarov pointed directly at me with his right.

The screen showed us exactly as we stood or sat in the room in real time. Our movements were photographed by a camera set high above the door, aimed at our backs. Ambrose occupied the edge of the frame on the sofa.

'This shows nothing.'

'You have to rewind it first,' I said, in that patronising way my daughter Eva speaks to me when I don't get something technical right first time.

Matthew pressed the rewind button and we watched as the fast rewind showed Ambrose rising from the sofa to be zapped by Matthew's stun gun, Ambrose pulling his punches away from Matthew's vast belly, and then lowering himself quickly to adopt his pathetic pneumonia-ridden posture.

'Why is there a cross in the middle of the picture?'

'No idea,' I replied. 'It was only set up last night. Probably needs adjusting.'

'How do I delete the footage?'

'I'm not telling you that,' I sneered. 'You may kill us both, but the evidence is stored remotely. It will be retrieved and you will die in prison.'

'I still have an ace up my sleeve.' Matthew smirked.

'Really. I would have thought you were right out of cards, aces included. Ambrose and I have nothing to lose.' Out of the corner of my eye I saw Ambrose stirring himself. He didn't look like someone ready to die just yet.

'I hold information that would be of great interest to the Ministry of Defence.'

I knew only too well where this was leading.

'Information about the Secretary of State for Defence's true parentage,' Matthew continued. 'The identity of his father, I mean. We all know who and what his mother is.'

'What are you talking about?' Perhaps he didn't know everything.

'Some weeks ago a certain Belarussian oligarch was taken fatally ill. He was moved to a private hospital for emergency treatment. Sadly he succumbed to his sudden illness. Some sort of poisoning we believe. That kind of thing is a Russian speciality. There was really nothing the British government could do but express its condolences.'

'What's that got to do with the Secretary for Defence?'

'For your son Bernard, a great deal, as it turned out. You see, in the cases of sudden deaths of people of interest, important but dubious foreign nationals, there's a standard procedure we carry out. It's highly secret of course, but it is Ministry of Defence authorised, which is ironic, don't you think?'

'Get to the fucking point, will you?' By this time I was in half a mind to rush him, even if it meant a bullet, and let Ambrose finish him off.

'The point is that we always take a DNA sample when we can, compare them to what we have in our files, see if we can make useful connections that may be to our advantage.'

'You mean the Russians?'

'All sides do it.' He smiled. 'And who do you think was this oligarch's closest living relative?'

'Surprise me.'

'Your own son, Bernard. So close that they could only be father and son. What do you think of that?'

'You've already set this "scandal" in motion, haven't you?'

'I needed to be able to pressure you. But there's no real harm done. Only I have the evidence. For now. If you tell me how to delete this footage nobody else need ever know. His accusers will back down and your precious minister's career will survive.'

'If I show you how to delete the footage, you'll delete the evidence?'

'It's a fair bargain. Tit for tat.'

'Press the red button,' I said. Matthew sighed with more than a hint of relief. He had won. He raised the remote control and pressed the red button. We waited.

'Nothing's happening.'

'You're too close to the screen,' I said. 'You need to take a few paces back.'

Keeping me covered, Matthew slowly stepped away from the monitor. I waited until he was perfectly framed in the centre of the screen. 'Stop right there.' Matthew stopped.

'On second thoughts, why spoil a good thing?' he said. 'I shall send the DNA evidence directly to the prime minister. I may even get a knighthood out of it.' The cross on the monitor exactly marked the middle of his broad back.

'Try pressing again,' I said.

Matthew pressed the red button and the loud crack startled us all. Matthew stumbled forward, then regained his balance. Even a close shot from the gun that Aaron had rigged above the door was not enough to knock his great bulk off his feet. Matthew lowered his gaze to his chest, where blood was spreading from his open bullet wound. He stared at himself on the screen, then turned around to observe the smoking rifle barrel pointing directly at him. He tried to speak but a torrent of blood gushed from his mouth and nose. The bullet must have passed through a lung and pierced his heart, because he toppled forward, quivered for a few seconds, then lay still.

53

'YET WHO WOULD HAVE THOUGHT the old man to have had so much blood in him?' Ambrose quoted as we did our best to mop up the mess.

'Steady on,' I retorted. 'You were the one looking distinctly old just half an hour ago.'

'I thought I played my part rather well, all things considered.'

'There were a few moments when I was quite taken in. How did you manage to look so pale? We both had fairly good suntans when we left Athens.'

'That was all with the help of that young lady Sarah-Azizi Ryan, who was sent to do your makeover. Wonderful way with a make-up stick. Pity we had to lose her.'

'Lose her?'

'Uhuh. They were waiting to arrest her the moment she finished making me look as if I were ready for the grave. Glad you told me about that second polaroid. Very much gave her away. You should have been more careful, you know.'

'I suppose it was my new look, it distracted me.'

'She gave the polaroid to Matthew, and he somehow got it to Aleksi.'

'He wanted me dead,' I said.

'Rather clever of Matthew, getting Aleksi to do the

executions. They found a DNA match on Raikes' clothes. By the way, did you have a plan B if the first didn't work?'

'My first plan didn't work. It was the coffee. Drugged.'

'Mine too?'

'I'm afraid so. In case Matthew switched cups. He would have killed you too.'

'No doubt.'

'And destroyed Bernard's career.'

'I didn't hear that.'

'You're not going deaf, are you?'

'Just a little tinnitus. But Bernard's secret is safe with me.'

'I'd like to know where he's put that information. It's dangerous.'

Ambrose reached into the breast pocket of Matthew's jacket. 'You mean this?' He produced a small envelope. I opened it. It contained the DNA samples and the names of Bernard and his natural father.

'You clever old thing. Do you think there are copies?' I asked.

'Most probably. But I noticed Matthew feeling his jacket pocket a couple of times on the way over, so I knew he kept something important there, and that he was worried about losing it. So perhaps this is the only record.'

There was a ring on the doorbell.

'Who the hell is that?' I asked.

'Clean-up service, come to get rid of Matthew for us.'

'Who's arranged that?'

'I did. As soon as Aaron told me about your idea last night.'

'He promised he wouldn't!'

'I don't think he did, actually. If you play back the conversation in your head, you might remember that he avoided making that promise.'

He was right. Aaron had simply changed the subject. The sort of thing I would have done. Crafty devil.

'Aaron is the most trustworthy person I know, present company excluded,' continued Ambrose, 'but he and I go back a long way, and he knows how much I value you. It was all done for your safety. Now hadn't you better answer that door before they get worried about us?'

I buzzed them in: two men wearing hoodies and a calm and very efficient-looking young woman. I recognised one of them as the man who had pulled me back from the brink of the tube platform.

'Are you my guardian angels?'

'You could say that. We've been watching you ever since you moved in here. But you gave us the slip a couple of times. In fact, I'd say you've given us more of a runaround than anyone I've ever known.'

Well, that gave me a little boost of pride.

The doorbell rang again, twice.

'That'll be the boss,' my rescuer said. He went to open the door. He returned, followed by an old friend.

'Percy!' I exclaimed. 'How glad I am to see you. What brings you here?'

'Hello, dear lady. How good to see you safe and well. We owe you thanks for helping us flush Matthew out. Now get your bags packed. I've come to take you home.'

There was one thing I had to do before I could put this whole series of events behind me. While his people cleaned up the safe house and disposed of Matthew's body, Percy had his driver Pete take me up to Hampstead. There we picked up Emily Charamboulos. I had phoned her on the way to tell her that her brother George could come out of hiding, as all danger had passed.

As I had discovered, Emily had known exactly where her brother was all the time. She was clearly made of sterner stuff than I had thought.

We drove down to a little Benedictine priory in Surrey. George Charamboulos had taken recourse to the somewhat medieval method of self-preservation by claiming sanctuary at the priory gates. The monks had been only too willing to take George in, on the understanding that he would, between meals and rest, offer up prayers for the redemption of the souls of his tormentors.

The reunion between brother and sister was touching. They held each other in a long embrace, and many tears were shed by both of them.

As for the monks, after a few weeks of George's ever-more alarming and paranoid tales of persecution, they were only too happy to see him leave.

54

WHEN I WISH TO RELAX and contemplate, there are few better ways to occupy myself than pottering around my cottage garden. It had, by force, been neglected for far too long. As the days shortened towards the equinox, I had been cutting back the roses, extirpating the brambles and mowing the grass.

In the undergrowth I found an upturned flower pot, cracked and with a section of one side missing. Inside I found a huge toad, as big as my fist. It studied me with a haughty expression, the sort that Matthew would adopt when presented with a bill which he had no intention of paying. A toad this fat would have to be female, but its resemblance to Matthew gave me cause to think back over the last few weeks with more than a tinge of sadness.

I could only imagine how Matthew must have panicked when he realised his deception and treachery was about to be exposed. How clever of him to put together a team of former agents, the smartest people he knew, and get them to find and root out those who posed the most danger to him. But how incautious to try to silence me with threats to expose Bernard's parentage. Matthew, never a parent himself, had been ignorant of how far a mother – even one as bad as I – might go to protect her young.

The doorbell rang. I had connected the bell-push at the front of the house with a loud bell at the back, so that I wouldn't miss visitors. Well, I hadn't done the electrics myself, Aaron had. He had come down to my little corner of West Sussex to collect payment for the apparatus – the electronic materials and the sniper's rifle – that he had installed in my safe house. Very sporting of him, waiting until after it was all over. Matthew might very well have killed both Ambrose and me, and Aaron would have had to whistle for his money. I offered him a little extra as a thank you, but Aaron refused to take it. Instead he did a couple of little jobs that needed doing – the sort of stuff Dennis used to carry out around the house – and bought and fixed the external garden bell that was summoning me now.

I opened the front door to find Bernard, my son, waiting on the doorstep, his ministerial limousine purring in the street.

'Hello, Ma,' he said, giving me a peck on the cheek, 'may I come in?'

He gave his chauffeur a wave. The limousine moved off quietly.

Bernard and I sat in the garden, enjoying the sun, sipping our tea.

'I can't stay long. My chauffeur will be back for me in twenty minutes.' Bernard fully expected me to voice my appreciation for his visit and acknowledge what a very busy man he was. I did not indulge him.

'I'm expected at Chevening in just over an hour,' he continued.

'Lovely place.' Chevening was the Foreign Secretary's country residence.

'Oh, you know it?' Bernard looked deflated that I hadn't been as impressed as he would have wished.

'Been there several times. Once I even stayed the night. Anyway, it's just as well you're not staying, I'm having a friend to tea.'

'A friend? Who?'

'Bella Walsingham. Perhaps you know her?'

'Name rings a bell.'

I was sure it did. Bernard had an excellent memory for names and faces, and must have been scanning his enormous brain's own version of Wikipedia as we spoke. His eyes lit up as he remembered Bella, but he said nothing.

'And on the weekend,' I continued, 'your sister Eva and her wife Silvana are dropping little Alice off to me.'

'I thought they were going to stay for a long weekend.'

'They've changed their plans. Silvana has to go to Milan for a conference, so they're flying out together from Gatwick. I shall have Alice all to myself.'

'How do you think you will manage?'

'Perfectly well, thank you,' I responded tartly.

Bernard shrugged, then gave me a sideways smile.

'Well?' I asked. I wanted to know what his visit was about.

'My enemies are vanquished. I have cut off those who harass me, and destroyed all them that have afflicted my soul.'

'Isn't that from one of King David's Psalms?' I had no idea how I knew this. The nuns must have drummed something into me after all.

'A paraphrase.'

'I heard the news about Grant Byford.' Byford, Bernard's under-secretary, had resigned his post at short notice, announcing that he wished to spend more time with his family. A day or so later his wife had responded by announcing that she was divorcing him, and that his family had no wish to spend any more time with him. She was quoted as stating, 'I married him for better or worse, but not for lunch.' It was an old joke, but a good one nonetheless.

'The moment I confronted Grant, he crumbled.' Bernard had regained his self-righteous, bumptious self. 'And any rumours he had been spreading, any sort of coup, suddenly evaporated. There was nothing in it at all.'

'Did my mentioning his name help?' I asked.

'Of course, I'm grateful that you steered me in the right direction. But it was nothing I couldn't have worked out myself.' Bernard bestowed his most benevolent look. 'Really, Ma, I'm perfectly capable of fighting my own battles myself.'

'Of course you are, dear,' I replied. 'More tea before you go?'

Acknowledgements

Back in 1994 I wrote and directed a film starring, among others, hell-raiser Richard Harris, Maryam d'Abo, Julian Fellowes and Jerry Hall. We took the film to Cannes the following year and when *Variety*, the Hollywood trade magazine, gave me a glowing review we achieved international sales for the film.

My prime investor, who later became a very good friend and confidant, said this to me: 'Mark, all my friends in the Greek shipping community warned me not to get involved with you movie people. They said you'd take my money, that I'd never see a penny back, and that the only creative element would be your excuses for not paying me back. Yet I've already recouped my investment before the film has even been released. To show my appreciation I want to invite you and Jenny aboard my yacht this summer.'

Our three weeks aboard his yacht was a wonderful experience. After visiting the first thirty islands on his itinerary I stopped counting. Although in business a formidable negotiator, our host proved to be remarkably relaxed, good-humoured and generous. After our holiday I had my photographs developed and printed. When I went to pick them up the printers said I couldn't leave until I told them where this fabulous place was. I explained that it wasn't one place or one island, but more than sixty islands and that I had taken just a couple of shots from the best vantage points in each one.

I heartily recommend a Greek islands cruise. It is one of the best holidays one can experience. Each island has its own character. In each modernity and antiquity combine to create a timeless charm which completely infuses the senses.

To our host, who wishes to remain anonymous, and to his wife, we extend our heartfelt thanks for so many extraordinary experiences and for their continued kindness and generosity.

I also wish to thank former ambassador Giles Fitzherbert and his wife Alexandra, who gave me valuable insights into how a British embassy functions, and my old schoolfellow Nicholas Armour who was the Head of Chancery at our embassy in Athens in the mid 1980s.

Special thanks also to my wonderful editor Carolyn Mays and her team – Polly, Claudia and Victoria – at Bedford Square Publishers, and to my agents Jason and Joanna at the bks Agency for their painstaking work.

Also a special thanks to Arabella and Johnny de Falbe of John Sandoe Books, whose team supported me so well at my first book launch at the Chelsea Arts Club.

And many thanks to all the book reviewers, book bloggers and readers who gave my debut novel such very generous reviews, in print and online. It is those validations that encourage the writer to keep on writing.

Among the reviewers I make special mention of Barbara Norrey, whom I met at the Capital Crime Festival. She has been a marvellous support and champion of my work.

And above all, I wish to thank my lovely wife Jenny who read my manuscript first and inspired new ideas and better dialogue.

About the Author

Photo credit © Jenny Chartres

Mark Ezra was educated at Ampleforth College in Yorkshire and studied film production at university. He first entered the film industry as an editor, and eventually became an accomplished film director, producer, and screenwriter. He is the author of several picture books for young children.